About the Author

Alex Frost is an imaginative author whose passion lies in crafting grandiose tales of good and evil. With a boundless imagination and a flair for storytelling, Frost weaves intricate narratives that transport readers into captivating worlds filled with vibrant characters and epic conflicts. His love for creating these larger-than-life stories stems from a deep appreciation for the timeless battle between light and darkness. Through his vivid prose, Frost immerses readers in a tapestry of moral dilemmas, exploring the human condition and the power of choice. With each page, he invites readers to embark on extraordinary journeys that challenge their perspectives and ignite their sense of wonder.

Custodes: Origo

Alexander Frost

Custodes: Origo

Olympia Publishers
London

www.olympiapublishers.com
OLYMPIA PAPERBACK EDITION

A CIP catalogue record for this title is
available from the British Library.

ISBN: 978-1-80074-667-1

This is a work of fiction.
Names, characters, places and incidents originate from the writer's
imagination. Any resemblance to actual persons, living or dead, is
purely coincidental.

First Published in 2023

Olympia Publishers
Tallis House
2 Tallis Street
London
EC4Y 0AB

Printed in Great Britain

Dedication

I dedicate this book to my mother and to 2020. My worst year and my greatest strength. It is because of all the bad that happened that year, along with my mother's encouragement, that motivated me to write this book.

Acknowledgements

I would like to thank my friends for getting me out of the house when I had writer's block. I'd like to thank my family for all of their support over many years.

Prologue

There are three things in life that cannot be stopped: Life, Time, and Death. These three things are inevitable: everyone is born, they get old and they die. But there is one exception to these three states and they are called legends. What do we do when someone so great, so powerful, passes and we never want their story to go unheard? We make them legends and legends never die. The definition of a legend is a story coming down from the past; regarded as historical although not verifiable. But people think of this saying in a literal sense every civilization has tried to remain relevant but life, time, or death had all but wiped them out. But what if these stories were true? What if there was more to these stories than just the tales told around a campfire or a pub much like this one? What if there was more to the world than you could ever imagine?

The stories I could tell you would make your head spin, tales of battles with dragons, demons, and all literal hell breaking loose.

"Oh please, next you're going to say unicorns, fairies and nightcrawlers exist. Just another drunk telling his tales," says a very large ginger gentleman in a white-collared shirt as he sits down, loosening his tie. "Monsters aren't real, bigfoot doesn't exist and the Loch ness monster is just a camera smudge. Bartender! My usual," says the large man. That couldn't be further from the truth, my very large sun-deprived

11

friend. The beings you'd call monsters are no more so than you or our lovely bartender here. You know there was a time when people believed in the supernatural. There was a time where people thought every woman was a witch, and men became monsters with the changing of the moon. Most of those people were stone-cold sober. Religious zealots? Maybe. Cultist? Could be. No way to know for sure.

How about this? If you indulge me for a bit, not only could I change your mind but I'll pay your tab for the night. Deal?

"So I get free beer and all I have to do is listen to another drunk guy drivel on about some nonsense? Well, I hope you're loaded because I didn't come alone and you'll be paying for my friend's drinks too."

Then we have a deal. Gather round, ladies and gentlemen, for I will tell you my story and the story about a people the world forgot.

"Well, get on with it already."

Chapter 1
Quis custodiet ipsos custodes?

I will tell you a story about a race of people called Custodes, an ancient race of people who watched over this world when others could not. But throughout the centuries beings mythic and human alike have simply referred to as guardians. They say a guardian is a warrior created by God to protect humanity from supernatural beings and maintain balance; others say they are merely the bastard offspring of angels or a bunch of fanatics that claim to be of divine beings. No one knows our true origins, some of it is still hidden even from us. We have been around since the dawn of man and creature alike. We are beings in a class of our own, unlike other creatures that walk this earth. There are the ones that say we are hybrids of humans and a primordial being from bowels of purgatory created long ago always protecting from the shadow. I have no idea if the first part is actually true but it is the more creative of the lot. Whoever our powers come from and whatever we truly are we are protectors and we save lives. It's our job. We didn't ask for it, it kind of fell in our laps. I look at it like this, if you're practicing a skill eventually you'll get good at it. You keep practicing and you'll one day become an expert then others will come to you when they need help. That's us, the Custodes got really good at breaking up fights. "All the power of a deity without the fragility of a human," my father's favorite saying.

"And that's why it's our job to protect them," my mother would add.

Though my father would say it, I never believed we were gods. For Guardians are not truly immortal as gods are meant to be. While there are few things in existence that can kill us we can be killed, our own weapons are lethal to us for they are forged from our souls. The venom from Aranea in morte, large spiders that stood over thirty-five feet tall when fully grown. With the strength to topple even the mightiest of castle walls, and a hide almost as strong as diamond small arms wouldn't stand a chance against them. Hell, a tank wouldn't be able to scratch them. This spider is a very old breed of monster that would lay waste to any that got within its path. It was decided that they posed too great a threat to the world at large, so they were long hunted to extinction during the third war of the beast in 1291 A.D. It was the last time that humanity and the mythicon banded together.

The sole purpose of a guardian is to be a peacekeeper among all things natural and supernatural. There is one guardian that was admired by all but one day he gave his life to keep the world safe from demons thus putting an end to the gnaw of hell and its offspring. Vestigium Titano Rgis, he was my grandfather, he was two thousand five hundred years old. "One of the greatest guardians to ever exist ever." He died during King Henry the seventh's time, long before I was born and I was named after him to honor him, lucky me. But I prefer my name translation, Trace Titan King, for it doesn't come with the expectation of greatness. Especially since I was born without any powers whatsoever. To be born utterly powerless, to hear, "What a shame, he's not worthy to bear that mantle," haunted me my entire life and, as a child, I hated the constant reminder of what I could never be.

For those who are wondering how much time has gone by since the passing of legend himself, it has been five hundred and four years. For those who don't want to do the math on that, the year was 2013, the day I and my twin sister Caeli graced this earth. I have to say living up to the "Greatest Guardian Ever" hasn't been the easiest to do. Honestly who can live up to the world's savior? And I'm glad I'm not the only one to share in the torment. My sister is named after our grandmother, Caeli, though we had never got the chance to meet her it is agreed that she too was a complete badass to rival even my grandfather. One day she just disappeared without a word, my mother searched for years and never found a single trace. Can't find someone that truly doesn't want to be found I guess. That leaves my three-year-old sister, Luna, she definitely got off easy. She's named after the moon, although the moon is important and if those damn moon cultists had their way it would be the only thing we had, it's still nothing compared to what we had to go through.

It wasn't till that day, the day hell broke loose and brought all his friends: death, destruction, and sorrow. Before that day I was nothing and no one. I hadn't shown any abilities whatsoever. Could you imagine that? I, the heir to the throne was nothing more than a glorified human. I had no super strength or speed, no heightened abilities, no conjuration, or shapeshifting skills to speak of. I didn't even have my weapon and you're practically born with one. I had nothing. I was a guardian in name only. I would have taken anything at that point, even turning into a bucket of water. But all I got was a

15

name of great power and prestige that surpassed even the mightiest of monsters. Fate had dealt me quite the hand. On that day all I could do was be a spectator in the destruction of my home. But that one unfaithful day we saw firsthand the terrors of war and that day changed us all and made us stronger in the process.

On July fifteenth, the day of our seventh birthday, it started out peaceful just like any other day. People from all over came to see the royal twins and shower them in gifts, little did I know then it was more so all of the bureaucrats could try to cozy up to my parents and the elder council. But it was fun to play and laugh with my sister, cousins and the other children of the kingdom, while the adults talked and watched. There was a carnival with games and prizes and a circus with dragons that breathed fire and ice and unicorns that could fly as they created rainbows in their wake. It was truly a sight to behold and that day will go down in history but for all of the wrong reasons.

I saw my parents slip away to talk but my mother didn't look too happy with the conversation they were having. With everything that was going on at the party, no one noticed me follow them. I overheard my parents arguing during the party.

"Ira, you can't ask that of him he's only a child."

"He is our child, Aiyanna. He's not a baby any more, he can take it. Know that I wouldn't ask that of him if I didn't think you could handle it. He was born for this"

"Ira, don't do this to him."

"Trust me, Aiyanna, I know it will work."

"Please don't do this to our son. It will only hurt him in the end."

"Or it will give him the push he needs to awaken his powers."

"No, Ira, I can't have this conversation with you again and I won't let you hurt our son."

"I would never dream of hurting him."

"Then drop it!"

"Let me just ask you this one question?"

"Fine, Ira."

"How is it fair for him to go the rest of his life without powers?"

"I'd rather him not have powers than subject him to that."

"Don't we owe it to him to try? Every year he wishes for the same thing and every year he gets more and more disappointed. He's not happy, Aiyanna."

"You don't think I can see that, Ira, but it's too dangerous."

"Why don't we just let him decide? What if he says yes?"

"No, Ira, and that's final. Even if he did say yes and we put him in it he may never wake up. Could you live with that?"

"That wouldn't happen. Ves is strong, a lot stronger than you give him credit for. I know he'd make it out there."

"No! Please let it go, Ira. It's their day and we should be there celebrating it with them."

"Okay. I'll let go for now. Let's head back to the… Oh, Ves, what are you doing here? Were you listening to our conversation?"

"Yes but only a little. Mom looked upset and I wanted to check on her."

"Always the observant one aren't you, sweetie? You know it's not good to eavesdrop."

"I know, Mom and I'm sorry."

"How much did you hear?"

"Most of it. What is it that you guys were talking about?"

"It was nothing, Ves, just deciding when the best time to start opening your gifts would be. How about we do that now? Let's get back to the party."

After hours of playing and running around and it was time to cut the cake and open presents, my mother called everyone over to watch the spectacle and sing us happy birthday. They told us to make a wish, my wish was to get my powers and someday surpass my grandfather so when people spoke of me his triumphs would pale in comparison. As we started cutting the cake my father, King Titan, received news from one of our scouts that monitors energy abnormalities. The scout came to warn us a large wave of energy was coming toward us and that there was an impending attack on our home by demons and within a matter of minutes, the capital was flooded with demons and just like that the balance of the world had been shifted. The war that had been over for over five hundred years was back on. My father's orders were for all of the royal children to be taken away from Eden and one adult to watch over them. Sometimes I think my mom drew the short straw to take care of the three of us and our five other cousin half of which were no more than four years old at the time.

I know most of the others were too young to remember or repressed it but I remember it all. The destruction and disarray we saw while fleeing away from the place we called home. Seeing the enemy advance and fires spread through the city. The last thing my father said to me before we left was, "My son I am passing the responsibility of protector of this family on to you. Your mother is going to need all the help you and your sister can give her. You are a guardian, my son, so promise to protect everyone."

"But, Dad, how can I do that? I'm weak and I don't have any powers."

"You are not weak, Ves, you are the son of Ira the relentless and Aiyanna the avalanche. Weakness is not in your blood. Ves, listen to me, my son we only have so much time. I know this is no small task. Promise me. Ves, we are Guardians so a promise is more than just words to us. Once you make this promise you can never break it and are bound by it."

"I promise to protect them, Dad. I will protect my sisters, my cousins, and my mom. I promise to defend them with my life."

"Ves, my son, the world can be cold and heartless but don't get discouraged. There are always lights at the end of the tunnel you just have to look."

"Lord Ira, the enemy is closing in."

"Right! Just one more minute, I need to say goodbye."

As we were saying our goodbyes, men in cloaks burst through the doors and attacked us.

"Get far away from here, Aiyanna and don't look back. Be safe, all of you. You are all you have. Goodbye, Aiyanna, Caeli, Ves, Luna, Aster, Hope, Leo, Willow, and Griffin."

"Goodbye, my love."

"Goodbye, father."

"Goodbye, uncle Ira."

The guards and my father intervened and told us to flee as they held them off. As we fled the hall, sounds of my father shouting to his soldiers. "All right, men the enemy is here! We will hold this line, no one shall pass through these halls. If the pale rider comes for us on this day show him that we are Guardians and we are not afraid! We do not run! We do not hide! And we will not go quietly. Stand and fight until the end."

After we got out of the hall we made our way to the airship listening to the sounds of explosions and the booming roars of thunder that chased close behind us. We escaped unscathed or so we thought.

While my father and the soldiers were fighting off the cloaked invaders we got ready for take-off. *BOOOOOOMMM.*

"What was that? Ves and Caeli stay with the others. I need to untie us from the dock." As my mother opened the door to the plane, one cloaked figure shot out of the smoke and onto the ship. The cloaked figure pulled out their weapon and attacked my mother. It looked like an oversized mail opener and it was covered in this blackish-green ooze. Stay away from our mom. My mother shouted, "Stay back! The venom on that blade could kill anyone of you. I can handle this."

While they were struggling a second cloaked assassin entered the ship and approached me and my siblings with his blade drawn and the same ooze on his blade. I could feel a burning deep within my chest. The only way I can describe it is as if something from within me was trying to claw its way out. A fire had been lit and all I wanted to do was to protect my family. The voice said, "If you want to protect them, hold your hands and I'll take care of the rest this time."

As the assassin lunged at us with his blade I put my hands up to block and a large smoldering shield appeared in and around my hands and fire erupted from it into the assassin and blasted him into the other assailant then my mother conjured an ice blade stabbing the assassins in their chest and when the frosted blade pierced their bodies they exploded into ash. As fast as it came that rush of power fled from my body and the strange lights faded away. The shield still giving off heat began to crumble in from the edges but my hands were still trapped inside it. "Vestigium, where did you get that shield?"

"It just appeared in my hand, now it's stuck to me."

"How? Put it away before you melt the hull of the ship."

"I can't it won't go away."

"Hold on I'll try to freeze it off." My mother placed her hand on the shield and froze it solid immediately. Steam started to come from the frozen shield. "The ice is melting already? Hold still." She punched through the shield and shattered it. As it shattered around my hand a blade began to reveal itself. A wave of heat began emitting from the blade getting hotter and hotter.

"Mommy, the floors are starting to melt."

"Ves get a hold of yourself or you're going to destroy the ship." My mother placed her hand over the sword and made a sheath of ice. "That should stop it from melting everything."

You gotta love traumatic experiences; they tend to bring out your hidden potential. Nothing was the same after that day, my mother said we had to move on and try not to think about all the people we left behind, my family and friends all gone. "It's best not to dwell on what we cannot change for if we do it will consume us and only leave darkness," said my mother. But that feeling, the feeling of fleeing from your home while the others stay and fight, it sticks with you, but I doubt there was much I would have been able to do anyway. After that day, we all made a promise we would return to Eden. One day we would help reclaim what was once ours and guardians always keep their promises.

Chapter 2
Flash

After that day we went into hiding as much as we could while still gathering information on our attackers. Eli, an old friend of my dad's, helped get us to safety. He even helped us conceal our identities and gave us one of his safe houses to stay in Bruce Crossing, Michigan. You may ask why there? The Ottawa national forest, one thousand five hundred and fifty-one square miles of lush green forest. Eli said it would be the safest place for us. "It will be perfect for young guardians to run wild and free," he said. I assume he meant just in case one of us should transform on accident, the locals would just think we were bears or wolves, and some cases even bigfoot. The safe house was an underground bunker with a small shack on top of it. No one ever suspected a thing when a woman and eight kids went in and never came out. But why would we ever want to leave the place that had nearly everything we could ask for? A training area with a pool and a range, a huge kitchen, library, barracks to sleep in, a workshop, six of the places I spent the majority of time in. A garden, small farm so we could be self-sufficient, even a war room. Mom would even let us use the projector in there for movie night. When we first got there the place needed a little bit of work but we made it our own. With that being settled, my mother made sure I trained every day to get stronger and when I wasn't training I was studying. I graduated from college when I was thirteen with P.h.Ds in computer and mechanical engineering, they called me a child prodigy. It's funny to look back at it, now those past six years had been a blur of books and coding. Long days spent studying and even longer nights training and when I got bored of that, movies. Lots and lots of movies. Marvel movies were my favorite, the Avengers movies were gold. The whispers of what was happening back in Eden was what kept me going all those nights. After I graduated I decided to become a full-time guardian fighting demons, vampires, shape-shifters and anything else that went bump in the night.

Over the last few years, my mother and I have been working on a system to help us keep tabs on the supernatural community. While it's still a work in progress, codename: Hun73r or Hunter as mother calls it, is a device programmed to help guardians keep track of each other, other supernatural energies, and is a codex of known creatures. I'll need to put an asterisk on known creatures, it means so long as there is information on the creature pre-entered into the database or if it has been encountered firsthand. So basically any information gathered from cases, or stories that were passed down through the generations, is in there. Basic tactics, locations, and the weaknesses of demons, devils, ghosts, vampires, werewolves, giants, wyverns, dwarves, etc. are in the codex.

"So wait a minute. Your family hunted mythical creatures for years, and no one bothered writing it down until you created this codex thing? Sounds like your people weren't that smart," the large ginger man says.

"Shut up, Davlin, you can't just interrupt a story with your stupid comments. It breaks the immersion."

"What are you talking about, Miranda, I'm just pointing out the flaws in the man's story. Instead of chastising me, how about the beer I ordered twenty minutes ago? The story isn't that interesting to keep you from doing your job."

"Fine, I take it, that'll be another round for everyone else as well?"

Yes, Miranda please get the rotund gentleman and his friends another round as I explain the effects of war.

So, to answer your question, there was a codex of a sort written down. There were hundreds, maybe even thousands of them at one point. All passed down through the generations.

"And what happened to them, if you don't mind me asking?"

Burnt to a crisp!

"What?" says Davlin.

"What do you mean?" say a few of the others at the bar.

Well as I stated before my home was ravaged by demonic troops and war. So the libraries in Eden at the time were either burned down or closed to the public. That and we were too busy running for our lives to be concerned with books. We had to start from scratch, so we decided we should condense that information into something portable. Are you happy with that answer? Can I continue the story now?

"Wait, I got a question ?"

Yes, Miranda?

"Sorry, but how does the codex get new information on things it hasn't encountered?"

That's simple, the Hun73r observes and records everything you say and do, then it compiles that data and adds it to the codex.

"Does it record you pooping?"

"Of course, it doesn't, Phylis, what kinda dumb question is that?" says Davlin.

Actually it does, and before anyone asks why. The program keeps track of everything you do: your temperature, weight, diet, vital signs, energy levels, sleep or lack thereof, and any and all bowel movements.

"But why?"

It's to make sure the wearer of the device is who they say they are and that they are, for a lack of a better term, normal or at least normal for themselves. Are we done with the questions?

"Bu—"

Good! Back to the story: where was I?

"You were talking about the Hun73r device and the codex."

"Right! Thank you, Miranda. A device with tons of different programs and information combined into a wearable piece of technology no bigger than a smartwatch. Inconspicuous, light, and ever-evolving, the hunter system was a huge help where training was involved. It allowed us to run countless simulations on mythicon we hadn't encountered. I spent hours inside them studying each and every creature trying to learn everything I could."

"You know that I am glad you've taken the initiative with your simulations, Trace. But they are only just that, at some point, you'll have to try real combat."

"I know, Mother, knowledge is only a third of the battle."

"Then what are the other two?"

"The other two are; One being able to act on the

information you have, and two, having a backup plan if the original doesn't work."

"Well, look at you, you've been doing more than sleeping during our lessons."

"Of course, I have, I want to be able to go out on my own as soon as possible and won't always have you there to give me advice."

"That is correct. That is why I made you this program for your hunter device."

"What is it?"

"I'll send you the program and you can install it."

"Okay? What's the program's name?"

"Her name is Minerva and I think you'll like her."

"Her? What kind of program is it?"

"Just install it, Trace."

"Okay. It's installed, Hunter! Run program: Minerva!"

"Engaging program Minerva!"

"Sooooooo? You gave my hunter gear a voice. Oooookkkkaaaaayyyyy."

"I'm more than just a voice, think of me as your guardian angel, I can analyze any situation you get into and suggest the best course of action."

"Oh! look another babysitter. Thanks, Mom, you're the best."

"Your sarcasm is adorable."

"Wait! does that mean you're gonna let me go out on my own now?"

"No."

"Awwww. Why not?"

"Because it's far too dangerous for a child to be out by

himself. Also, when you eventually go out on your own you'll have someone to talk to and get advice from."

"Uuuuugggggghhhhhhhhhhhh."

"That's enough out of you." My mother laughed. "Instead of being a pouty teenager try being as appreciative as your siblings."

"Minerva, deactivate the simulation."

"Yes, Aiyanna."

"Mom, did you give him the program?"

"How'd he take it."

"I bet he pouted like a baby."

"No, I bet he took it like a man, a manly man."

"I bet he likes it, it's sooooooo coooool."

Included with the barrage of questions stood four children in the doorway. "Pouted like a baby!"

"See! I told you, Caeli."

"I'm sure she's joking, Hope."

"No Way! Trace would never pout; men like us don't pout. We're too manly."

"We get it, Griffin, you're super manly."

"You mean it, Aster?"

"Sure do."

"Everyone got the babysitter program?"

"It's not a babysitter program, and yes everyone got a version of the program tailored specifically to them. Minerva is yours and yours alone. She's programmed to handle your pouting and sarcasm."

"I wasn't pouting! I was yawning."

"All of your programs are still in a beta phase and need you to test them, so use them as much as possible. On that note,

Caeli, where are Luna, Leo, and Willow?"

"I don't know? Hey Aceso, where are my brothers and sisters?"

"Locating siblings... their A.I. said they went to race by the lake and then went further into the forest. Hmmm. Odd. I detect two dark roots closing in on their location. They are all roughly three miles away."

"They're doing what? Um, Mom they're... where'd she go?"

"Her and Trace ran real manly like out of here. While you were talking to your program. Probably went to go fight the dark roots, like men!"

"We get it, Griffin, enough with the manly stuff and follow them."

"No time, Caeli, TO THE FOREST!"

"Minerva, what's the fastest way to them?"

"The fastest way is always straight."

"What? That is not helpful at all."

"Oh, sorry, my sarcasm dial is turned to seven out of ten."

"Seriously, now is not the time for that my brother and sis—"

"Boreas, lead me to my children."

"Yes, ma'am right away. Locating... Head straight ahead for a mile and a half then go right at the waterfall for another mile and a half. If you've reached the dark foreboding pit then you've gone too far."

"Come on, Trace, we have to get to them now!"

"Right!"

We ran through the forest, jumping over logs, through

bushes around the lake and over a hill.

"I see the clearing up ahead!"

"Help us, someone, the monsters have my brother and sister!"

"The children are straight ahead, Mrs. Aiyanna and they're in danger."

"Thanks, Boreas didn't notice! Trace, protect Hope and I'll get Luna and Leo. Hastam Glacies!"

A spear of solid ice appeared in my mother's hand and she threw it at the creature's roots freezing it in place, shhhink. Not to be shown up I unsheathed my blade and yelled out, "Ignis" and my blade became engulfed in flame, booosh. I charged full speed at the twenty-foot moss-covered tree person in-between me and Hope. I swung my flaming blade and shouted. "Hey, firewood leave my little sister alone!"

The first attack left the dark root reeling in pain and gave Hope enough room to run.

"Hope, stay behind me I'll handle it." The dark wood regained its composure and swung its large tree trunk arm at me. I braced my sword for the swing and when the branches made contact with my blade they burst into flames. To stop the fire spreading, the dark root ripped its burning arm off and sprouted another one. "Sorry about the arm, I'll aim for your heart next. Where exactly is your heart by the way?"

"A dark root's heart resides in the core of its stump."

"Thanks, Minerva, pretty sure I could have figured that out myself."

"Then figure out what you are going to do about those five wood spears flying toward you."

"I'll just dodge those."

"Yes, but can Hope?"

"Fuck." I raised my blade and swung at the spears, as they hit my blade they burned to ash.

"That all you got?" The dark root roared and shot more spears from its hand, this time it tripled the amount.

"I don't think I can block all of those, Hope, you need to run." As we turned to run, an ice wall shot up from the ground.

"Hope, stay behind the wall it will protect you. Trace, You can do this, stop playing with your foe and beat it already."

"Yes, Mother, I was just holding back because I didn't want Hope to get burned is all."

Now that I didn't have to worry about Hope I could go all out. "My turn, monster. This time I can put my back into it. RAAAHHH!" I charged the dark root. The dark root started its spear assault again, I swung my blade, burning some of the spears and deflecting the rest as I was halted in my tracks. "These spears are getting tougher to deflect, is this thing getting stronger?"

"I can't detect any change in the density of the material of the spears, this creature has had no change in its power."

"Then why are only some of the spears burning?"

"I don't know, Trace, I can only share my analysis of this battle. I have noticed the heat of the fire on your blade has decreased several hundred degrees after the first few attacks. I also noticed a large decrease in your energy and speed as well."

"What are you talking about? I feel fine, Minerva, your sensors must be busted. I just... I just lost my concentration. **Ignis**!" *Booosh.* The fire reignited on my blade. "Let's end this." I dashed to the base of the dark root, dodging wooden spears and slicing through the vines trying to grab me.

"Cripple the roots, Trace."

"What do you think I'm trying to do?" I slashed at the roots and cut halfway through the monster's leg, causing it to stumble backwards and burn. I dart over to the other leg and cut through it. The dark root falls on its back and I climb on top of it and stab my blade into its chest. "**Ignis!**" *Boooosh. Crackle.* The red fire burned brighter, spreading up my arms and burning a gaping hole into the dark root exposing its smoldering core. As the core started to burn out, the leaves started to turn yellow and fall from the tree.

"All life signs of the creature have ceased, you have achieved victory. Yay! Here, some digital confetti for your efforts'."

"Minerva, enough, we don't want this victory to go to his head. Trace, your technique was sloppy and your power had begun to fluctuate. If I hadn't stepped in when I did, you and Hope may have been a pin cushion. But you did do a few things well. You showed no fear and faced your enemy bravely. You also did a great job of using their weakness against them. As for your last attack, truly impressive, I've never seen a flame quite like it and that war cry was magnificent. I was all the way over here and it gave me the chills. So, I say an A+ for spirit. Now, if you could keep your energy output as consistent as your last attack they would have been no match for your fire. I give you a B- for the fight."

"Don't be so hard on him, Mom, Trace still saved me and that's what matters right?"

"I'm not being hard on him, Hope, I am giving him my opinion of his battle. I'm trying to make him a better fighter.

As for the rescue I have to give you a D+."

"A D+, really? That's not fair, it wasn't that bad was it?"

"Yes a D, it's what's fair. While you did save your sister you immediately put her and yourself back in danger. You should have focused on taking her to safety instead of the enemy. I was here with you, you could have asked for my assistance."

"Okay, Mom, I get it. Do you always have to make everything into a lesson? It's never good enough to just win with you."

"Trace, while I am happy that you won, that is only part of a Custode's job. The other part is to protect people, it's kind of in the title."

"Don't listen to her, Trace, you did great! You get an A+ for saving Hope and being awesome." I hear from my siblings on the sideline.

"Yeah, Trace, you fought that tree like a MAN!"

"Trace you're definitely my hero and thank you for saving me."

"Enough, we better burn the rest of them and get out of here before someone finds them. Trace, will you do the honors?"

"**Ignis!**" *Boosh, crackle.* The flames engulfed both of the trunks.

"Let's go home and get cleaned up." We made our way home, got cleaned up and had dinner. All through dinner I could only think about what my mother said about my shortcomings. Even my brothers and sisters trying to cheer me up didn't help. After dinner, my siblings headed to bed and I went down to the training room for a few hours. As I went to leave my mother stopped me at the door.

"Trace, all of the mistakes aside, you did win. I know I can be hard on you, but I want you to improve as much as possible. You need to think about the world around you. You get tunnel vision in combat and forget about everything else. Do you see the difference in simulations and real combat now?"

Yes, Mother, I do."

"One last thing, Trace."

"Yes, Mother?"

"Good job, take a few days off, absorb what you learned from your first true fight and try to get some rest. Good night."

"Good night, Mom."

Chapter 3
Caught at the Crossroad

Even though it was buried in critiques, my mother said I did good, that small compliment made me feel accomplished. Over the next few weeks, I went with my mother on every single investigation she worked. She would criticize every move I made, every misstep I took but I learned a lot in the process. I got to see firsthand how powerful she was. When she would let me help she would tell me how to better utilize my powers and how to fight someone with similar powers as myself. As those weeks flew by we both realized that one day soon I would have to be out here on my own. I'd have to start doing more than just helping set up traps, looking over clues, and being the lookout. I'd have to start doing my own investigations and I would have to fight monsters. Since the siege only whispers about Eden and its people are heard once in a blue moon. Are they alive? If they are, they are being tortured and how much longer can they hold out? The only information we have comes from one of my mother's contacts Eli. Eli is an information broker and has been friends with my family for years. He had helped us expand the Hun73r network and in exchange for having access to it, and he would try to get any information he could on Eden. A dark energy cloud surrounded the island making it hard to get any intel. . Eli did find out that there were people still alive there and were taken as slaves but that's all he could be sure of at the time.

Around that time, I had started researching similar energy sources in a town in New Mexico. It was because of that similarity I figured whoever was causing it would have more info on Eden. I brought my findings to my mother and asked if she thought it could be the same people who attacked us? She replied, "Shouldn't you be in bed instead of looking for trouble? Whatever it is we can talk about it in the morning. As for you, shorty, get some rest otherwise your stubbornness won't be the only thing you share with dwarves."

"But?"

"But nothing, Trace, go to bed."

"You didn't even look at it and I've spent days working on this? You don't even care."

"Do I not care that people dying or that there may or may not be a clue to who attacked our home? Of course, I do, more than you could ever know. And I am more than aware of your late-night extracurricular activities. We will talk about all of it in the morning, now go to bed!"

"But?"

"One more but out of you and I'm going to punt yours into the next county, young man."

I had decided it was in my best interest to not continue the matter tonight, by the serious look on her face I knew my mother was far from joking. "Okay, okay. I'm going, see you in the morning."

First thing the next morning I got up bright and early to show my mother what I had found. "So, Mom. It's the morning, Mom. It's the time you specified, Mother, it is time for our discussion. The discussion involving the—"

"Trace, enough! just show me what you have."

"Let me show you the energy readings I found as well as the unexplained deaths and disappearances."

"Go on."

"It started with the all the abnormalities: power surges, satanic markings on walls, and then possible possession of peepaw with his trusty pitchfork trying to skewer teens partying at some farm in Moriarty a week ago. Who knew that a seventy-five-year-old man would be more than a match for a high school football team? The report said Old man Harold was off his meds, that's why he attacked the entire starting lineup and several other drunk teens and brutally murdered them. After talking, Harold doesn't recall the incident but one of the people to have had a first-hand encounter with the hay-slinging slasher and survived confirmed the tale. After the attack and questioning by the police the teen suffered a mental breakdown and had himself committed to a mental ward in the same hospital Harold was currently in. Also, several houses all over town burst into inextinguishable flames out of nowhere five days ago, the news blamed the houses on a faulty gas line that caused a leak. As for the church, they didn't even try to cover it up that well. Apparently, they all drank and partied themselves to death. You heard me right, over one hundred people died from alcohol poisoning."

"Okay, Trace, where do we go from here?"

"Excuse me?"

"If this were your investigation how would you proceed?"

"I'd go to Moriarty and talk to the locals to see where the cover-ups end and the truth begins. I'd also try to find out what brought the demonic present there."

"What about why this demon is being so brazen with its escalation of events? Clearly it wants someone's attention, the question is who?"

"I didn't think about that, I thought maybe it got sloppy or was just an ass."

"It's a possibility but not likely. Most demons try to stay in the shadows and make their side deals."

"So we need more information?"

"We need to get a closer look at these events."

"We need to?"

"Yes, we. This is your case, you gathered the information and have done all the work thus far. However, I will be at your side and we will work together until the fighting starts. This demon of whatever it is could be dangerous. You have to let me handle it, deal?"

"I'm sure I could handle a demon in a fight."

"Trace what did I say? I will fight the demon, you do the investigating got it?"

"Okay, okay."

"Then pack your stuff we'll head out tomorrow."

"Yes, ma'am. Hey, Minerva, I need two train tickets to Moriarty, New Mexico."

"Already done."

"I'll make sure everything is taken care of here while we're gone."

I went to my room and packed the essentials; holy water bombs, blessed crosses and yes there is a difference, the blood of a saint, don't ask how we got that. I also grabbed this new invention I'd been working on. It's a portable devil's trap, instead of having to draw the symbols all you have to do is throw this ball of powder and it makes a perfect pentagram. I wanted to bring my new armor but it was still in the test phase. The suit fully integrates our A.I. into a hud as well as synergizing with our powers. I'd bring it next time for sure. Another day passed and my mother and I got ready to depart. But first I said my goodbyes to my siblings.

"Trace, be careful and do what Mom tells you."

"Okay, Caeli."

"Be sure to show those demons who's boss, big bro."

"Thanks, Aster."

"Yeah, show them you're the man."

"I will do just that, Griffin."

"Don't let the demon impel you with a cross and try to sacrifice your soul."

"Oddly specific and I'll try to avoid that, thanks for the advice, Luna."

"You ready to go, Trace?"

"Um, sure. Ready to go!"

"Good. Bye, everyone we'll see you in a few days and call you when we get to the hotel."

We headed to the train station and got on our train. It was a long ride ahead of us, to New Mexico, and the closer we got the more nervous I got. Maybe it had to do with what Luna said or maybe it was because this would be the first time my mother let me help her with a demon? Either way, I knew it would be something I would never forget.

When we got to Moriarty we immediately got to work, we started talking to the locals and we went to visit the two guys that got possessed. Mom went to talk with Harold, and I the football player. Perks of being a teen, I told the nurse that I went to school with him. Max told me that from what he remembered the old man sprouted horns and was spewing fire from his hands. He also mentioned that the other players started acting weird and instead of running as he did they tried to fight Harold.

"They were like mindless drones, they got stabbed and set on fire but the kept fighting," to quote Max. Could there be other demons? If so why would they fight another demon? I thought to myself. After our talk, I left Max to rest and drew a devil's trap on the door of his room. I went back to the hotel and waited for my mother to return. When she got back we exchanged information. She said that Harold was a wealth of information and was a member of the church.

He was saying that the church had gotten into some weird practices when the new preacher showed up. Harold said that he went to a gathering at seven p.m. and from there everything was flashes of blood and screaming. He did say before he blacked out that he heard a voice saying something about making deals for bastard souls.

"So there's a crossroad demon taking the souls of people whose parents weren't married?"

"That is not what a bastard soul is, it's actually far worse than that. A bastard soul is when a person barters for someone else's soul without their permission."

"How is that even possible? How do you sell another person's soul?"

"It is not as difficult as you may think, you just need a person to be considered your possession. Like when people sacrificed their firstborn for riches. The other way would be to find a demon that knows a spell to bind a soul to them.

However, the spell itself was forbidden even by other demons. Crossroad demons have a code, they always keep their deals."

"That would explain why the other demons would have tried to take this demon out."

"It's clear that this demon is pretty powerful, so this is where you get off, Trace."

"What do you mean?"

"This demon is clearly too dangerous to have you help any further."

"If it is as powerful as you're making it seem then you'd need backup, right?"

"No, Trace, you will have no involvement from here on."

"It's not like I can say no, I already agreed to stay out of the demon fight, and I will. Do you need help scoping out the church?"

"Nope, already did that."

"Well okay, then when are you planning on going in?"

"Tonight, before they even know what's coming for them."

"Okay, then good luck and be safe. Before you go, take some of my devil's trap devices."

"Thanks, they may come in handy. I'm going to get ready then leave."

Five minutes later, my mother headed out, but something was off about this whole scenario. It's not like her to rush into a fight without taking time to plan everything out, this demon must be a big deal. I waited for about thirty minutes, but I still couldn't shake this weird feeling. I know I should trust my mom but something was wrong. Another hour and a half went by, that's when I decided I would go to the church to check things out myself. Things seemed way too quiet for a demon fight to be taking place. I circled around the building looking for all of the entrances and I put sigils on all of the doors to make sure the demons inside didn't escape. I made a second pass around the building and entered the backdoor.

When I got inside the church the place was empty. I looked around for any signs that anyone had been there. "Minerva, scan this place for demonic energy. Minerva? Minerva! answer me." That was when the hairs on the back of my neck stood on end. I needed to get out of there. I ran for the door and it disappeared. "Oh shit! what the hell is happening here?"

"What is happening here, my boy, is that as we speak your soul is being drained from your body," a voice said echoing around the room. "I will admit, you put up quite the fight, you have quite the resolve. Makes me curious, what are you? Clearly not a human, and definitely not a demi-god you don't stink of pegan energy."

"When I get out of this I am going to fuck you up!"

"Hahahaha. You won't be getting out of this. You're gonna die here."

"You got that right." I pulled out my knife and stabbed myself in the heart.

"No! If you kill yourself, you'll—" The world started to melt around me and I woke up in the church strapped down to an altar surrounded by the church parishioners.

"Minerva, execute guardian angel." A bright light shot out of my Hun73r watch. I used my strength to burst out of the straps and get to my feet. "Who's first?" I shouted. As soon as I said that they parted and a man in a robe walked through them.

"Well, well, well. Very impressive, child, you shattered the illusion, unfortunately for you that was me giving you a quick and painless death. So, child before I kill you, would you like me to show you the difference between you and I?"

What is this guy? Every cell in my body was screaming to run away. I could feel the power oozing from this man. I just had to stall until my mother got there. "Okay, you satanic piece of shit, let's dance. Minerva, I need my weapons."

"I detect your sword one hundred and fifty feet south of you, probably in that confession booth." I went to run to find my weapons and before I got five steps away the priest was in front of me.

"Where do you think you are going, child?" How is he that fast? He reached his hand out and slapped me one hundred feet across the room. I slid across the floor and hit a wall.

"Your weapons are now two hundred and fifty feet away. Try getting slapped closer next time."

"You are so helpful! What do I do here?"

"Remember the lessons your mom taught you."

"Gee thanks, Minerva." She wasn't wrong I had to think, I have trained for this. Remember the lessons.

It was then I could hear my mother's voice in my ear reciting her combat rules. "Mom, is that you?"

"No it's a recording of her lessons, I thought it would help you remember. Would you like me to stop?"

"No, let it play." I got back to my feet and readied myself.

"The rules of combat are simple, lets get started.

Basic Rules of Combat

•Rule number 1: When fighting an unknown opponent

don't underestimate them. Don't underestimate the strength, intelligence or desperation of an opponent or you'll end up eating pavement. So be prepared for anything."

First things first, I needed to get around this guy and get my weapons. I ran at the priest head on and dodged to the left to get around him. I reached for the door of the booth, and felt a hand grab my arm and pull with enough force to yank it out of its socket, then slam me into the ground. "You can take a hit, kid, this is kinda fun." The priest lifted me up and punched me square in the chest knocking the wind out of me. "Definitely not a human. Those bones would have broken immediately."

•"Rule number 2: Don't let them bait you. It's one of the oldest tricks in the book, they pull you in and use your emotions against you."

"If I had my weapons, you wouldn't be having so much fun."

"Is that right? You sound pretty confident. Okay, I'll bite. Go get your weapons." The priest threw me at the booth and I went crashing through it.

"Your weapons are zero feet away."

"Thank you, Minerva." I shambled to my feet and grabbed my sword.

"Are you really going to fight me with one arm?"

"Trace, you should relocate your shoulder before you fight this guy." I set my sword down and grabbed my arm and yanked my shoulder back into place.

"Now that is pretty metal, kid."

"Fuck off you sack of demon shit!" I picked up my sword again and yelled, "*Ignis*!"

"Ooooh a flame sword, I'm so scared."

"You will be soon!"

•"Rule Number 3: Know your limits. This rule is the most important, you don't want to try to fight a demon as your first real taste of combat because you will not walk away unscathed."

I lunged at the priest with my sword drawn and he dodged the blade and punched me in the face. "Oooh, so close that time. How about this, for your next attack I don't use my hands to block it?"

"Do you think I'm going to fall for that?"

"You come here." He took his sash from his robe and had one of his followers tie them behind his back. "See I can't use my hands at all. It is your move."

"What game are you playing? We both know that doesn't stop you from doing anything."

"Oh darn, he didn't fall for my trap. You're right, kid. I don't need my hands to beat a weakling like you." He vanished before my eyes and appeared next to me, then kicked me in the jaw and into the cross above the altar. If this was how the rest of this fight was going to go, I don't think I could take much more of this. Where was my mother?

"Trace, your energy levels are decreasing at a rapid rate. You need to run."

"That's probably not a bad idea, Minerva." I got back to my feet bloodied and bruised. But I wasn't done yet. This demon hadn't seen anything yet. I'd never told a more obvious lie in my life.

I charged again, this time he grabbed my arm and said, "I thought you said the fun would stop when you got your weapon, funny I'm still having a blast." I started trying to free my arm. "Kid, I like you, I'm gonna give you a break." *Snap!* No sooner than he said that my right arm shattered.

"Aaaaaaaaaahh!"

"Ha ha ha, see, there's a break. Isn't that funny? Did I mention I like puns?"

"You bastard! I'll kill you I swear it."

"Oh I highly doubt that." He slammed me into the ground again and again and again. "But I do have to admit you are durable. There are demons that can't take this level of beating. Like, even I would have given up by now. You truly are a marvel kind. What are you? How are you? I've never seen anything like this." He threw my limp body into the destroyed pews. At this point I was barely maintaining consciousness. This guy wasn't even trying, and here I was laying in my own blood. I had one last trick up my sleeve. The priest slowly approached me and said. "You dead yet, boy? I hope not because I'm not done with you yet. Boy?"

Mumble mumble.

"What did you say, kid I can't hear you?"

Mumble mumble.

"What? You're going to have to speak up or did I break your jaw too."

"I said just a little closer!" I rolled over and thrust my blade into his stomach, "***Mors ignis***!" A pillar of black fire exploded forward and sent him into the altar and the roaring flames consumed him. I beat him, it charred my right arm to a crisp but I did it. Mom, I know you said never to use that attack because of what it requires but the sacrifice was necessary. I really didn't have a choice in the matter.

"If you follow these rules then you have an eighty percent chance of winning the battle and beheading a demon or any other supernatural creature. If you are completely outmatched by your foe, these rules will not help you in any way. Abandon all attempts to fight and run like hell. Because you will lose and most likely die."

"That's what you get for underestimating me. That was a close one, I nearly bit the big one." *Clap clap clap.*

"Well done, child." *Clap clap clap.* "If I hadn't transformed at the last second that might have done some real damage," I hear coming from where the altar once stood. A horned monstrosity steps out of the fire with a charred cross in hand.

"I will give it to you, I'm sorry I underestimated you. You have the raw potential to be something truly amazing, but you lack the experience, the instinct that extra umph that separates the men from gods. If I had a power like yours, I would be unstoppable.

"I surely wouldn't have needed to steal all those souls if I had you. Man! I can just imagine the power boost I'm going to get from this. I would say try better next time but I don't want to give you false hope."

There was barely even a scratch on him. I was out of moves, I had to run. Come on body. Just get up and move. I mustered up the strength to stand and I turned to run. *Sshhluck!* I felt a sudden sharp pain in my back. I looked down and there was part of the cross sticking out of my chest. "To see such potential squandered breaks my black shriveled heart. But this little game of ours is over, kid, thanks for the exercise. It's been fun." The demon hoisted me up and planted the other end of the cross in the ground. "You will die here and your soul will be mine."

As I lay there with a stake in my chest staring at the painting of Saint Francis Borgia I could feel the life leaving my body. At that time all I could think was; is this really how I die? In a church to a preacher. I never saw this coming. I started to feel an extreme cold rush over my body. This must be it, death had come for me. *Booooom!* I saw a flash of light burst through the door.

"*ALTA FRIGIDUS!*"

"Trace, she's here, your mother is here. Just hold on a little long—" Thank god. The world went dark after that.

I woke up in my bedroom, with no recollection of how I got there. I looked around and my sisters Caeli and Luna were laying on the right side of the bed. This had to be a dream. I tried to move and all I felt was pain shooting through my body. Caeli and Luna immediately woke up.

"He's awake," they said in unison.

"I'm going to get Mom and the others, you stay with Trace, Luna."

"What happened? Where's the demon?"

"Calm down, Trace, Mom will be here any second and she'll explain everything. Everyone was so worried; they'll be relieved to know you're up. Do you need anything?"

"No. There is one thing I want to ask you about, Luna. What you said before we left for New Mexico? How'd you know what would happen? How did you know I was going to get stabbed?"

"Uuuum, I don't know? I mean, I guess I wasn't sure if it would happen or not."

"What does that mean?"

"Well, I had a dream about you. In the dream, I saw flashes of you in battle, there was an explosion, then I saw you bleeding with a wooden cross impaled through your chest. I thought it was just another one of my bad dreams. It's my fault you're hurt. I'm so sorry, Trace I should have told mother and you would have never gone with her."

My sister Luna has had nightmares since her powers first awakened when she turned five. Three years later and they'd only gotten worse. Pretty much every dream she has comes true in one form or another. My mother says that Luna was gifted with the oracle's sight but from the screams at night I would say it is more of a curse than anything else.

"It's okay, Luna. It's not your fault, you told me and I should have taken it more seriously. I never mentioned it to Mom and if I were stronger none of it would have mattered anyway."

"Trace!" I heard coming from the hallway, a slight rumble could be felt approaching the door. Seconds later an avalanche of children came crashing into my room.

"Big brother, you're finally awake."

"Of course, he's awake, he's a man ain't he?"

"Welcome back to the world of the living, sleepy head."

"See everyone you were all worried for nothing. Trace is too strong to be taken down by a demon. You were out for quite some time though."

"That's because fighting that demon head on took a lot of energy. Isn't that right, big bro?"

"What are you talking about? That wasn't much of a fight?"

"That's not what mom said, she said that the demon was pretty much beat by the time she got to you. She said whatever you did weakened it a lot. She said he practically fell over when she started fighting him. You have to tell us about the battle, we want to know all of the details spill it."

"Yeah, you have to tell us!"

"That's enough, guys, one at a time, give the demon slayer some room to breathe. Glad to see you're awake, my son, after sleeping for two weeks I bet you're ready for some more training?"

"What are you talking about? Training? Demon slayer? Is this some type of joke? Am I still dreaming? That's not what happened? I didn't beat the demon, I lost. I didn't even stand a chance. We weren't even on the same level."

"What are you talking about, Trace? Mom said you really stuck it to that demon."

"Oh, trust me, if anyone was stuck it was definitely me."

"Okay, everyone, I think that's enough questions for one night. Trace still needs his rest. Let's leave him be."

"I wasn't strong enough. If I had been stronger, I wouldn't have needed to be saved. I shouldn't have needed to be rescued like some defenseless kid."

"Big brother, what are you talking about?"

"I thought I was a Custodes but after that I'm just trash."

"What do you mean, big brother, you are a Custodes? You're one of us!"

"No! No, Luna I'm not, I'm a joke, a failure. Look at me! Do I look like a demon slayer? Why am I the bloodied and bruised one? I had to sacrifice my right arm and for what? If I was such a big help why was I laid up in a coma for two weeks? That doesn't sound like a Custodes to me. I'm too weak. Always have been. I'm done, there's no point in trying anymore."

A look of sorrow fell on all of their faces. "Mommy, what is he talking about? You said he helped beat the demon."

"Yeah you said he played a critical role in pummeling that demon, aunty Aiyanna."

"We will discuss it later, everyone leave us, I need to speak with your brother alone."

"Yes, Mother."

"You'll get to spend more time with Trace tomorrow."

"So that's it, huh? One loss and you quit? You can't quit. What example does that set for your brothers and sister?"

"What example does being beaten into a bloody pulp set? What example does lying to them about what really happened set?"

"You do t get it, they look up to you."

"Why? I'm weak and every single one of them is stronger than me. They don't look up to me, they pity me."

"That is not true, Trace, they look up to you because you have never given up."

"Never say never."

"I'm not joking, Trace, what do you think they see when they look at you, Trace."

"They see failure. Everyone else has grown more powerful with each passing day, while I struggle to even come close to keeping up. I can see it y'know."

"What are you talking about?"

"I can see how much they hold back when I'm around. I can see that I am just an anchor slowing them down."

"Yes, they are stronger than you now but you're wrong, you are not an anchor. You are their entire reason to push themselves. They see how hard you work and all the effort you put into your training. They see that you push yourself to your limits every day. All they ever say about you is how you motivate them, and even though you have to try harder to keep up with them, you keep pushing. You are their idol, you always have been."

"If I'm their idol they have really low standards. I am the oldest and yet I am the only one that hasn't awakened his Ego."

"You are so much stronger than you realize, Trace. Why do you think I push you harder than the others? I know you can take it and I've seen your potential. We all have, you're just a late bloomer. Just like with your powers, you need more time. So you can't give up. I won't let you. Trace, if it wasn't for you they would have given up hope of ever going back to Eden. I know you've realized it and seen it too. When they are down they always talk about you or come to you. When you're not around they pretend to be you. They call you their hero. You're their Superman. They all say that it's you that will get them home. That they want to be like you when they grow up. That it is you that will save the world. Not them, not me, not anyone else. You. Trace if you give up it is not just you that will pay the price for it. It would shatter them."

"Why is it my responsibility? I never asked for that nor do I want it."

"No one chooses to be someone's hero, Trace, and people don't look up to them because they win every time. They look up to them because they keep fighting and even if they fail they don't give up. It's about character and your resolve. Trace, I know you are stronger than this. Don't let one defeat define you. Who you are matters and what your will become matters more than you know."

"Fine, I won't give up. But what am I supposed to do?"

"The same thing everyone else does when they fall down. You get back up."

"That's it, those are your words of wisdom?"

"Yeah, that's it."

Okay, I'll do it for them, are you happy now?"

"No, but I don't have much say in the matter, Trace. Take a few days off. Relax. Maybe we'll all go for a run around the lake. I know everyone would love that."

"Sure, that sounds like fun."

"Try and get some rest, okay. I am here for you and will do whatever it takes to help you. Whatever you need I will get for you."

"How can I rest when I feel so empty? Like the wind has been taken from my sails. I don't think even you have the ability to fix that."

"You will get past this. You have to get back out there. Once you go back to work you'll forget all about one simple loss compared to a mountain of victories. But only after you are completely healed."

"I'll try it your way. I just hope it works."

"It will, trust me. We've all lost before; you just shake it off. Rest your arm."

"I will."

"And, Trace?"

"Yes, Mother?"

"Please don't use that death flame any more, it's too

dangerous. If it wasn't for your healing ability you would have lost that arm."

"I really didn't think I had a choice."

"I know. But don't do it again. Goodnight, my son. I love you and I'll see you in the morning."

"Goodnight, Mom and thank you."

As I lay there trying to sleep the only thing I could see when I drifted off was that demon's face. His smug grin and his red eyes that pierced my soul. And his words, I know I said I wouldn't give up but in the back of my mind, from then on there was always something eating at me. Doubt, maybe? I am nothing, how can I have ever hoped to take back Eden when I'm this weak? I'm no guardian, I'm a failure. That demon may not have taken my life but I wish he did. I tried to shake it off but that was my first true loss. I should quit and give up. But I can't, at least, not right now. I am both bound by that promise that we made so many years ago and my brothers and sisters need me to keep fighting. If I can't give up then I have to get stronger, I have to surpass my limit. I will fight, for them and get strong for them. In the morning I would start anew.

Chapter 4
Den of Beast

"Whoa, did that really happen?"

"Did what really happen?"

"You getting impaled?"

"Yeah, it was the first time and certainly not the last."

"Didn't you say that guardians can only be killed by like two things? So how could that demon have nearly killed you?"

No. I said there are only a few things that can kill us. And that is mostly reliant on our healing factor. If something can mortally wound us and we can't heal fast enough it can kill us. We have to focus our energy on our healing, it doesn't just happen on its own. At least not for me.

From then on I become far more serious about training. Nothing like getting some humility knocked into you to put your priorities in order. If I'm honest my hubris came back to haunt more times than I can count and it definitely is the reason I'm stuck here. But I'll get back to the interesting stuff. Now, where was I? Oh yeah, another hunt. You see, after having a lesser demon teach me a hard lesson my mother, in all her sage-like wisdom, had the notion that I was not ready for solo hunts.

"Even with all the promise you've shown you are not ready to head out on your own. I have gone far too easy on you, my child." "I agree, you've gone easier on me more than my siblings, with fighting and all the other important stuff. Which is why I need to go out on my own." Beep Beep Beep. You have an alert coming in. A friend of the family contacted my mother telling her that there had been a few wild animal attacks in Baltimore, Maryland and wanted to know if she could look into it.

"An animal attack? That sure sounds like a waste of your time."

"Your point, Trace?"

"I mean it's pointless for someone of your caliber to go investigate a measly animal attack. I mean you're so powerful it would be overkill."

"Trace, your point?"

"Okay. Okay. How about you send me instead? This is such a minor job anyone could do it. And you are always saying that the only way to improve is by gaining real life experience. So how abo…"

"Okay, fine."

"You have to let me fight on my own at some point."

"I said okay."

"I mean it's not like I'm a baby anymo— Wait, what?"

"You can go, but you have to promise to listen to Minerva and if she says it's too dangerous you contact me. Got it?"

"I promise."

Assuming that this was just an wild animal attack with the amount of bodies stacking up would be ridiculous. But if it was truly that simple the humans could handle it and I could go sight seeing. Doesn't hurt to check it out. Not knowing what was behind the animal attack, I packed for any scenario. I will admit I met my fair share of fearsome opponents over the years

55

but you never forget your first solo. I didn't take long for me to figure out what was causing all the ruckus. I snuck into the coroners office to check out the bodies.

"Minerva scan the bite and claw marks to see if they match with the local wildlife."

"On it. Hmm. This is weird. These bites and claw marks don't match any bears, or mountain lions, cougars and any other big cats. There's hardly anything of them to call them bodies"

"That's what I was thinking as well. Did you notice that dried yellowish-green stuff around the mouths and bite marks?"

"I would need a sample to analyze what it is."

"Or we could read the toxicology report. Mind pulling it up for me."

" Done! Let's see here the tests show that it is some kind a paralyzing agent in the system. Similar to that of a cone snail, but way worse. It seems to get more potent the longer its in your system. At first it just slows you down and then you lose motor controls and become defenseless. But even before the does finally kills you the predator eats you whole and you feel every single bit of it."

"Are you saying that these people may have still been alive while they were eaten."

"I'm afraid so, but not for long. I'm sure they either passed out from the pain or died from the shock."

"That doesn't make me feel better Minerva. Can you find in the report where the bodies were found."

"The bodies were found not far from here near a popular set of caves and trails."

"Caves you say. That could narrow down our list of suspects. Make a copy of the examiners reports and see what the cops think about this."

"Already on it. I also took the liberty of getting you a room at the nearby motel."

"How many stars?"

"Does it matter? Not like you're going to be sleeping anyways."

"Fair enough."

I made my way to the motel to go over all of the information we got. I spent hours going over each of the reports and all signs pointed to more than just a wild animal attack.

"Minerva bring up the codex."

"Hun-Seven-er Codex activate."

A giant holographic library of creature covered the walls of the room.

"Hun7er not Hun-Seven-er, do you not know leet speak."

"I am unfamiliar with this leet language you speak. What is the dialects origin?"

"It comes from... you know I actually don't know. Just say hunter. Pull up every predator that uses some sort of paralysis, on it's prey."

"There are over five hundred creatures in the codex that use paralysis in their hunting."

"Okay let's narrow it down. Show me the ones that would have fangs and claws that can match what was left of the bodies."

"Narrowing... There are still over one hundred creatures that fit those parameters."

"Get rid of all the creatures that don't live in caves and prefer warmer climates year round."

"Narrowing... That leaves five creatures that it could possibly be."

"Start the roll call."

"We have Wendigo's known for eating humans as they stem from cannibalistic curses."

"That can't be it, if it were them the only things left would be bones at the most. Remove."

"Next we have a wereplatypus."

"Wereplatypus are extinct, besides not of the corpses that were intact came back to life as a giant furby. Remove."

"Okay what about this one. The razorback."

"Razorback huh? The beasts of Baltimore has a nice ring to it. All right, I can handle that. Summerize"

"Razorback: A large greyish-black beast covered with sharp quills that can be fired at will. It also has six-inch claws, and fangs that ooze a paralyzing agent. These creatures can be confused with werewolves from a distance but they are actually much larger, stronger, and faster."

"And to top it off silver can't hurt them, doesn't even slow them down, which can make them hard to kill without the proper equipment." So, these Razorbacks are dangerous monster?

In my opinion? No, these beasts aren't exactly savage, they are known as gentle giants that normally don't leave their caves or forest unless they are disturbed so we leave them be. But every so often there are the ones that get a taste of blood, people blood, those are the ones that you have to worry about, if you don't stop their transformation in time they become something else entirely. Razorbacks have the tendency to move closer to the Midwest or the North where there are mostly large open space or mountains where they can live in peace. However, rogues prefer places like campgrounds and cave systems where people can go missing and go unnoticed.

Tracking them is fairly easy because of their size and the bodies they leave behind in their wake, but it has been my experience to talk with the locals for extra information on the area. After narrowing down what I was looking for, I needed a place to start. The reports said the bodies were found around the caves and trails. That could mean they moving through the area migrating north. Which means this can get a whole lot worse before this is over. Let's ask around maybe the locals know where to start."

"Trace, it's eleven p.m. no one is awake and or wants to talk to you at this time of night."

"Fine! I'll do it the hard way. Give me a map of the area with were all the bodies were found."

"The majority of the bodies were found here, here, and here."

"On the trails? Okay, what caves are in this area?

There are a few there is lion cave, Beaver Run and deathdrop cave."

"Which one has had the highest concentration of bodies over the last forty eight hours."

"Lion Cave with a group of five being attacked."

"Then that's our target."

After tracking the razorback to Lion Cave in the northern

Baltimore area, I had figured I had a long night ahead of me but I was prepared. It was around midnight when I had finished prepping for my mission. I headed out to the cave. It is well known that razorbacks have an amazing sense of smell and sight, which helps them navigate in the dark. Making this the perfect place for our little showdown to take place. Making sure there were no civilians around I stood at the entrance of the cave. Now looking back on that day I would have been more cautious when I entered the cave, and gave it more thought that there might be more than one of these monsters waiting somewhere in the darkness of the cave. Hell, I might have even considered calling for backup.

Nothing could have fully prepared me for what came next. I continued into the cave and the smell of rotting flesh and blood was in the air. I slowly walked into the cave, not a single sound, it was very dark and eerie I pressed further on into the cave. I heard something in the distance. I paused for a second and the hairs on my neck stood on end and I felt them, watching me wait for my next move. I took a few more steps and I heard bones breaking under my feet. As I took another step several large shadows started to shift back and forth. I could see their movements, they were coming.

"Brace yourself, one's attacking head on."

I tried to stand my ground but I couldn't get any firm footing, the beast took a swipe at my head with its large claws. I evaded its attack. I had stumbled upon a whole nest of rogue razorbacks. It was originally believed that the rogues preferred to live on their own away from their own kind, but no one understood why so, at the time, this had never been seen before. Imagine my surprise, being the first to discover this fact was no longer true.

Fighting one or two of these beasts was hard enough to do on the best of terrain, much less six, an impossible feat especially for someone that had only read about these things in a book. "Well, impossible for a normal guardian that is, these things must not know who they're dealing with," I thought to myself.

Have you ever wondered about, if you could go back in time, what would you change? I'm having one of those moments right now starting with my arrogance. The battle before me was like uncharted territory that no one wanted to chart.

"Let's do this! Bring it on demon Furby's!" And yes, Minerva had a battle cry. The fight I had been waiting for had begun and before I could draw my sword one more charged knocking me off balance. And, as if on cue, the first one attacked again. There was no time to dodge, I could only try to block as much damage as possible. The beast rammed me head-on, throwing me several feet away. With my guard down, the second one came from behind and I couldn't turn fast enough and it cut me across my back with its large claws. Blood poured out of the wound, which only increased their bloodlust. These things moved as one, where one failed the others did not.

Knowing that I only had a small amount of time before the venom set in, I tried to focus on healing and slowing it down.

It was at this point in time where I started to have one of those feelings, you know one of those good in theory and bad in practice moments, I could feel the venom slowly creeping through my body. I needed to act, but my body wouldn't move. Trying to remember something to help me keep calm, but nothing came up. Then I heard a voice, and at first, I couldn't make out what it was saying, it was saying, "Minerva, is that you?"

"Is that me what?"

"What are you waiting for a fightback already?" That eerie voice echoed in my head I'd heard this voice before.

I remembered this voice this feeling, the numbness that creeps down your spine it was like that time with the assassins.

"Trace! Focus, the venom is making you hallucinate. Have you forgotten everything the codex said about fighting razorbacks? You need to think, use your combat awareness. I can help you I know their weaknesses."

"Minerva, shut up for two seconds!" I had no control of my body and I was trying to focus on the voice. Was it just a hallucination? Then I heard the voice again

"Don't let these things push you around, you are a Custodes not some defenseless pup. These beasts are nothing, stand up and fight back because if you don't stop these beasts here and now more innocent people will die. YOU WILL DIE! So get up and fight for them, you're a guardian, right? Protecting people, saving lives is what you do." And just like that the pain and fear went away; I could move once more.

"Minerva, I have a plan but I need some space."

"Oh, do I have permission to speak now?"

"Now is not the time for this. It's still hard to keep up with all of them at the speed they're moving. I need you to be the eyes on the back of my head."

The most important tactic to remember when fighting a

razorback is to render their heightened senses useless, the easiest ones to go after would be their sense of smell and their sensitivity to light.

I looked around but there was no light to be found, the beasts had stopped attacking and they knew this fight was pretty much over. With no other options, I reached for my sword and the voice said, "Concentrate and try to focus all your energy into your sword. Then repeat after me: *turbine ignis flammae!*" echoed throughout the cave. A tornado of fire erupted from my blade high into the air. It wasn't the light I was looking for but it did the job. Blinded by the light from the flames the razorback retreated a few steps giving some room to breathe. "Good," I heard the voice say. "They have backed off now we need to go on the offensive. I don't have much power to spare but I can give you just enough to beat them."

"Then I'll have to do my best with what you give me. I'm not going to get another chance at this especially with their venom inside of me."

The razorbacks went into a frenzy. I clenched my sword focusing all the energy I had into it ready to unleash the torrent of flames upon them. All of the razorbacks jumped into the air trying to avoid the flames. But their lack of sight caused three of them to crash into each other and fall back to the ground in front of me. The others managed to dig their claws into the ceiling of the cave and keep their distance. I guess I'd take the three stooges on first. I dashed to the first three as they started to get up. I sliced the first one down the middle and it burst into flames. The other two tried to scramble away. I waved my sword at them and the tornado of flame consumed them. *Rawr*

rawr. The beast cried out as they burned to ash. The other three let out these huge roars.

"Oh did I upset you? How about you come back down here and do something about it, you oversized porcupines?" As if they understood my challenge, one after the other they dropped from the ceiling and rose from the shadows. With the flames growing behind me they all began to approach from the front. With all of them gathering so closely I could wipe the rest of them out all at once. No more holding back, it was time to let it all out. I focused solely on the flames.

"Feel the heat emanating from within you and your sword. This is your true power. I cannot hold on any longer, end this now."

"Right!" With my vision starting to get hazy I raised my blade one last time and let out a huge firestorm that took the shape of a great wolf. As the flames engulfed the beast all I could hear was their howling in pain as the fire washed over them. The sounds quickly faded and they all turned to ash, the only thing left to do was to clean up the mess and ge... *Thud.* Before I even finished my sentence the venom had taken effect.

"You dead yet, boy? How much more of a beating do I have to give you? Why won't you break."

Thump thump, thump thump. "Wake up, Trace!"

Hours had passed when I came to; I stumbled out of the caves and through the darkness. As I limped through the woods I saw a small house with a white fence and green grass. It was like something out of a movie, I thought to myself that this couldn't be real I must be hallucinating. I walked through the fence and walked up to the door, as I went to knock I collapsed again and the door opened. I saw a large shadow surrounded by light, was this the light they speak of, was this the end? Right before I passed out I heard a voice and it said, "What do we have here?"

Chapter 5
Friend or Foe

I felt like I was hit with a ton of bricks.

"You're up! Finally. Aiyanna has been calling nonstop, and I have been stalling for hours. You need to call her."

"I will, but first I need to figure out where I am."

"Well, you're in a cabin in the woods. You know kinda like that one movie about teens in a cabin in the woods. I can't seem to recall the name though."

"Hey, Minerva?"

"Yes, Trace?"

"Can you focus please? Your ADHD is acting up again."

"Shut up, dummy, AIs don't have ADHD."

"Yeah but they also aren't sarcastic dicks that state the obvious either."

"Touche."

I looked around the room for any clues about this place and the thing that lived there. A very nature-centric room, everything looked like a tree or a tree byproduct. The bed was stuffed with leaves, the blinds were made from vines. The walls were made of logs and who decorates with moss? There was moss and dandelions everywhere.

"We're in the house of a serial killer. One that murders their victims with allergies."

Knock, Knock.

"Hello, child are you awake in there, may I come in?" It was the woman's voice from before.

"Crap, the murderer's at the door, what do I do? Minerva, what do I do?"

"I don't know, be murdered I guess."

"Minerva, I really try my best with you and you give me nothing."

"Fine, clearly whoever brought you here doesn't mean you any harm, they brought you back into their home and gave you a place to rest so I'd say you're safe."

"Wow, that was surprisingly insightful."

"Or I could be lying and they corrupted my data and you are about to be devoured by a golem and its master."

"Annnddd there it is. Can you not be serious for two minutes?"

"Can your face not suck a butt?"

"What does that even mean?"

"It means you're a butt sucker, you butt sucker."

"I hate you."

"Is everything okay in there?"

"Yes, ma'am. Sorry, you can come in now."

"Good to see you finally awake. You gave us quite the scare. A child can get hurt in the woods alone. I'm glad we stumbled upon you when we did. We saw the claw marks and blood on your clothing and thought you were hurt. I had Thain carry you to the bed, he thought you were some homeless kid raised by wolves. Ha ha ha ha, but that only happens in the movies?"

"Riiiiight, only in the movies."

"Would you like to join us for something to eat and maybe

you can tell us how you ended up outside my home?"

"Sure, but if you don't mind me asking, where am I?"

"Follow me and I will explain everything while we eat."

We head down this long hallway with green carpet with leaves on it and the walls are covered with paintings of nature. I follow the woman to the dining room table covered from end to end with food.

"Please sit, my child. Once Thain gets in here we will explain everything. Are you hungry please feel free to start eating."

"Yes and thank you." The food looked amazing. They had steak, pork chops, mashed potatoes, corn on the cob, macaroni and they even had pie. As I went to load up my plate and take a bite, a very large stone-like man walked in and sat at the table.

"Looks like the little hobo is awake, how are you feeling?"

"I'm fine, sir, not to sound ungrateful, but maybe you can tell me who you two are and where I am?"

"Oh right, where are my manners? It's been too long since we had guests. I'm Celeste and the boulder of a man is Thain. What's your name?"

"I, um, Trace. My name is Trace."

"You don't need to lie, kid, you can trust us."

"I'm not lying, and what's wrong with my name?"

"Oh, how unfortunate. Your wolf parents couldn't come up with something better."

"Thain, don't be rude to our guest. I apologize, sweetie, Thain has the filter of a bucket riddled with holes, Trace is a wonderful name, dear. Apologize to the boy, Thain."

"Yes, madam, my apologies for making fun of such a silly name, little vagrant friend. Why not Woof or Bark maybe even Grrrr."

"Thain!"

"It's not a big deal, Ms. Celeste, I have been called way worse."

"I couldn't imagine why anyone would call such an adorable child anything other than that."

"Well, honestly look at my clothes, clearly someone doesn't like me."

"Speaking of which, how did your clothes end up like that?"

"Isn't it obvious? My clothes were mauled by a bear and that 'blood' you saw was raspberry jam which attracted the bear to begin with."

"That was impressively cunning for a child."

"Ouch. Sarcasm hurts too you know."

"Don't waste your time lying to me, Trace, I know the smell of blood well and I have seen the claws marks of many beasts. I know for a fact that those marks are from no bear. They belong to a creature far more deadly and spikey. I say again, how did you end up in your situation, child?"

"I could tell you the truth but you wouldn't believe me anyway and why do you know what blood smells like?"

"Answering a question with a question. Madam, I think he's trying to deflect to avoid answering the question."

"I can see that, Thain. Maybe it's a trust issue. You don't know who we are or what we are so it's natural to be guarded. How about I share a few things about us and you can share as you like."

"That's fair."

"I've already told you my name but allow me to tell you who I am. I am Celeste the witch of the wilds. I have lived for many years roaming the world with my companions and creations like Thain. We are also aware of the 'animal attacks' or should I say razorback attacks that have been happening in the area. What I really want to know is who you are and how did you manage to defeat those beasts? I've never met a human capable of keeping up with their speed. Especially after getting a dose of their venom. I also don't know of any humans that have ever recovered from it without the antidote. Their venom is strong enough to kill six adult elephants. What I'm getting at is that I know you aren't human. But I can't quite figure out what you are."

"That's, uh, pretty straight forward."

"Well, it's better to be up front how else would you trust me?"

"I'll answer your questions but I will have a few of my own. What do you mean Thain is your creation? If you knew about the attacks why didn't you do anything about them?"

"Simple enough, fighting monsters isn't my job anymore and what I mean by my creation, that is just as simple. Thain is a golem made of stone to resemble a man, his sole purpose is to help me with the day-to-day chores and to keep me company."

"Okay, can I see proof that you are a witch? You could be a crazy lady calling herself a witch." She waved her hand and a finely detailed staff with a gem in the center of it appeared in her hand.

"I take it you are satisfied with your answers. How about you answer mine?"

"I'm a monster hunter, but only the bad ones that hurt people. My partners and myself find them, track them down, and kill them. I was hired to find those razorbacks and kill them."

"What about the blood and the claw marks, clearly they attacked you but there isn't a single scratch on you? There aren't many creatures that can heal that fast and the amount of them that are humanoid are even fewer. Makes me curious about what you are. You're not a warlock or a vampire, that's for sure. Maybe some type of shifter; a werewolf. How about a demon? They heal pretty fast. Is that it, kid? You a demon?"

"No, I am not a vile demon how dare you even suggest it."

"It seems you struck a nerve there, madam."

"Seems like it."

"I'm a demigod of a sort. A kind of guardian if you will."

"Not possible."

"What do you mean not possible? How else would you rationalize my healing and being able to fight all those monsters?"

"It's not possible because most, if not all, of the demigods died off years ago at the hands of devils. The ones that didn't went into hiding. And the Olympians, Æsir, Roman, Egyptian, Yoruba Orisha, Aztec and all the others shut their gates and haven't been heard from for a hundred years. Who were your parents?"

"Aries and a demon hunter."

"What was her name? Maybe I've heard of her."

"Wanda. Wanda Maximoff."

"Never heard of her."

"You may know her as the scarlet witch."

"Nope. Let's say you're telling the truth for even a second. Why would you tell me? I could have a grudge against your kind or be on the side of the demons?"

"I'm a pretty good judge of character and I can sense that you two are good people. Well one of you is, and I don't sense that you have any intention to harm me even after I told you what I was. Am I wrong?"

"You're an interesting kid, you know that? You're right but that was a bold move. I'm glad to see that the rumors weren't true, a world without people like you, the world would plunge into chaos. Are you the only one?"

"Yes, my mother escaped with me but she was injured."

"Escaped you say?"

"Yes, it is like you said some people hold grudges against the gods especially the ones of Olympus and would love to take it out on them. But since they can't, their kids will do. My mother and I originally left from Greece and were headed to Eden for safety but the demons attacked us on the way there. My mother was wounded as we fled during the assault. We were given shelter by allies but the wounds she sustained were too much to heal from and she died a few months later. I was given to a family for safekeeping until I was able to defend myself and now I hunt monsters."

"Hmph. Interesting. I am impressed, kid."

"Impressed with what?"

"I'm impressed with how fast you came up with that story."

"What do you mean? What story?"

"I know you're not a demigod and that you're not the son of Aries and your mother isn't the great scarlet witch."

"It was the Aries thing wasn't it? I should have said Hermes. No one cares about him."

"Among other things but I'm not going to press the matter. If you put the effort into hiding who you truly are I have trust it is for a reason. Either that or you don't know yourself. I will respect that for now."

"Do you know what I am then?"

"I have my ideas but again there's no need to go into that now. For right now I'm fine with you being Trace son of Aries."

"Really?"

"Yeah really. I don't really have much interest in prying nowadays. Your past is your own and You'll share as you please. It is a fortunate surprise to see someone of your kind out this way. I am glad you are safe. The world needs hunters, maybe you can fix what has been broken. My dear child you have a lot ahead of you. Since you are a hunter I'm sure you have heard of what has been happening all over the world. Ever since Eden was invaded the creatures of this world have become bolder. Attacking humans in broad daylight, migrating to areas they don't belong, possessing humans and causing massacres. The legends of the Custodes used to keep them in line, if this were a few hundred years ago monsters wouldn't have broadcasted their attacks. Things wouldn't be as messy as they are now. I miss the peaceful days, and the balance of powers. But after Vestigium passed there was only a power vacuum waiting to be filled. His loss was something they never truly recovered from and yet they used him; the love, the fear, the name, his very essence and the respect, they so desperately held on to that was no longer theirs. Maybe it was the arrogance that didn't allow people to see the changes coming, without him war was inevitable. The king and queen of Eden knew this was coming and should have been better prepared. They shouldn't have depended on the legend. But it wasn't just them, it was the covenants and other allies that were caught off guard. The vampires and werewolves reignited their civil wars. Some want to rule over humanity as gods and others just want to want to coexist. You also have the gnomes fighting dwarves, orcs fighting the elves the blood feuds never end. Don't even get me started on the humans, they are too busy fighting themselves and starting more civil wars across the world than all of the other factions combined. But they have only made the same mistakes all the others have before them. They are young, foolish and oblivious to the creatures around them. Sometimes I wonder how it all would have turned out if the Custodes never stepped in the first time. If the world hadn't become so dependent on them. Would they have gone to war sooner? Would they have been ready for the coups?"

"Coups? What coups? What are you talking about? The attacks on Eden were out of nowhere. The king and queen had no idea that a war was going to break out. To say they knew and stood by and let it happen, how dare you insinuate such a thing."

"Think about it, my dear boy and it'll all make sense. In the world of politics there really is no blindsiding. Their alliances were failing, their army weakening, becoming complacent and the amount of supernatural occurrences near

Eden and all over the world had been increasing over the years with a huge spike happening a few months before the invasion."

"The attack in Eden was just one of many, my child. There were other assassination attempts on the other mythicon Leadership. With the world still in shock from Eden, others enacted coups. Several disappearances happened around that time leading up to and after that day. Replacing the leaders with power-hungry simpletons with no idea how to wipe their own ass let alone lead an entire people. Which has caused more chaos for everyone? The war of beasts is raging on but this time demons are at the helm of it. Pushing all the right buttons and whispering in the ears of fools. They tell them what they want to hear and they are gullible enough to believe them. The devils are only out for themselves and always have been. But no one knows what they truly want. They could be after the souls of the fallen and trying to gain strength. Or they just want chaos and the world to end."

"That can't be it. While they are demons, they realize if the world were to end it would only hurt them. And chaos for chaos' sake is more of the style of a singular demon or a very small group. But by the organization of their attacks this group is very large and has a much more nefarious plan in play.

"Right now no one can say. But someone has to stop them and sorry to thrust this upon you in this way but that responsibility falls to you."

"This can't be true! How could you know all of this? What are your sources?"

"I have had my ear to the ground and unlike the rest of the world I actually listened. The demons have been out recruiting for years. The Custodes had nearly as many enemies as they did allies. I just wish that they had been more aware. They could have prevented all of this."

"No. It can't be possible. The royal family is strong, caring and they are loved by everyone. No one would have dared to go against them."

"You are very naive, there are tons of creatures that preferred the old ways of the world. The time where vampires could feed and leave bodies littered throughout the hold."

"The time when humans made offerings to beasts for protection or when humanity worshipped them as gods. I'm sure your father could tell you a thing or two about that."

"My father? Oh, right, Aries. Yeah, he'd know all about it. Many wars were waged in his name."

"As could be said for most of the gods. They fed off the hate, the love and the prayers of their followings. But the Custodes stopped all that, or rather Vestigium did, even when he lost the support of everyone, he held on to his goal of uniting the species. The Olympians much like a lot of the others lost a great deal of power and control when that happened. They saw it as an act of treason against them but all Ves ever wanted was equality and he died to get it. He was a great man with a noble vision."

"You speak so highly of him and in such a personal tone, you two were close then?"

"We fought side by side in many a battle, I respected him."

"If you respected him then why didn't you help his people? Why didn't you try to warn them? Why would you allow his family to be slaughtered?"

"Don't you think I tried? I sent warning after warning but

there was no saving them because they did not want to see the truth. The skeletons in their closets are many. If you don't believe me I am sure you have sources that can verify what I have told you. But, Trace, I do warn you that delving into that ocean isn't one to do lightly."

"I refuse. I refuse to believe that everything that went wrong with the world started because of what happened on Eden. I don't believe that it was because the royal family was too blind to see the truth in front of them. I can't believe that their own hubris caused the downfall of our army. It just doesn't make sense."

"I am sorry to be the one to tell you this, child, but it is true. And I am even more sorry for what I have to tell you next. Since the Custodes are gone, no one can restore balance to the world. Without the guardians there will never be peace. The world will fall into chaos."

"Then I'll do it!"

"You really think you alone stand a chance where they failed?"

"Yeah, why not? I'm just as tough as they are!"

"You might be right. Or you could be wrong. You being who and what you are. There may be a chance. You have huge shoes to fill and if you accept that task. You won't be able to as you are now. You are too frail and weak to do it now. But I have a feeling you already knew that already, your soul reeks with doubt. Deep down."

"Maybe, I can't. But it's better than sitting in a cabin secluded from the world doing nothing and letting everyone else suffer for it. I need to be excused."

"It is a hard truth to accept."

"I don't and I won't". I stormed out of the house to get

some fresh air and to think.

"I need to call Mom, Minerva."

"On it." *Riiiiiiinnnng. Riiiiiiinnnnnnnggg. Riiiiiiinnnnggg. click.*

"Hello."

"Trace, what happened to you? You were supposed to check in hours ago, are you okay?"

"Yes, Mom, I'm fine."

"Are you sure? I'm coming to get you."

"No, you don't have to I'm fine, the mission went fine, I'll explain everything when I get back home."

"I was worried about you, when you went to investigate the cave I was monitoring your vitals. I saw them drop for a few minutes. But they then surged off the charts. I think there is some malfunction in your Hunter gear."

"I'm fine."

"Fine, but you better get home soon, everyone's worried about you."

"Mom, before you go, was there anything weird leading up to the attack on Eden?"

"That's a weird question. What do you mean by weird?"

"You know, like increases in supernatural occurrences. Where there any clues that there was going to be an attack?"

"Those are loaded questions."

"So, is it true then? You and Dad knew there was an attack coming?"

"Where is all of this coming from, Trace. Are you okay?"

"I do not know yet, you haven't answered any of my questions. My feeling will be determined after that."

"Trace, this is not a conversation to be had over the phone. We will talk about it when you return."

"That's always your answer. It's always later, in the

morning or when you get home."

"Trace, enough! We will talk about it when you return. I promise."

"Okay, I'll be home soon."

"Be safe, my son."

"Always. Goodbye."

"Goodbye." *Click.*

"Someone's an angsty teen today."

"Shut up, Minerva, I'm not in the mood right now. The witch might be telling the truth. I need to get home. I've rested enough."

Creak.

"Did your walk help to clear your head?"

"Not really, it just led to more questions."

"Sorry to hear that. Child, if you need any other questions answered just ask."

"As much as I'd like to stay and talk I need to head home."

"Was it what I said? That spurred this hasty decision?"

"No, it's not. I was only supposed to be gone a few days and I have reached my deadline for this job."

"Ah I see you're a busy kid with better things to do than hear an old lady dawdle with tales of the old days of peace and conspiracies."

"No, it was helpful information and thank you for helping me and looking after me while I was passed out. I'll get my stuff and head out now."

"By yourself? It's almost night time, it would far too dangerous for you to travel on your own."

"I highly doubt that this area is that dangerous. I think I'll be able to handle myself."

"Nonsense I will have Thain lead you out of here and to the nearest station. It's the least I can do for the good job you did for taking care of those beasties and the company."

"Okay then, Thain, lead the way then."

"Right this way, pup, time to find your way back to the wilds."

"Ugh. Let's just go."

Chapter 6
Runaway

Thain showed me the way out of the woods and gave me directions to the station. Before we parted ways he gave me a blank piece of parchment.

"What do I do with this?"

"When the time comes it will guide you to your destination."

"Okay? Well I appreciate it and thank you, Thain."

"Goodbye, little wolf. Stay out of bear traps. Say hi to your pack for me and howl at the moon a few times."

"I wasn't raised by wolves and I'm not a wolf, granite head. All aboard! I better get going then. Bye, Thain."

"Hi there, young traveler, what brings you to the train at this time of night?"

"I'd really rather not talk about it."

"Sure. But I do have a question for you. Trains are for runaways, kid, and you don't look like a runaway?" said the conductor.

"No, I'm heading home actually."

"Well, good for you, I'm sure your family will be happy to see you."

"Oh, I'm sure they will, I'm going to go to my seat now."

"Sure do you have a ticket?"

"Sure I do let me just get it. Crap. I lost my ticket."

"That's okay, kid, this ride's free anyway. Hop on."

"Um. Thanks."

"Enjoy your ride, young man." The train ride home had a new feeling to it, I couldn't quite describe it.

I don't know if it's the shame combined with the hatred of being weak. Or is it the feeling of loneliness and all of the new questions I need to have answered. But I don't know if anyone can. What am I supposed to do or be? Am I just a shadow of a legend? Will I be able to fix what's broken like Celeste said? Do I even belong in the same category as my grandfather. No. I never have. Everyone around me is growing so fast that I can't keep up anymore. Maybe I'm wrong and it's just in my head. I'm going crazy.

Ding. Ding. Ding. Now arriving at Bruce Crossing station next stop Land O'Lakes, Wisconsin.

"Hey, kid isn't this your stop?"

"Yeah I should probably get home."

"Not there yet but you'll get there eventually. It'll take some time but you'll find your own way."

"Okay. I'm going to go now."

"I'll see you soon, Trace."

"Sure?" Wait, I never told him my name. Hey how…

The train had already started to pull away from the station before I could ask him how he knew who I was.

That was weird. It should only take twenty minutes for me to run home.

"Trace, over here."

"Mom? What are you doing here?"

"We came to pick you up. You seemed kind of weird on the phone."

"We?"

"Me and Luna. She said she had a dream that you'd need us to be at the station at this time so here we are. What do you know she was right."

"It does save me the walk I guess. I'll have to thank her."

"She's in the car waiting so grab your bag and let's get home. This way."

"Sure. Mom?"

"Yes?"

"You remember what we were talking about on the phone before?"

"Yes and I will talk to you about it tomorrow."

"Tomorrow it is."

"Trace! You're okay. I was worried when I had a dream monsters were attacking you."

"No, I'm fine, Luna, it takes more than a few beasts to best me."

"Y'know, I've been having a lot of dreams about you lately. There was this one I had a few weeks ago about you surrounded by burned down building."

"Interesting, I haven't been around any burning buildings recently."

"By the way, Trace, who's the old lady in the woods that helped you?"

"How did you? Never mind."

"You didn't mention that you had gotten help from anyone, Trace. Who is the woman?"

"She was no one. Just a kind old lady that let me stay at her place when she found me passed out."

"Did she seem suspicious of you or ask any questions?"

"No, I told her me and some friends were making a movie for our class about werewolves. I said I had narcolepsy and fell asleep while filming. I'm sure she bought it."

"I hope so, we don't need to draw any more attention to ourselves after the church incident. I'm sure someone might have noticed a demon that powerful disappearing overnight."

"I think you're worrying too much. That demon was being hunted by other demons. No one would miss him. He's dead and gone."

"You're right. But it doesn't hurt to be more cautious and lay low for a little while."

"Yeah, you're right. That was my fault for getting caught and needing you to save me. We could have taken care of him way more quietly."

"That's not what I meant, Trace."

"It's okay, Mom. I get it."

"We made it home, big brother, everyone will be happy you're back. C'mon let's go inside."

"Trace. We will talk more about this later."

"Yes, Mother."

Creak.

"Look everyone Trace is here! I'm glad you're back big brother I have so much to tell you."

"Is that right, Willow?"

"Yeah."

"Yeah, Trace, Aster did something super manly the other day. Not nearly as manly as you but still manly."

"As descriptive as ever, Griffin. Remind me to get you an encyclopedia for your birthday."

"Pssshhh. Books aren't manly."

"Oh but they are. They can show you tons of things. They even can tell you stories about super manly men."

"Really!"

"Yeah, like your favorite heroes Hercules and Thor. Both super manly, cunning and smart. And they also read books."

"No way."

"Yeah, totally I wouldn't lie to you."

"Maybe reading can be sorta manly. If you and those other strong guys did it."

"Super manly."

"Don't you start that too, Trace, one person shouting manly all day is plenty."

"You have nothing to worry about, Caeli. Where's Aster and the others anyway?"

"The training room."

"Well, then what are we standing around here for? Let's go to the training room."

"YEEEAAAHH! Follow meeeeee."

"Why is Griffin always so loud?"

"Leave him alone, Willow, he's just excited."

"He's coming! Trace is coming. I can sense him."

"No duh, Leo, we can all sense him."

"Shut up, Hope, no one asked you."

"Trace!"

"Hi, everyone, I can see everyone is excited today. This must be big. Hey Aster! I heard a rumor something cool and manly happened while I was away. Care to show me?"

"Well, it's not that cool. Everyone is just making a big deal out of it is all."

"Aster?"

"Yeah Trace?"

"They're not this excited for no reason so show me what you got."

"Okay. Stand back then." He takes a few steps back and gets down on all fours. *Crack. Crack. Crack. Growl. Crack. Crack. Crack.* White hairs started to sprout all over Aster's body as it contorted and bent. His nose extended to a snout and claws started to grow from his hands. *Growl.* His eyes turned completely black. *Rooooaaar!*

"Aster, you can shift?" It was no longer my little brother that stood in front of me, but a large white polar bear.

"I told you, Trace! Super manly."

"Yes, Trace, Aster managed to shift the day after you left. I told him to wait to show you."

Roar. Crack. Crack. Crack.

"I'm sorry, Auntie Aiyanna. I really wanted to show him. I wanted Trace to think I was cool. What did you think, Trace?"

"It um. It was. It was super cool, little brother. I'm so proud of you."

"See, Aunty, Trace thinks it's super cool."

"At this rate you'll surpass me in no time."

"No way, Trace, you're super strong and you get to go fight monsters. I don't think I'm anywhere near your level."

"You'd be surprised. All of you have grown so much over that past year. I'm proud of all of you. You've gotten so strong so fast. Soon you guys are going to leave me behind and won't even need me anymore."

"That will never be the case, Trace, who else is going to protect us from the tree people?"

"Luna, I'm sure you guys can handle yourselves at this

point."

"But your fire magic is super strong against them."

"So was Mom's ice magic."

"But?"

"That's enough showing off for tonight, everyone. It's almost midnight and you all should have been in bed two hours ago. You guys have to get to bed."

"Yes, ma'am."

"Trace and Caeli, make sure they are in bed in twenty minutes. There's something I have to get from the workshop."

"Yes, Mother."

"All right, everyone, off to bed."

"Aye, aye, Captain Caeli."

"Trace, why are you just standing there aren't you coming?"

"I can't."

"What do you mean you can't?"

"I can't come with you guys this time."

"Oh right, you probably want to get changed first right?"

"No that's not it, Aster, he's probably hungry, he was on a train all day."

"No, Leo, that's not it either."

"Then what is it, Trace?"

"I can't. I can't come with you because—"

"Because he's leaving us."

"Ha ha ha. Very funny, Luna. C'mon, Trace, stop joking and come on."

"It's not a joke, Aster. She's right. I have to go."

Sob.

"What do mean, Trace, you can't leave."

"I'm sorry, everyone."

Sob.

"It's my fault isn't it. This is why Aunty told me not to shift."

"No, Aster it has nothing to do with that or any of you. This is all me. I have been lost for so long now. I need to find my place in this world and I need to get stronger. The way I am now I can't keep our promise we made all those years ago."

"Trace has his own path to walk, his own trials to undergo."

"Luna, what are you talking about? You knew about this?"

"Yes, Caeli, I knew this day would come. I dreamt about it. I didn't know when it would happen I just knew it would."

"Why didn't you tell me or Mom?"

"You and Mother would have tried to stop him."

"Of course, we would have. He's our brother, he can't leave us."

"He doesn't have a choice, the world needs him to go."

"But we need him more."

Sob sob.

"I know how you all feel but in my dreams I have seen what Trace becomes. The lives that depend on him outweigh us all. Could you ask him to stay knowing that?"

"Yes. Yes is what I want to say. But you're right. We can't make him stay no matter how much I want to go run to tell Mom. I can't do it."

"Trace, your path will be a long one, brother. It will take you far from here and it will be filled with hardships. Some that you may believe impossible to overcome. But you will be stronger for it."

My siblings all rush to hug me. "We don't want you to go."

Sob.

"Why can't you just stay here forever?"

Sob.

"Who am I going to do manly things with now?"

Sob.

"I'm sorry. I—"

"Don't be sorry, Trace, just promise us you'll come back to us in one piece and that you will never give up until you do."

"I promise I won't give up. I promise to get stronger. I promise to get our home back. I promise to come back to you and make you guys proud of me."

"We are proud of you already, dummy. Just go already."

"Hope!"

"What? I am proud of him and he is a dummy for not knowing that."

"What she means is we love you, Trace. Go find what you're looking for. We'll be here when you get back."

"Thank you." *Sob.* "So much. I'm going to miss you guys and I'll try to call you as often as I can. "

"We know you will and if you don't. We'll have Mom hunt you down and drag you back here."

"Ha ha ha. Fair enough. I love you. Watch each other's backs. Caeli you are the most caring and selfless person I know. You see the good in every living thing, look after these degenerates. Aster, you've always followed in my footsteps and just like I have to find my path I know you'll make your own. Hope, you are the most stubborn and blunt person I have ever met. Never change for anyone because honesty will always be hard to come by. Griffin, please take some time to read a book and learn at least six other words for manly by the time I get back. Jokes aside, Griffin, you are bold but know this, there is a time to fight and a time to withdraw. Sometimes the best option is to retreat. Willow, you've always been the quiet one, don't be afraid to make your voice heard. Little Leo, you are bigger than you think, size means nothing if you don't have the skill to back it up. You are a lion, never forget that. Last but not least, Luna, you are so special and wise beyond your years. I wish I could see the world as you do. One day everyone will look to you for the answer and I am sure you will be there taking a nap and when you wake you'll have a story to tell. You seven are the best brothers and sisters I could ever ask for. I wouldn't change that for all the power in the world. Goodbye everyone. I will see you again and when I do I'll have stories to tell and I'll be strong enough to take back what's ours."

"Bye, Trace, we'll miss you!"

As I walk down the hallway and out the front door I hear Caeli say, "All right guys time for bed."

Creak. I could just imagine them groaning and sighing. "Aw do we have to." Every night it was the same thing. First the pouting then the excuses and the buts, I'm gonna miss all of it. *Wumpth.*

"So that's it you're just going to leave? Just like that. Without saying goodbye?"

"Yeah. That was kinda the plan. Not that it would even matter you won't even notice I'm gone."

"You can't be serious? You can't mean any of that."

"I can't take it anymore. I don't belong here with you or them. I don't deserve to even be a part of this family. I am nothing more than a ghost."

"Stop it. Stop it right now."

"Stop what? Telling the truth? Everyone can see that I—"
Smack.

"Vestigium Titanos Rgis. How dare you think any of that much less say it. Not a single word of it is true."

"It's okay I get it and I understand. I know it's hard to admit. You'll be happier this way, everyone will be."

"No, Trace. I won't be, none of us will. I don't like seeing you like this. And I'm not just talking physically, but mentally as well. I don't want to ever see my child broken and beaten; I wish I had never taken you with me. I wish I had gotten there sooner. I wish you didn't have to go through that. I know you are suffering, and I know you feel alone but you're not. I am by your side and I will do everything possible to help you grow."

"You can't help me anymore, I can't do this as I am now. I'm tired of losing or winning by the skin of my teeth. How can I ever fulfill my promise if I can't even defend myself. I'm a mistake, a broken guardian that shouldn't exist. My name is a mockery of what I can never be. I will never leave my grandfather's shadow."

"Trace, I have tried my best to help you over the years, I've tried to be nurturing, to give you everything you needed and even let you change your name to make you more comfortable. All of us have been trying to help you carry that weight and I am so sorry for ever putting that on you. You are not a mistake, you are my son. You mean the world to me. I just want you to be happy, how can I do that? I would go to the ends of the earth for you and your siblings. What do I have to do?"

"Stand aside and let me go. If I succeed I'll come back to you. Better than I am now, stronger than I am now."

"If not?"

"Then I don't deserve to be a part of this family and I won't return."

"How could you ask me to do that?"

"Because one way or another I'm leaving. I have to do something other than sit around. Being here, I'm stagnant. I will not resign to my fate, I would rather die than continue with this. I won't get stronger here. I would appreciate having your approval on this."

"You can't ask me to just let you go off and not know when or if you'll ever come back. What about your sisters and brothers? You'd just desert them?"

"They already know and they don't like it anymore than you do but they understand. I've already said my goodbyes to them."

"Okay, I have faith in you. But I have one condition if you want my blessing. Promise me that when we meet again, no matter how long it takes, that you will find what drives you and make your own way. Don't be me, don't be your father or your grandfather. Don't let our problems be yours, Trace."

"I promise."

"Two more things. For the record I didn't name you Vestigium because I wanted you to be him. I named you that because I knew you were destined for greatness like him. I love you, my son, you are a guardian in every way possible."

"I love you too, Mother and goodbye for now."

"Trace, before you go. I want to give you something. I have been working on it for quite some time now." My mother reached out her hand and gave me a small cube.

"What is it?"

"It's a guardian suit. Like mine. When you are ready just channel your energy into it and it will transform around you. Usually, I'd be giving it to you once you turned eighteen, as is tradition."

"Thank you, Mom. This means a lot."

"Thank your sister. Luna had said she had a feeling you'd need it sooner rather than later. And with her gift she is rarely wrong."

"Thank you. I really appreciate it."

I hugged my mother one last time, it was a different feeling this. Not like leaving for a hunt or a simple farewell. It felt like the end of one chapter and the beginning of something greater. I started walking through the forest and I pulled out the paper that Thain gave me. "Okay, paper, do your stuff. Show me what I need to see." I waited for a few seconds and nothing. "What the hell? Is this thing broken? Minerva?"

"Yes, Trace?"

"Would you know how this works?"

"Scans show it's a magical item so you could try a magic word or incantation."

"Okay let's see. Abra-kadabra, ala-kazam." Nothing. "You have anything, Minerva?"

"Ummm. *Ignis*!" Nothing. "Darn I really was hoping that would work."

"Why would that have worked on the paper? And why

would it work when you say it?"

"Ooooh, you meant the paper. Hahahahaha, I thought you were talking about your sword. For a second I thought you forgot how to use it."

"How are you an A.I.?"

"I'll show you, that parchment you have just needs you to channel your energy into it."

"That's it?"

"Yeah, genius. It's super simple."

"I can give it a shot but that's never been my strong suit."

"Focus, focus, fo-cus. FOCUS!"

"Jesus, Minerva, stop yelling I can't concentrate."

"Whoops, sorry just trying to help you focus."

"I appreciate it but I need some quiet."

"Focus," she whispers one more time. I poured a small amount of energy into the parchment and the once blank piece of paper revealed a location. You've got to be kidding.

"Hey, isn't that the—"

"The old lady's house? Yeah, yeah it is. If all this thing did was lead me back to her she could have just said that. I guess we're going back to Maryland, to the train station we go."

I made my way back down to the station, the same conductor was there waiting for me.

"Oh, you're back, young traveler? Running away again?"

"No, well, yes I guess. Is it running away if your parent knows you left?"

"Do you plan on going back home?"

"Eventually, maybe."

"Then no that doesn't count, that's more of a field trip. Where are you off to this time?"

"Back to where you found me last time I guess. By the way, why are you so interested in me? Why so many questions? And how do you know my name?"

"Just curious about your story. So many people get on and off this train every day, from different walks of life. They always seem to be running away from something. Most never say a word and go about their way. I often wonder where they are off to or what their life is like. You, you're different, I feel like you're not running away but running to something. Something special."

"You could say that I guess. I'm trying to find what and who I'm supposed to be. What drives me and gives me strength? What is the plan for my existence?"

"That's some deep stuff for a kid to think about."

"Well, I'm not a normal kid, I have goals. Big ones."

"I can see that much."

"Thanks, I guess."

"You are very welcome, young man. You should get to your seat; the train is taking off."

"It was nice talking to you, sir."

"You as well."

I arrived in Maryland but before I disembarked, I waved bye to the conductor and he shouted, "Your mother was right to put her faith in you, you're going to go far, Trace, I can sense it. You'll definitely surpass him."

"Wait, how do you know about that? What kind of conductor are you?"

"I'm not a conductor, kid, I just like trains. Farewell, I look forward to seeing how your story plays out in real time."

The train takes off again before I can ask another question.

"What a weirdo? That guy's totally a predator, watch your back, Trace."

"Thanks, Minerva. Off to the old lady's house, just got to follow the map." An hour later and we made it. I don't remember the walk taking this long when I was with Thaine.

"Yeah it does seem to be further, it looks like we're almost there. Should be around here somewhere."

After walking for another fifteen minutes I still had not found the witches house.

"None of this looks even remotely familiar. The Map says it should be here but I don't see it."

"Maybe you're reading it wrong?"

"It's a magic map I don't think anyone can read them wrong. Maybe the place is cloaked?"

"Like the letter?"

"Yeah, can you scan for the witch?"

"Sure, scanning, scanning…. Nothing. Maybe I can find the rock man? Scanning, scanning."

"Why do you do that?"

"Do what?"

"Narrate the things I ask you to do?"

"Do you not like it?"

"Not in the slightest. It's weird."

"You're weird."

As me and Minerva argued over who was weird the home of the witch had appeared in front of me.

Let's see what's in store for us this time. *Knock. Knock. Knock. Creak.*

"Hey, Madam Celeste, the little hobo is back." I would take offense to that but I am kinda homeless right now.

"Thain, invite the boy in."

"Yes, Madam, come this way hobo. M'lady is in the den.

"I knew you'd come back."

"How could you not? Your rock puppet over there gave me a map that leads to you."

"No it doesn't, silly," she said laughing. "It takes you where you need to be, that's the magic of it. I had no idea it would lead you back to me."

"Suuuuurrree you didn't. Okay, now that I'm here, can you help me? I need to get stronger so I can stop getting my butt kicked."

"Why?"

"Why what?"

"Why do you want to be stronger?"

"Well, because I need to."

"Need or want?"

"Both I guess."

"I can't help you."

"What? Why not?"

"Because you're not being honest with yourself."

"I am too."

"No, you're not. If you were simply seeking strength because you don't like losing fights there isn't much I can do for you. So, I say again, why do you seek power?"

"Because I, uuuuuh…"

"If you can't admit it to yourself then you can never grow as a person much less stronger."

"Okay, I want to grow stronger because ever since I was born I have been a burden. I'm supposed to be a hero that people look up to like my father and grandfather. I want power to protect the people I care about and so I can save the world and junk. Happy?"

"It's a start. For this to work I will have to look deep inside your soul."

"Okay and how do you do that?"

"You have to lay down and I have to cast a spell on you. The spell will show me your innermost desires and from there I will find out how to pull out your true potential."

"Is it going to hurt?"

"Only if you were lying about your reason for seeking power or who you truly are."

"What?"

"The spell looks into your heart and if you can't be honest with yourself this spell will cause excruciating pain. You may also lose the power you do have. You may become a vegetable and never wake up again. Are you ready?"

"Why does that sound familiar?"

"If you need time to think—"

"No, I'm ready now."

"Okay then, my child, lay down on this couch. Thain, get the straps, make sure to hold him in place. The last thing we need is for him to thrust around and hurt himself."

"Yes, Madam Celeste."

"What are the straps for?"

"They are enchanted and they limit one's powers and help prevent soul-severing during the spell."

"So without these I would loss my powers or soul?"

"No, these only help lower your chance of that happening."

"By how much?"

"Um, how about we discuss that after? Okay, Thain are you ready?"

"I mean I could use some water, maybe a snack."

"Thain!"

"Yes, ma'am. I am ready."

"Trace, are you ready?"

"Yes, I am."

"Okay let the blood sacrifice begin. Mwahahahahahahahah…! What? Nothing? I get no reaction from that?"

"Not really, no."

"Wow, and I thought Thain was the stone man. Let's start. *Somnus!* Sleep my child. Listen to the sound of my voice, as you drift off, let it guide you. We will reach deep into your soul and find your power." My eyes started to get so heavy, I couldn't keep them from closing. "Tell me what you see and feel."

"Darkness. Pitch black darkness is all I see and I feel an emptiness."

"Hmm, that is odd."

"What's odd?"

"Your inner world shouldn't be pitch black. Nor should it be empty. This will be more difficult than I thought. I'm sensing a weird energy within you."

"Wait, I see something! Off in the distance, I see what looks like a small fire, fading in and out."

"Wait, don't go to it."

"What do you mean it's just a fire, I'm immune to it." As I reached it the fire turned black and exploded into a raging flame and a demonic hand reached out and grabbed me.

"You are weak, boy, and your soul belongs to me."

"What is this? It burns."

"Trace you need to get away from the fire."

But I couldn't move. The fire was spreading toward me and up my body. "AHHHHHHH! IT BUUUURRRNNSS!"

"Oh God, I'm pulling you out. *Expergisci!* Awaken my child. Come back to us."

"SOMEONE HELP ME IT BURNS!"

"Madam, its not working."

"Dimittere! Release him dark one! Thain, I'll have to send you in with him."

"Yes, madam."

"*Somnus!*"

"Let him go, monstrosity. The Lady wants her vagabond back this instant." I felt Thain's hand on my back pulling me out of the fire.

"Return to me child. *Redi!*"

"It burns so much, please help me!"

"Come to me."

An elegant staff appeared out of nowhere. "***Aquarum Calentium Exundatio!***" Glowing green water flowed from the staff and covered my entire body.

"There are burns to seventy five percent of your body. These waters will help heal the damage and negate some of the pain. Rest, child, let the waves wash over you."

As I began fading in and out of consciousness, I could only hear bits and pieces of the conversation. "Madam, that thing, that monster inside the boy's soul. What is it?"

"A demon has left its mark on this child and tainted his soul."

"Can you get rid of it?"

"No."

"So what will happen to him?"

"The darkness will consume him." The pain finally started to pass and the world faded to black and I was able to sleep. "Your soul belongs to me," and "the darkness will consume him," echoed in my mind. It got louder and louder.

"No! I won't lose to you demon, stay out of my head! Stay out!"

"Wake up, Trace! Wake up!"

"What? Where am I? You're in the hotel you're here with me, silly."

"Mother?"

"I think you've rested long enough, don't you? Get up, and get moving sleepy head. We have to get to the hospital remember? Harold and Max, this ringing any bells?"

"Oh, right sorry, I'll get ready. You know, I had the weirdest dream last night. There was this huge fire and—"

"Trace we don't have time for dreams, let's go."

"Okay, jeez what's got you in a rush."

"Sorry, just excited to get started I guess."

"I can see that, I'm ready to go."

"Great! Time to move out." We headed out of the hotel and made our way to the hospital. So who do we approach first? Harold or Max? "Hmm. How about you talk to the old man, Trace, and I'll talk to Max."

"Don't you think that's a little weird?"

"What's weird about that?"

"A kid going to see some old man and you a random woman going to see a high school kid?"

"Why would that be weird? I could be a concerned teacher checking on her student. And you are the old man's grandson."

"Okay? There is a small problem with that besides the obvious we don't look alike and are two completely different races. What about his wife?"

"What about her?"

"Don't you think—"

"Trace, that's enough. As your mother, I don't appreciate you questioning me. Do as you're told."

"Yes, ma'am." She's bossier than usual. I went to the counter to speak with the nurse. "Excuse me, ma'am?"

"How may I help you, young man?"

"I'm looking for my grandfather, Harold. You know the one that attacked those teens on that farm?"

"Yes, Harold is on the third floor, room 318. You can take the elevator, just follow this counter and it will be on your left."

"Okay, thanks." I made my way to the elevator.

"Going up." I can't believe that worked, this will be easier than I thought.

"Third floor, please exit the elevator." Okay, which way is 318? I look at the sign on the wall that says 300–310 to the left and 311–320 to the right. Right it is.

As I start walking down the hallway it just dawns on me, won't there be a cop at Harold's door? He did just murder a bunch of people. How will I get past the officer? I stop at the corner of the nurses station and look around. Weird, no police in sight. Maybe they don't see him as much of a threat? I walk up to 318 and I reach for the door. *Boooooooommm!*

"Your soul belongs to me!" A torrent of hell fire explodes

102

from the door sending me back on my ass.

"Hey are you okay, kid?"

I turn to look at the voice and say, "The fire, we need to get everyone out of here."

"What fire? Did you fall and hit your head?" I turned back around and the fire was gone.

"Do you need help?"

"No! No, I'm good." I got back to my feet and walked back to 318. I knocked on the door. "Come in," I hear from the other side of the door. "Oh hello, my dear boy, it's been too long. Harold wake up. Our grandson is here."

"Hmmmm, huh, what? Trace, my boy, is that you? It's been ages. How have you been?" What did I just step into? Why do they think I'm their grandson? How do they know my name? I guess I'll have to play along if I want any info. "Well what are you waiting for? Come give Grandma and Grandpa a hug."

"Sorry, I was just taken back because it's been so long since I last saw you two."

"You've gotten so big," Harold and Margret said as they embraced me.

"Yeah, been eating my vegetables so I could get big and strong just like you, Grandpa."

"I can definitely see that, you look like you could bench press a car."

"Speaking of strength, Grandpa, I saw the news that said you got into an altercation with some high school kids?"

"That I did, they tried to mug me on the way home and I gave them what for."

"Wow! you took on nine people more then half your age.

How?"

"My time as a marine may have been years ago but the training stuck with me. I remember the days in the hot Texas heat and drill sergeant Payne yelling in our ears. He was right, the muscle memory would be with us for the rest of our lives."

"That's my Harold showing them what's what."

"So, you defended yourself, but how did they all die? The news said you killed all of them except for one of the teens."

"Oh, I don't know, after the fight they were alive and I left."

"Then a few hours later, the police showed at our house saying I killed them and they shot me. Then I woke up here."

"Hmm, doesn't that seem weird to you?"

"Okay, that's enough questions for now. Grandpa needs his rest, Trace. How about I give you the key to our place and you can wait for me there?"

"Okay." Margret digs around in her pockets for a key. "Oh no! I seemed to have misplaced my keys. Maybe they're in my purse."

"And where's your purse?"

"Oh, seems like I misplaced that too."

"Where did you last have it? Retrace your steps."

"Well, after Harold was shot I came to the hospital with him. They weren't sure he was going to make it so I went to see the pastor so he could pray for him. Then I came back here."

"So your purse is most likely in the church?"

"It could be. I'll look around the hospital and you can go check the church."

"I can do that, I'll call you if I find them. I'll head over there now." I shut the door behind me and started to leave the hospital. Maybe I should tell my mom I'm going to the church. What if she's still talking to Max? I won't interrupt her, I'll just go to the church and come right back. "Minerva? Can you message Mom and tell her where I'm going?"

"Will do, sir."

"Sir? When did you get so formal, Minerva?"

"My apologies, how would you prefer me to address you?"

"Never mind that's not important. Let's just get over to the church, it's not that far of a walk from here. Minerva? Does this situation seem a little weird to you?"

"What do you mean, Trace?"

"Harold and Margret? They addressed me as their grandson, the fight, and the murders. Something's off here?"

"They are old, and old people can have memory issues and if you combine that with poor vision then you have the answer for the mistaken identity."

"And what about the fighting?"

"PTSD. Harold said he was a marine in his youth so maybe he had a flashback and it gave him the strength to fight those football players."

"And the murders?"

"There is clearly a serial killer roaming around town and he happened across the teens as they were recovering from their fight with Harold and killed them."

"That all seems like a stretch and one huge coincidence. Harold couldn't possibly have bad vision or memory; he talked about his training with sergeant Payne in Texas like it was yesterday. And unless he was daredevil a man with poor vision wouldn't have stood a chance in a one on one fight let alone a nine on one. Something is definitely weird here."

"We have arrived at the church, Trace. You should go find the old lady's purse. That way we can search the house."

"Yeah, sure let's get back on track."

"This looks familiar. Why is this place so empty? I'm sure someone has a prayer or two to say today. Oh well. Since the place is deserted, let's look for that purse."

"So what does the purse look like?"

"Uuummm. That's a good question, Margret didn't say. It can't be that hard to find. I doubt that many people forget their purses in a church. I'll check the pews." Fifteen minutes later and still nothing, not even a wafer. "Where else could it be?"

"Maybe it's in the confession booth over there."

"Good idea." I walked over to the booth and reached for the door and the hairs on the back of my neck stood on end. I sensed a darkness in this booth. I grabbed the handle and flung the door open. BANG! the sound of the door slamming against the wooden booth.

"What do you see?" There it is. A pitch black purse with chains for straps and covered in spikes. Kind of a weird purse for an old lady, maybe it's the wrong one? I search around in the purse for any identification. Bingo! An I.D. with a picture of Margret Senkrad and her house keys. I should call the hospital and let her know I found her stuff.

"Quite the commotion out here. I am the pastor of this church. How can I help you child?" A man in white and black robes stood at the altar.

"Uh, no thanks, just came back for my grandmother's purse is all and I think I'm just going to head out now." I turned

106

to leave and the man was standing in front of me.

"You sure about that, my son?" He reached for my throat and I tried to move but my legs wouldn't work. "You'll be going nowhere, boy. Your soul is MINE!"

"No! Get away from me!" I went to draw my sword but it disappeared as I reached for it. He grabbed me by the throat and lifted me off the ground.

"Time to die, boy!" The pastor transformed into a demon and reeled back his fist. "I'm gonna enjoy ripping your heart out."

Right as he was about to make contact with my chest I'm shaken awake by Thain. "Little homeless boy wake up you're having a bad dream."

"That's enough shaking, Thain, stop before you cause more damage."

"Yes, Madam."

"Are you okay, Trace? You were talking in your sleep when Thain came to get me, you had started screaming about demons."

"Yeah I was having another bad dream, it's been nonstop since New Mexico."

"What was your nightmare about?"

"It was about one of the cases I worked. There were demons possessing old people and high school football players. But everything was off, nothing happened like it did in real life. It was almost like—"

"Like it was told from someone else's point of view. Like someone that didn't have all of the information you had?"

"Yeah, exactly and the ending always changes each time more different than the last. How'd you know?"

"It all makes sense now."

"What does?"

"The darkness in your soul and the demon Thain described when he pulled you out of the trance. I thought maybe it was the spell that caused you the pain because you were hiding your true motives but that was not the case."

"I'm still at a loss here."

"The demon you fought did it die, did you kill it?"

"No, I didn't even come close. But my partner did."

"And you're sure they did?"

"Yes. I am hundred percent sure she did."

"I have good news and bad news. I will tell you the bad news first. You have been cursed by some sort of joining spell."

"So, what's the good news?"

"Well since we know that you were cursed by a joining spell this shrinks the number of spells that could have been used."

"Does that mean you know how to fix me?"

"Weeeell, no. At least, I can't say for sure that is. There are certain creatures that have the ability to cast these types of spells and the strength of them are based on two things; what cast them? A demon obviously. And what they used to link the two of you."

"How do we find that out?"

"It's pretty obvious when a demon casts a joining spell on you. Do you remember any funny feelings or glyphs appearing on you or the demon?"

"No, there was none of that. I just remember getting my butt kicked and stabbed through the chest. I don't remember much after that happened and I passed out before the demon died."

"How unfortunate, it must have done it while you were unconscious."

"So that's it? We won't be able to figure out what the demon linked itself to me with and I'll have a demon inside me forever."

"No that wouldn't be the case, the demon would eventually overpower you and devour your soul and take over your body." '

"Oh great, that's even better, might as well kill me now."

"Let's not go that far, there is still a way to find that information out but you are not going to like it."

"What is it?"

"To know what bonded you to the demon you'll have to relive the moment it happened."

"But as I told you I was unconscious, so I didn't see anything."

"You didn't, but your soul did."

"I'm sorry but what?"

"To better explain, your soul is like you but not like you. The major misunderstanding about souls is this, most think souls simply reside inside your body. This is wrong, your soul surrounds you and can be manipulated to do a great many things. You can expand it to sense beings around you, shrink it to conceal your presence and tear parts of it off and put it in different objects."

"Like a stone golem."

"Exactly right, you catch on fast. Another misconception about souls is that if you are dying your soul weakens and fades away. Actually, when you are dying or near death your soul's awareness heightens."

"Why do you think people always talk about things being different after near death situations or their lives flashing before their eyes? It's because your soul awareness is so heightened that it overloads your brain with specific memories that resonated with it even if you have forgotten it yourself. You were pretty close to death wouldn't you say?"

"Sure."

"There is a technique that has been used for generations to pass on information from the living to the dead. It is called soul scrying. It allows the users to see what the soul witnesses. Your soul was more vulnerable and responsive because you were on death's door and because you and the demon now share a connection it should help us figure out what he did."

"So if I get what you are trying to say, even though I didn't see what happened after I passed out with the demon, I can actually use that to see what happened?"

"Exactly!"

"Are you aware how crazy that sounds?"

"Trace, you fight monsters and demons on a regular basis and are practically immortal. How is soul scrying where you draw the line?"

"You know what? You have a point. How do we do this?"

"We have to teach you to get in touch with your soul. Learning to communicate with it will allow you to manipulate it to its fullest extent. To do that you will need to go into another trance. But this time we will put up blockers to prevent the demon from resurfacing and taking hold of you. Once you establish the connection to your soul, you can began scrying into the past."

"Okay, let's get started now."

"No."

"Why not?"

"Your body and your soul are out of sync right now from the trauma to your psyche. The healing water spell I used on you should help with that but it will take a few days for it to stabilize, the time should also give your body the rest it needs."

"My body's fine, the burns are almost all gone."

"Regardless of how fast you heal it's the trauma you took for the first dive, it's not good for you to put yourself under so much strain. And I won't cast the spell on you anyway so just take the break while you can. You might not get another for a while, maybe you should call your family or partners to let them know you're okay."

"Yeah I'll be sure to tell them I'm being consumed by a demon."

"No, your soul is being consumed by a demon. You on the other hand will just fade into oblivion doomed to exist in a world where you can never die if we do nothing about it."

"Splitting hairs now huh? I guess I'll give them a call."

"We'll leave you to it. We're going to make some breakfast so join us when you're done."

"Minerva, call home."

"Right away, calling mommy." *Riiiiiiiinnnnng. Riiiiiiiiinnnnnnnngggg. Riiiiiiiiiinnnnnnnngggggg. Click.*

"Hello?"

"Hello, Trace, is that you? I didn't expect to hear from you so soon. Is everything okay? Are you safe?"

"Of course, I am! Just training and getting in touch with

myself. You know the typical spiritual journey."

"Well, that's good to hear. Have you learned anything so far?"

"Um nothing yet just meditating and battling my inner demons."

"Mom, is that him? Is that Trace?"

"He's off being manly and fighting monsters like a man isn't he?"

"Yes, it is."

"Can we speak to him, Mom?"

"Of course, you can. I'll connect you two."

"Big brother!"

"Hi, Luna. Hi, Griffin."

"Sooo when are you coming home? It's so boring with you gone."

"Griffin! You know you're not supposed to ask about that."

"Sorry, Aunty."

"It's okay, Griffin, to be completely honest I don't really have an answer for you. Like I said before I left, when I'm strong enough to protect you guys and get our home back I'll come home."

"But I want you to come back now!"

"I'm sorry, Leo, but that is not possible for me right now."

"You guys. We've already talked about this. Trace is on his own journey and we can't force him to stray from it. No matter how much we want him back with us. No matter how much I miss him, I can't. I mean we can't ask him to come home."

"But he's going to come back right,?"

"Yes he will, Leo."

"You promise, Luna?"

"Yes, , I promise".

"Trace, can you call back later? I need to get everyone else up for breakfast."

"Yeah, I can do that. Hey, Mom, let everyone know I love them. okay?"

"I will. Stay strong, my son, I'll be here whenever you need to talk. Bye."

"Bye, Leo. Bye, Griffin. Bye Luna." *Click.*

I didn't think they would take me leaving so hard, Mom did it all the time. When she went on hunts and investigations. It was always just the eight of us in the bunker. Why is it so much harder for them this time?

"Trace, they can handle it, you are doing this for them."

"You're right, Minerva, I'm getting stronger for them. I want them to have their home back and their old lives back. I'm doing this for us. Thank you Minerva I needed that."

"It's what I am here for." All right, I can't get distracted right now. Just need to focus on the task at hand. I have a demon inside of me and it's trying to take my soul. I can't be there for them if a demon takes my body over. Maybe Celeste can tell me more about soul scrying and sensing. I'll head downstairs, maybe the food is ready. I head out of the room and back down the hallway to the dining room. Celeste and Thain are setting the table.

"For there to be only two of you, you sure cook a lot of food."

"Oh dear, Trace, we don't usually make this much food. Only when we have guests. You're a growing boy and you definitely will need the energy so eat as much as you can."

"You don't have to tell me twice, what's for breakfast anyway?"

"You know the usual; bacon, eggs, sausage, pancakes, ham, steak, hashbrowns."

"You know if someone asked me what I thought a witch and golem in the woods ate on a regular basis I would have never guessed normal people food."

"Normal is different for everyone, and sorry to disappoint you we don't eat children or people's cats."

"Not disappointed, actually pleasantly surprised."

"That is good to hear then, you can't judge a book by its cover."

"That is very true. Which is why I have a few questions for you."

"Let me guess, about scrying?"

"Among other things. Like why do you know so much about so many different forms of magic? And why can you cast like me? Who are you, really?"

"If I refused to tell you what would you do? Would you leave your only chance of survival behind?"

"No, I just really felt like asking some personal questions. Honestly it really is your own business and I can only assume that you have a good reason to hide who and what you are. It's not like I've told you everything about me either. We'll share if and when we're ready."

"You are an odd one. You ask such personal questions just for fun, not knowing what my reaction might be. I could have decided to throw you out or even kill you just for prying."

"Ha ha ha I doubt that. I knew you wouldn't have gone

that far."

"How do you figure that?"

"Despite the cabin in the woods and the whole witch thing you don't come across as that kind of 'I kill teens in the woods' person. Clearly you are a very kind and caring person. You have some maternal instinct to help me in my time of need. And for the most part you've been open about most things from what I can tell."

"Those are a lot of assumptions."

"Yeah I have a feeling that you are a good person."

"It's time, Thain."

"Yes, Madam it is."

I felt a very hard hand rest on my shoulder as Thain walked up behind me.

"That feeling may be your last mistake, child."

"Would you like a muffin, my transient friend?"

"Yeah totally! Wait a minute. What kind do you have?"

"I have chocolate, banana nut and blueberry."

"Blueberry please and thank you."

"Damnit, Thain! I was building the tension."

"I thought you said no cursing."

"Yeah no cursing for you, I'm an adult, I can say whatever I want. Did you at least buy it a little bit?"

"Not even a little. Like I said before I can tell neither of you want to hurt me. My feelings are usually right and I'm okay with you not telling me all of your secrets. As long as you can help me get stronger it doesn't bother me one way or the other."

"I will try my best to do that, but I make no promises. But I can promise you that we will try our hardest to get that demon out of you."

"I sure hope so otherwise I'll end up in purgatory and be forced to watch as a demon takes over my body."

"You're a good kid, with so much potential you don't deserve such a fate."

"Are you sure about that? I'm sure there are a few monsters that would say different."

"Perhaps. But your kind has always been hated by true monsters. You are the bane of their existence. If your people weren't around, this world would be a free for all. That's why they attacked you I imagine."

"That reminds me, you know you never told me the other reason you knew I was lying about who I was. If you know who I'm not then does that mean you know who I am?"

"I know you're far above a demigod and if I had to guess I'd say you are a Custodes."

"You sound very sure of yourself for that to be a guess. How'd you know?"

"It was your energy. It's very distinct and old."

"What does that even mean?"

"Your people are ancient beings so the energy you give off is that of an ancient one. Most people would not notice, but I've spent plenty of time with your people, not to mention your grandfather. You're a lot like him."

"I don't get it, since you knew I was lying, why are you helping me?"

"If I didn't help you I would be damning us all to oblivion. I meant what I said, the world needs someone to restore the balance and with everyone else out of commission it falls to you.It is actually your job to fix it, you were born for it. But

116

like I also said before you are not ready to do any of that. As you are you can't help anyone, but I will help you and train you for that. You will need a lot of strength to hold the demon within you at bay."

"But since we can't start on the actual training can you tell me more about soul scrying and the other techniques?"

"Like I said before there are many things that your soul is capable of doing and combined with your powers you could truly be a force to be reckoned with. Your power and soul are particularly unique. A Custodes soul is stronger than normal because within your soul lies your ego. A manifestation of your true powers, in this manifestation; your abilities are heightened, senses even more intense, durability boosted and raw power increased. For some a transformation can take place and others can make the world around them bend to their will, the power of one's soul is limitless. Your soul will create a world within itself while you are there. It is the best way for you to tell if you and your soul are in sync. As of right now your soul and energy are in disarray and is being suppressed by the demon. So I will have to join you in your trance to stop the demon from overwhelming you again."

"So does this mean that after we get this demon out of me I'll awaken my ego? I know or at least I think I've come close to it before."

"There is a chance of that, but it is not a guarantee. And sure, you may have used your egos power but that is because it lent it to you in a time of need. Awakening it is something truly different. An awakening can take years to manifest if at all, how about we work on one thing at a time? Demon first, ego second."

"One more question for now, why was my inner world pitch black? That's not necessarily my idea of a great place to be. Why would my soul create nothing?"

"There are a few reasons that could cause a soul to make an empty world. The obvious is the demon, its presence is disrupting your soul and stopping the soul from making anything other than an endless abyss. The second reason is that there is a world there but you just can't see it. Rather, your psyche, your feelings and inner turmoil are preventing you from seeing the world."

"Fine, then. That's all of the questions I have for you right now."

"Good, finish your breakfast then go meditate and relax while you can."

Chapter 7
Mirror

Over the next few days Celeste told me more about the soul trance and brought me some of her books so I could read up on it more. There are a few dangers to using this technique, the biggest one is being trapped in the trance permanently. Many people have gone in seeking the feelings of their past and have gotten lost in them, trying to right wrongs that have been set in stone. "Don't chase fantasies or what ifs because everything will play out the same way and doing so can send you into madness," is what one of the books said.

"Hopefully this isn't a one-way trip."

"Yeah I don't think your mom would appreciate you becoming a vegetable."

"Insightful as always, Minerva."

Celeste made me meditate with Thain to hasten the "resyncing" of my soul and body. I do not recommend taking meditation advice from a golem, they are unhelpful. They are all soul and stone so sitting in place for hours comes naturally to them. Thain said that the meditations was helping but I couldn't really tell, just had to take his word for it. Not like I could do much else besides that and reading, since sleep was out of the cards for me. Every time I'd try to sleep, I would keep having the dream about the pastor and the church. I definitely had enough of Groundhog Day for the time being.

"Since you already understand the basics of energy channeling, we can start with energy sensing. This will allow you to be more aware of both yourself and the world around you. However, where energy channeling mostly relies on touch, energy sensing relies on the other five senses; sight, hearing, taste, smell and last but not least feeling."

"Wait aren't feeling and touch the same thing?"

"One might think so, but no they are not. Touch is the physical aspect where feeling is more of the spiritual side that allows you to sense what goes unseen."

"Okay, I think I understand."

"Good, back to the similarities of channeling and sensing. They are relatively the same thing in theory so think of it as channeling your energy into your weapon but instead you will focus your energy on a person, it's simple."

"That's what everyone says." *Yawn.* "If it were that easy, I would be able to do it already. How about I just go back to bed and we continue this later?"

"To be completely honest, this should be second nature to you. Custodes have some of the best sensing abilities. I need you to cast a spell."

"But it's five in the morning and I barely got three hours of sleep. It is way too early for this."

"Didn't you say you wanted to get that demon out of you?"

"Ugh. Fine, let me go get my sword. *Mumbles* Old lady making me do stuff this early. What and I a navy seal?"

"Are you saying something dear boy?"

"NO, JUST GETTING MY SWORD! She's worse that mom."

120

"She's only trying to help you, you know. And you did chose to come here."

"I know, I know."

"Took you long enough, you got lead in your shoes or something."

"Oh, I'm sorry I'm not a stone golem that's just ready to fight and cast spells at a moment's notice. Some of us need sleep."

"Do you always complain this much? Just cast a spell."

"Okay. **Ignis.**" *Shhhink.*

"See how simple that was? You can channel energy without thinking. We need you to do that but with your senses."

"Yeah that's probably not going to happen."

"Why not?"

"Because my sword is the only thing I can use my power on. I can't use them in any other way."

"So, you're saying you can't cast or channel without a conduit."

"Correct! I can't do that."

"Why can't you?"

"I don't know I just never have been able to."

"Never? How'd you get your weapon then? Didn't you summon it?"

"I don't know. I just never have been able to and by summoned do you mean dropped in my lap? Because that definitely happened one time when I was a kid but I don't think that counts."

"Well, no that isn't a summoning. A summoning is when a Custodes speaks with their ego and requests a piece of its power, it is done through a sacred ritual. The ritual requires the Custodes to forge a dagger from their own energy and to plunge that dagger into their heart."

"That sounds kinda dangerous and deadly."

"Under normal circumstances, yes, but this dagger serves as a totem of a sort, it is harmless to the wielder and is meant to establish a connection. Once the blade pierces the heart of the Custodes they dive into their inner world and come face to face with the source of their power, their ego."

"Oh, yeah I totally know what you're talking about and my answer is still no I never really summoned it, it just appeared that day I really couldn't control it and nearly burned down the ship we were using. It had to be sealed in ice as a safety precaution."

"Really? There was nothing. No heart to heart with a spirit or a vision of any kind?"

"I mean not that I can really think of. There was no talk of a contract or mention of spirit stuff."

"So the summoning wasn't done properly so that means your bond never had a chance of fully forming with your weapon. Then that means it was still in its shifting phase. That explains the disconnect you have with, well, everything. A Custodes' powers draw on their emotions and that creates the link between them and their ego. That's what creates the weapon in the first place."

"Does that mean you know how to fix me?"

"That depends. I need you to explain how you got your blade. What did you feel? What was the cause?"

"An assassin wanted to kill my family and a voice spoke to me but she didn't really say much. She just said to hold my hands out and she'd take care of the rest."

"Hmm, a voice told you to. Has that voice ever talked to you outside of that time?"

"One other time when I was fighting the razorbacks. I was getting my ass kicked."

"Language, young man, there will be no cursing out of you."

"Sorry. But like I was saying I was getting my butt kicked by them, I mean really torn to shreds there, blood everywhere. On the walls, on the ceiling, my shoes, their claws basically everywhere that wasn't in my body where it's supposed to be. You should have seen it, it was like a Kurosawa movie."

"Okay, Trace, we get it there was a lot of blood, please continue."

"Right, so they were cutting me up and then I heard this voice again. The same voice from before and it told me to fight back because if I didn't the razorbacks would hurt more innocent people. That time it healed my wounds enough for me to stand and I felt a surge of energy that I've never had ever, it made me so much stronger and I learned a new spell."

"Interesting."

"What do you mean by interesting?"

"Even though the connection between you and your ego was never correctly formed when your powers manifested, you still hear it and it can still lend you its power. You are a curious one indeed. Normally, if the original bond is never made or improperly formed, then the guardian loses all of their power. Their egos go into a deep sleep, never to awaken, the Custodes becomes a fallen. The emotions or desire that drive a guardian and that they draw on for power are shared. Like with most guardians the common emotions or desire that they draw on; happiness, anger, fighting for their beliefs and in some cases excitement of battle. But with the fallen that no longer resonates with them and they basically become a human just with a longer lifespan. or and even worse fate and that is the guardian becomes consumed by their ego. Not knowing friend from foe, becoming a true beast. But that's the odd part, you on the other hand still have your powers and can draw on them through your desire to protect people."

"Is that a good thing or a bad thing?"

"Honestly? I've never seen anything like it. It does seem that your sheer will and your desire to protect others has kept you and your ego's connection intact even if it's just by a thread. Which is unheard of. The only thing I can call it is a miracle. "

"Okay, so the voice in my head is my ego and I'm not crazy?"

"No, Trace you're not. Well so long as that's the only voice in your head. That voice you've been hearing is your ego trying to reach out to you. It's trying to connect with you through your emotions."

"Cool so do I stab myself and have my spirit quest?"

"No that will not work as made apparent when I put you in a similar trance and you nearly burned to death."

"Oh. Yeah, I remember that. It hurt a lot."

"Trace, you will need to get rid of the demon before you can even begin to connect with your ego. Or at least suppress it somehow. It must be in a defensive state trying to keep the demon contained inside you, that does explain why it hasn't taken over already. You are a strange kid even for a Custodes.

You remind me so much of him you know. Ves was a strange one too and stubborn to boot. He never knew when to quit."

"Gee, thanks for the compliment."

"It's not necessarily a compliment, that stubbornness drove him to the grave. You are more like him than you know."

"I have no desire to unite anyone or anything, I just want to take my home back."

"You do know they may be one and the same. I'm only telling you this in hopes you don't end up like him."

"Trust me, I have no desire to follow in that man's footsteps. His own desires killed him and left a void in his family that was only filled by the promises and responsibilities he left behind. Some even named their first born after him, more of a curse than a gift."

"Oddly defensive, are you speaking from experience?"

"No. My family was close with the royals and they would talk about him a lot."

"You only have secondhand information then? Yet I can hear hostility and anger in your words. You sure you aren't speaking from personal experience?"

"Can we talk about something else? Anything else?"

"If that is what you wish then fine. There is much to learn when it comes to mastering control over your soul. But you will need to control your emotions a lot better than you do now. They can reveal much more than you want them to and they can cause you to lose control of your power. Especially where your ego is concerned. Thain, can you go get the soul grimoire for Trace?"

"Yes, Madam right away."

"Oh great, another dusty old book. What's this one

supposed to do?"

"This dusty book, as you put it, is Soulbound and it will teach you ways to manage your feelings and powers then use them in a more productive way and how to focus them so your soul isn't in complete chaos. It will have the spell in there for the soul scrying and the aura sensing, they both can be accessed with a trance."

Thain returned with a flawless grey book with nothing on it. "Here you go vagrant and brace yourself."

I reached for the book. "Trace, before you take the grimoire, know that you cannot take this lightly and, Trace, if you fail, it could have lasting effects on us all. Do you understand what I am telling you?"

"I do. My life's at stake here, I will take this seriously." I grabbed the book from Thain's hand. The book became red, tattered and singed on the ends. The rock on the cover became a humanoid body with a black dot in the center of the body. "What happened to the book? Why is it so heavy?"

"It's showing you a reflection of your soul and its burdens. The cover is an illustration of you, swallowed from the inside by a darkness."

"Grrreat. Anything else I need to know about this book?"

"That grimoire is very unique and possesses magic of its own. Once you open it you will be pulled into it and it will test you to make sure you are deserving of the knowledge it contains."

"What is the test?"

"I cannot say for sure but it could be one of four tests with each having its own difficulty; it can be confronting your fears, it could be a scavenger hunt to find what was lost, it could be as simple as following a road to its end. It is whatever the grimoire deems is the right way to test you. The whole goal of this test is for you to conquer whatever is desyncing your soul. For you to gain something you have lost. The results of doing so will start awakening more of your abilities and power."

"Okay and what about the fourth test?"

"That one's a surprise that I won't spoil for you."

"Do I have to worry about burning to death?"

"No, it's not like going into a trance, this is a world within the grimoire itself. You will be in no danger but you will not be able to learn soul scrying or anything of that nature until you pass the test."

"Are you ready to open the book?"

"About as ready as I can be."

"Then you may begin. Open the book."

As I opened the book the pages began to rustle. All righty! Here. We. Go. "Oh, before I forget, you can't bring your weapons or gear with you. And you may not be in any real danger but you can still feel pain."

"Wait what?" *Swoosh. Thud.* Ow my neck. God, my ears are ringing, They could have warned me about the fall. Oh, good a forest at least this is terrain I understand. Okay, Trace, focus your senses, what's the worst this book can throw at me? Maybe I should go for the high ground and see if I can find any clues as to what my test is. As I try to come up with a strategy I hear something flying through the air. *WHOOSH. THUNK.* An arrow whizzes through the air and into my chest and the world fades as I am ejected out of the book.

"Back already? It's only been five minutes. Madam he's back!"

"Ow, what the hell was that?"

"You okay, Trace?"

"I didn't even get to defend myself. Just shot in the chest with an arrow."

"So, a battle test huh?"

"I'm going back in!"

"Good luck, little beggar friend."

Swoosh. Splaaaaasssh! What? This isn't the forest, this is a lake. *Woosh! Sploosh.* I know that sound. An arrow lands right next to me in the water. I'm a sitting duck out here. I need to get out of this water. *Whooooosssh!* Dive! What in the hell is shooting those arrows? Can't worry about that now I need to swim away from whatever it is. I need to regroup and recompose myself. This is just a simulation. And you've done hundreds of those.

Splash. Splash. Splash. Finally, I'm out of that lake. All right, Trace, look for a vantage spot to see if I can— *whoosh.* You've got to be kidding m— *Thunk. Swoosh.* Oh, come on. How is it even possible for that thing to find me that fast. "Fifteen minutes that time! A small improvement."

"Shut it Thain!"

Swoosh. Squish! Ah man did it have to be mud? *Whoosh!* Seriously I don't even get a second? Time to run. *Splat!* Ha you missed! At least my reaction speed is getting better. I need to circle around this thing, whatever it is and catch it off guard. But first I need some cover and something to block those arrows. That tree looks like decent cover. Okay is there anything around I can use to protect myself? *Whoosh. Thump.* The dirt isn't me, Hawkeye. That one wasn't even close, their aim must be starting to wane. *Whistle.* What's that sound? The arro— *Boooooommm!* A blinding white flash of light erupts from the arrow. *Thud.* Ouch. The arrows explode on impact if they miss too! And they're flash bangs! That's not fair. I don't even have my weapon. *Whoosh. Thump.* Oh no, not again. *Whistle... boooom!* Well, there goes my tree cover. On to the next one, I guess. I need to run. *Whoosh.* Give it a rest already, Legolas, we get it! Where is are they shooting from? *Whistle. Boooom!* The arrows are always coming from the east or the west of me somewhere. But why? Why have they only been on those sides? I need to pinpoint where or I'm going to be hiding behind trees all day.

I'll have to risk being hit by an arrow to get a better look at where they are coming from. I'll have to run into the open. I'll move after this next shot. *Whistle.* He shot another arrow without me knowing? Couldn't have, I would have heard it coming. *Whoosh.* Now! Where is it coming from? Ah! The sun's in my eyes. *Whistle. Thunk.* That's it! They are staying on the side where the sun is, so it's harder to see their location. That's something I would do if I was hunting someone. Pretty smart. Again. *Swoosh.* Okay where's the sun? It's to my right, so it's east. *Whoosh.* Not this time, Katniss, I'm ready for you. I'll just— *thunk.* They changed sides this time? What is going on here? *Swoosh. Whistle... boom.* More! *Swoosh. Thunk.* I'm not done yet. *Swoosh. Boom.* Just one more time I almost got behind them. Round fourty! Again!

"Wait a minute, mister!"

"Thain, let me go."

"Thain, don't let him go, at least not until he listens to what I have to say."

"I thought I was starting to get this guy."

"That's exactly what you are supposed to think. You, my friend, managed to get the fourth option for your trial."

"Is the fourth test supposed to be confusing?"

"No, just to out think you."

"What do you mean?"

"Like I said I won't spoil the surprise but I will tell you that you need to start thinking outside the box. Because hiding behind trees and getting shot with arrows won't help you."

"How did you know what was happening?"

"I opened the book while you were inside. Showed me everything. So before you rush back into the grimoire take time to reflect on what you have learned about your opponent."

"Okay, fine, what have I learned? The archer is skilled enough to hit nearly any shot, and they keep countering every move I make. Right when I think I'm going to reach them, their strategy switches up."

"Anything else?"

"Those stupid exploding arrows, they suck so much. They're clearly special arrows."

"What makes you say that?"

"Because they explode with white light, they don't even have explosives on them."

"What else is unique about them?"

"They make a weird sizzling sound when they shoot them and again before they explode."

"Whistling arrows?"

"Yeah, but that's not even the worst part it's the explosion and they are smart enough to use the sound cue to throw me off."

"I wouldn't give your opponent that much credit. That

whistling you're hearing isn't the explosions triggering or even the arrows themselves."

"It's not?"

"No, that's your senses attuning to the magic being used. You're subconsciously learning how to sense magical auras because the grimoire is boosting your connection with your soul."

"Really? So that's what you meant by the grimoire teaching me how to sense things."

"That's not bad for six hours of training."

"Only six hours? No I was in there for so much longer than that. At least twelve hours. How?"

"Time flies when you're having fun. How about we call it there for today, you should get some rest."

"Can I go one more time? If what you're saying is true then I should able to locate the archer if I focus more on the whistle, right?"

"With the progress you've made, possibly."

"So, I can go back in?"

"Sure, one more time. Just know I'll be watching your progress closely this time."

"Okay!" *Swoosh. Thud.* Great, I started in the forest this time. That tree looks good. Okay focus on the whistle. No trying to attack just listen. *Whistle. Whoosh.* Sounds like it's coming from the southwest this time. *Swoosh. Boooom!* Okay, I should move to the next tree. Wait for them to fire again. *Whistle. Swoosh.* GO! *Thump...* No explosion this time? Is it because I dodged? *Whistle. Swoosh.* Move. From the sound of the last whistle, they haven't moved much. I have a general idea where, I just need to try to get closer. *Whistle. Boooom!*

Whistle… Swoosh. Whistle… Swoosh. Two of them this time, getting serious, huh? Time to move closer. The trees on the right are a little further than I'd like but would be a good spot if I could move fast enough.

Thud. Thud. Booooooooom! Whoa! That was a lot bigger than I expected. Must have figured out that I can hear the arrows. Let's just hope they don't figure out I can hear them too. *Whistle. Swoosh.* To the bushes. *Whistle. Swoosh. Thud. Thud.* One lands twenty-five feet from me. Again? Why didn't it explode? Is it proximity based? One more time, I should move to somewhere more exposed. That fallen tree should be perfect. *Whistle. Swoosh. Thud.* This one lands only feet from me. Nothing, huh? If that's not what's causing them to explode could they be activating them or controlling when they explode? Ooh, I'm an idiot. I think I got what I needed out of this round. I'll just step out for this next one. *Whistle. Swoosh. Thunk.*

"Why did you let him shoot you?"

"I was done with the test, for now at least."

"You do realize you could have just said you wanted to leave right? The grimoire would have teleported you out."

"It can do that? Well, my way looked more badass."

"He does have a point, Madam, it did look pretty cool."

"Thank you, Thain, I appreciate that."

"So what did you learn for this last time in the trial?"

"The original whistle is from them using their power to make the arrows and the second whistle is them channeling that magic to make them explode. The archer was gauging my reaction with the last shots. They definitely know I can hear the arrows and know when they are going to explode. I know how to find them and dodging the arrows is getting easier."

"So you've finished the first part of the trial."

"First part?"

"Yes, this trial has multiple phases to it."

"So, there's multiple trials and inside those trials are more trials?"

"No, I lied earlier there is only one test the book gives you."

"Why would you lie about that?"

"I wanted it to be surprised. If you went in expecting, it to be a combat trial you would have just ran head first into battle. With me not telling you, you were more cautious and started honing a new skill. So what is the next step of your plan?"

"To get close enough to attack the archer."

"And how do you plan to do that? Once you are able to reach him that is?"

"Well, since I don't have my sword or anything I'll have to fight him hand to hand."

"So, from hiding behind trees to rushing him head on. You sure that's a good idea?"

"Why wouldn't it be? It's an archer, close-ranged combat is not their specialty."

"You would know what you are capable of better than I. If that is what you think would work then try that next time. As for right now you should go take a bath and wash up for dinner, you smell like a wet dog."

"I don't smell that bad."

"No offense, my homeless friend, but you do smell like a trash panda."

"Y'know just because you say no offense doesn't make it

any less offensive. I'm going to go take a bath now and by the way, Thain, I take great offence at being called a dirty racoon. I prefer sanitation engineer thank you very much and I'm not homeless, I have a home I just left it."

"My apologies, sir, I will keep that in mind."

"That's more like it. I'll just leave my stuff here and be right back."

After I retuned from my shower, there was another unnecessary cornucopia of food crowding the table.

"I see you guys went with the all part of the all or nothing approach again. But I'm not complaining. More is always better in my book."

"As I said before you are a growing boy and you spent most of your day training in the grimoire, you'll need the food to regain energy. So please eat."

"Thank you for the food and I will do just that. I do have to ask and I know you said why you cook so much but where does it all come from and how do you make it so fast? You don't have a refrigerator, a stove or an oven and I haven't seen a single animal around here."

"Very astute of you to notice, Trace, and the answer is simple. It's magic."

"That's it?"

"Well, what else do you want me to say? I am the witch of the wilds and conjuration magic is my specialty."

"So, you just make it out of thin air?"

"For the most part. The food I make is infused with my magic which is why your body and energy recuperates so much faster after eating it. Why do you think I feed you before you train or before I gave you the grimoire?"

"Hmm, I guess I never noticed, but now that you mention it I do feel rejuvenated. I guess I should thank you again for that."

"No thanks needed, Trace, I am just here to help you succeed. Speaking of rejuvenation, how was your bath?"

"Refreshing, I guess, I definitely needed it. I haven't been covered in that much mud in a while."

"Good to hear, and I see you've cleaned your plate again. Would you like thirds, there is plenty more where that came from?"

"No, I had plenty, besides if I ate anymore I might explode. Is it possible to go back into the Soulbound tonight?"

"I actually have another exercise for you tonight that will help you in your trial and to better understand your enemy's technique."

"Okay, what's the exercise?"

"This one will be easy and it uses some of what you've learned so far from your time in Soulbound. In this test you will have to find your weapon."

"What do you mean find my weapon, it's right here. Hey, where's my sword and the rest of my gear?"

"Well, I don't know, I had Thain hide it. Thain, where'd you put his stuff?"

"I don't know, Madam, you know I can be kind of forgetful at times. Must be my pebble for a brain."

"You've got to be kidding me?"

"No, I'm really not, I do have a pebble for a brain. It's more of a large stone but—"

"Not what I was talking about. How do I find my stuff?"

"As I suggested, to get your stuff back you will have to

use the new senses and knowledge you have gained. You notice that the archer is putting their energy into their bow and arrows to create them and make them explode. I want you to try and do the same with your sword but this time without having to hold it. I want you to channel enough energy into your weapon so you can hear it resonating like with the arrows. This should be easier for you because you are looking for your sword made from your own energy. Give it a shot."

"I guess I can try to, I'm not all that good with energy channeling."

"Nonsense, you do it every time you cast a spell and use your senses. It's second nature to you. You just don't think of it in that way. I'll even help you channel it this time. Give me your hands with the palms facing upward."

"Okay, now what?"

"Just imagine your sword in your hand. It is a part of you, you share a connection with it, focus on that."

"Right. Imagine my sword. It is in my hand. Hump."

"What is it?"

"I'm not really feeling anything."

"That's because you're overthinking it. Just imagine your sword in your hand that's it."

"Okay. I got this. Just using my imagination. Shut everything else out."

"Sir, may I suggest you stop talking so much you're going to psych yourself out. Try holding on to this stick, it should help."

"Thank you, Thain."

"Close your eyes and take a deep breath. In and out. In and out."

"I feel something. I feel heat and the weight in my hands."

"Good, Trace, now channel your energy into what you're feeling."

"Okay, I will try. In and out, in and out." *Whistle.* "I hear something." *Boosh.*

"Oh boy, didn't expect that to happen." *Splash.*

"What did you do that for I was starting to hear the whistle."

"Sorry, sweetie, but can't have you setting things on fire in my log cabin."

"Sorry, I didn't mean to."

"Not a big deal we will just need to take some precautions with you. Thain, get the fire extinguisher."

"Madam, you are the fire extinguisher."

"Right, well, then go grab something that absorbs heat better."

"I know just the thing. Be right back."

"While he's going to get whatever it is, let's talk about what just happened. What did you feel when you were channeling your energy?"

"It was like you said. It felt like the energy was just flowing to another part of me. And after that I could hear the whistling but it was really low."

"See, you are a natural. I could see your aura growing the harder you concentrated."

"I have it, Madam. Here you go, sir, a ceramic rod should hold the heat better."

"You ready to try again?"

"Yes ma'am." Deep breath in and out, in and out. Let my energy flow to my weapon. *Whistle.* "I hear the whistle again."

"Good now which direction is it coming from?"

"It sounds like it's coming from behind me like it's outside."

"Then open your eyes and follow the sound."

Creak. Chirp chirp. Chirp chirp. Chirp chirp.

"Now which way is the sound coming from?"

"It's kinda hard to hear because of the bugs."

"Ignore them and focus on the whistling."

"I know, I know." *Whistle.* "It sounds like it's coming from straight ahead."

"Then go to it." *Whistle. Whistle. Whistle.* "I'm getting closer, what's that strange glow over there? It's coming from behind that tree over there." *Whistle.* "There you are, I found you. Where'd the light go?"

"You found it, well done! You have progressed at an alarming rate. Soulbound's magic really pushed you over the hump."

"Thanks but how is this supposed to help me with the archer?"

"Is it not obvious? It was to help you to understand the process of channeling your energy into an object. You can now understand your enemy better and you may actually be able to find them next time. You did say something about a glow coming from the sword behind the tree, right?"

"Yeah and it disappeared when I got to my sword."

"Much like with the whistling you hear, that light you see is the energy being projected by your sword. The more energy you channel into an object, the easier it is to observe by others. Remember that when you are in battle next time. But for now get some rest and you can reflect on what you have learned today."

"I am pretty tired and thank you for all of the help. You too, Thain, even though you hid my stuff."

"Anytime, sir."

"I'm going to head to bed now and get a fresh start tomorrow morning."

"Maybe consider checking in with your family? It's been almost a month since you last spoke to them."

"You're right I probably could give them a call."

"I'll leave you to it then. C'mon, Thain, let's give him his privacy."

"Yes, Madam."

Riiiiiiiinnnnng.

Riiiiiiiinnnnnnnngggg.

Riiiiiiiiiiinnnnnnnngggggg. Click.

"Hello? Mom?"

"Hello? Trace can you hear me?"

"Yes. I can hear you."

"That's better. There was a little static so I couldn't really hear you. How are you doing, Trace? It's been a while are you okay?"

"Yes, mother, I am fine. And I know it's been a few weeks. I'm sorry about that. Just been really busy. It sounds quiet over there. Where is everyone?"

"They're all in bed. They spent most of the day running around in their beast forms, they're all getting really good at it."

"That's good to hear. I'm glad they're also improving."

"I'm sorry, Trace, I should have asked how your training is going?"

"It's going well. Starting to figure out that whole sensing energy thing you were trying to teach me years ago. I also learned how to channel energy into my weapon without having it near me. It's not transforming or anything flashy like that but I think it's pretty good."

"That's great! I can see your time away has helped you improve. I feel like maybe my being overprotective stunted you in some way."

"Not true at all I had some soul searching to do of my own and fighting with my inner demon before I could get stronger."

"You're just being nice, Trace. I know I could be overbearing at times. I should have trusted in your abilities more and let you spread your wings."

"No, that wasn't it at all. I was mentally and physically ready to learn everything you could have taught me but my soul was not where it needed to be. And sending me out on my own sooner would have ended in nothing but agony. But I'm getting there, slowly improving, one day at a time. I know that this was the right thing to do. Thank you for letting me do this and for trusting me to make the right decision."

"You're my child, I raised you. There isn't a terrible decision-making bone in your body. A know it all one for sure but I will always support you and your goals whatever they may be and that is a promise."

"I'll hold you to that when I augment my body and become a cyborg."

"You know what, I take back what I said about the good decision making."

"Thank you again, Mom."

"You're welcome, sweetie."

"I should probably head to bed now, going to be an early start to training tomorrow. Let everyone know I'm thinking about them and I'll call again sooner this time. I love you and them as well Goodnight."

"I love you too, Trace. Goodnight." *Click*

"Trace, why haven't you told her about the demon issue? It's kind of a big deal."

"I can't bring myself to do it, Minerva. How do I tell her that if I can't get through the Soulbound's trial, the demon she thought she killed will take over my body?"

"Like that I suppose."

"Sure, so she can blame herself for this happening. I couldn't do that to her, to my brothers and sisters."

"Dying and having your body be the puppet of a demon and them never hearing from you again is the better option?"

"No, it's not which is why that won't happen. I will pass this trial and I will get this demon out of my soul."

"How do you know you will succeed?"

"I promised them I would come back to them. So I will or die trying."

"Well, that goes without saying."

"Hey, Minerva?"

"Let me guess. Shut up?"

"No. Thank you. Even though you can be a douche you're my douche. I appreciate your company and advice even if I ignore it from time to time."

"Thank you?"

"You are welcome. Let's head to bed."

"Wake up, sleepy head, it's time for more training!"

"Thanks, Minerva. Time to get to work."

"You can do it, Trace, go kick that archer's butt!"

"Hell yeah! Soulbound, I'm coming for you! AAAAHHHHHHH!"

Swoosh. I landed back in the forest area, surrounded by trees and bushes. "All right, Green Arrow, let's dance. I will find you this time and kick your ass." *Chirp, chirp, chirp. Chirp, chirp. Chirp.* "Why is it so quiet in here? Where are you? You hiding? What are you waiting for?" *Whistle.* "There you are to the southeast." *Whistle.* "From the southwest now?" *Whistle.* Now, the north of me? *Whistle.* They've changed their tactics since the last time. Every improvement I make, they counter or adapt to it. *Whistle, whistle, whistle.* It's so loud now I can barely concentrate, how am I supposed to find him now? Don't get overwhelmed. It's just like last night's exercise. Take a breath. I need to focus on the arrows and the bow. Breathe in and out. In and out.

They have to channel their energy to make an arrow. Dodge until I find where they are, I just need to react fast enough to not get hit. Concentrate. *Whistle.* "Wait for it. Wait for it. *Whoosh.* They're to the west. I rolled out of the way at the last second and the arrow strikes the tree to the east of me. *Whistle... boooom!* "You know deforestation is a big issue nowadays and you're not helping!" Actually, destroying their hiding places might not be such a bad idea. *Whistle, whistle, whistle. Whoosh.* Here it comes again. They moved again. *Whistle... boooom.* They're definitely on the run and trying really hard to disguise their location. I won't be able to track them down if they are constantly moving and all these other arrows are making it hard to discern where the energy is

142

coming from . This has definitely thrown a wrench into my plan. I need them to stay still long enough to hone in on their aura. I won't be able to stop their movement completely but I can try to limit it to one area. Even though I don't have my sword I can try to channel my energy into the trees like I did last night. I run to the nearest tree. I really hope this works. *Whistle, whistle, whistle.* Concentrate on the tree. *Whistle, whistle, whistle.* Tune out the whistles. Focus. *Boooosh. Crackle.* Holy crap I did it. Not nearly as big as with my sword but it'll do. I'll start by going after the trees and let them think the arrows are distracting me. I'll set everything ablaze, It'll make it easier to pinpoint their location. I'll start running through the trees setting the inner sides of them on fire. I'll trap them in the circle and with a firewall at my back I won't have to worry about attacks from behind. Hopefully they don't catch on to my actual plan. *Whistle... Booooom. Whistle, whistle, whistle. Whistle... Boooom. Whistle, whistle.* They definatly are not letting up. But that's good they are definitely focused on me.

Just a few more trees and I should be good. I run to the last two trees setting them a blaze. *Booosh. Booosh.* Okay now that their movement is limited to this circle and most of the arrows have been taken care of I can concentrate. Focus. *Whistle, whistle.* That is so much better than before. *Whistle, whistle.* I close my eyes. Imagine the bow. Picture the archer drawing the arrow. *Whistle, whistle. whoosh. Whistle... booooom.* What was that glint just now? Was that them creating another arrow? I need them to fire again to be sure. *Whistle, whistle. Boooom, booooom.* There it is again. It's too quick. I need to get closer. There's the underbrush that's ahead of me. If I move I'll have to burn the area behind me so I don't get blindsided. But it will prevent my ability to retreat. I guess this will be all or nothing this time. Boosh. It's time to run for it. *Whistle, whistle. whoosh.* Another one. I dove into the underbrush with the arrow missing by a mile. Where is are they aiming? Is the fire throwing their aim off? That can't be it. *Whistle… booooom.* I should be safe here for a little bit. The tree should withstand a few explosions. *Whistle, whistle.* With the fire spreading inward this little area of ours will bring us closer and make them easier to see. I can try to focus more on them now. That last little flash hadn't moved that much from before so I know the general area. I just need to close the gap. And at the rate the fire is burning I'd say we have ten minutes before this whole circle is engulfed in flames. *Whistle, whistle, whoosh. Whistle… booooom.* Concentrate. Just like my sword. concentrate. *Whistle, whistle, whoosh.* I see an aura fifty feet to the northeast. Can't tell if it's just an arrow or the archer. Concentrate. *Whistle… Boooom.* Trace you can do this, you can do this. *Whistle, whistle, whoosh.* That's definitely the bow. That aura is so wild. It's like a tornado of light and dark. *Whistle… Booooom. Whistle, whistle, whoosh.* This aura feels so familiar but why? *Whistle… Booooom.* Can't think about that now. I need to come up with a plan to catch them off guard. I know rushing them won't work. *Whistle, whistle, whoosh. Whistle… Booooom.*

Whistle, whistle, whoosh. Whistle… Booooom. Those arrows are getting further and further off the mark. *Whistle, whistle, whoosh. Whistle… Booooom.* They are just shooting wildly. What's changed now? The fire is moving pretty fast; we still have six minutes left. It's like they can't see me any more… That must be it. The fire I made is created from my power and it's spreading all over this forest. That explains why they were always able to see me no matter what. They have been tracking my aura, now their blind, finally I have the advantage. With those last few shots I have a better sense for their energy. I can see their aura more clearly, it's like mine is consuming theirs. I know exactly where they are. I'll attack them from the side but I'll need more cover. I could wait for the fire to spread more. But with the rate they are firing those arrows there won't be much forest left to burn. *Whistle, whistle, whoosh. Whistle… Booooom. Booooom. Whistle, whistle, whoosh. Whistle… Booooom. Whistle, whistle, whoosh. Whistle… Booooom. Booooom.* Jesus that last one was way too close for comfort. I can't sit here much longer, time to make my move. There's only four minutes left, the pressure is definitely on. They pushed up a little more, only thirty feet between us. They might notice a move if I make a run for it. I guess I'll have to climb to stay out of their line of sight. *Whistle, whistle, whoosh. Whistle… Booooom. Booooom.* Yup, up the tree before he blows it to smithereens. With the fire climbing with me they won't notice my ascent. The roar of the flames continues as I make my way up the tree to look for a way to get to them.

Looks like I see a way to get behind them through the other trees to the left of here. I can make the jump, it's not too far away. Here's hoping they don't look up. On three. One. Two. Three. *Hmph. Whistle, whistle, whoosh. Whistle… Booooom. Thud.* That last shockwave nearly made me miss the tree. Okay, three more jumps. One. Two. Three. *Hmph.* Another. *Hmph.* Last one. *Hmph.* Made it! They are under that branch up ahead. It looks sturdy enough to hold my weight. *Creak creak*. They don't seem to realize I'm here. I have them now. One last jump onto their back. Here goes everything. *Hmph*. Look out below you archer bastard. *Thud!*

"I got you! Time to uncloak you!"

"You got me? Is that what you think, kid? Sorry to disappoint you. The cloaked man said."

"What do you me—" The cloaked man wrestles his hand free and grabs me. "Hey, let go of my arm."

"Nah, I think I'll hold on to it." He flips me off his back and slams me onto the ground. As he does that I manage to grab his hood and get a glimpse at the archer's face. No way. That's not possible. *Slam!* Ouch! That hurt. *Gasp*. Like a lot. *Gasp*.

"You gonna get up now? Or would you like me to slam you some more?"

"Nope, I'm getting up. That's enough slamming. Okay what is up with your face and why do you look like me?"

"Is it not obvious, Vestigium? It's because I am you. The true you."

"Excuse me? What does that even mean? This has to be one of Soulbound's tricks."

"It means exactly what I said. I am you and no this is no trick. The point of Soulbound's magic is to show you what you are truly capable of. It creates a sort of mirror of the person that enters this place, a person that can mimic you. Someone that knows you inside and out, your thoughts, your feelings and your reactions."

"Why? What does that have to do with learning about soul scrying?"

146

"To overcome your shortcomings. Yours are the fact you overthink every little thing, it distracts you and it blinds your senses. All the doubt and the fear you have is holding you back. You need to believe in yourself and your abilities. You are constantly putting your own self down and that is what's been holding you back. You are only limited by yourself, you have to break that habit. To communicate with your soul on the level you toned, your mind has to be open to it. Before this trial started you were unable to sense magic and channeling your power into anything other than your weapon was impossible. Yet in less than twenty-four hours in the real world you've become able to do both."

"Yeah barely."

"Doesn't matter. It's not the quantity but the quality. Look around you. This whole forest is burning and that's because of you. Your power has steadily increased since you started training."

"I doubt that."

"Cut it out! Did you not notice how much faster your reactions have gotten from dodging the arrows? Or your physical strength? You literally jumped tree to tree with ease. Think about it, Ves, you are improving you just haven't realized it."

"Celeste said something like that too. I didn't believe it though. But it's hard to argue with myself. By the way, sorry for burning the forest down."

"Then get rid of the fire."

"How do I do that? I don't have a fire extinguisher or water spells."

"The fire is made from your magic energy. The only

reason it spread this far is because you wanted it to do so. It is under your control if you want it gone, make it go away."

"Is it that simple? Just will it away?"

"Yep, all you have to do."

"Okay. Fire go away." All of the flames start to smolder and fade away.

"See, how easy that was?"

"I didn't know I could do that."

"How long have you been doing this again?"

"I know I'm an awful guardian."

"Not what I said. You are way too hard on yourself. You are doing the impossible as we speak. Even though this place is boosting your abilities you are performing better than most with their ego partially awakened. And yet you have done all of this without it. That is no small feat. Most people rely on their ego to heighten their senses, speed, strength and reaction time but you don't."

"Because I can't."

"Not the point. You have learned not to rely on anything other than your natural abilities. You are excelling, Ves, you need to see that. That is part of this lesson, you need to stop doubting yourself, you need to realize you are not like everyone else. You will grow at your own rate."

"Okay, I get it. Enough with the PBS motivational 'you're unique' talk. I do have some questions for you about the trial and about you…"

"Ask away."

"Why are you so old if you're supposed to be my mirror image?"

"Honestly, I don't really know the answer myself. I could

make the guess that maybe Soulbound figures this is the true you that you'll become."

"Why are you shooting exploding arrows and not fire ones?"

"Because you are terrible against ranged enemies. and who said they weren't? Who says I don't have fire powers?"

"You didn't use them at all and you seemed like you were afraid of getting burned. If you still had your fire powers you wouldn't have been worried about that and you would have put out the fire."

"What's your point?"

"I'm just saying your whole mirror story is starting to fall apart y'know. Clearly you are not my double."

"I didn't say I was the exact copy. I will tell you what the book told me. What you are seeing right now is you and what you may become eventually. What I've seen and done made me into who I am and it may do the same for you. But there is no way to tell for sure.. But to simplify it the best I can it may not today, tomorrow or even two years from now. But at some point you and I will be one and the same. Maybe not the exact image, but pretty damn close. This grimoire is not bound by the normal constructs of time and space as I'm sure you have learned. So it has the ability to pick and choose whoever or whatever it wants from whenever or wherever it wants to. Which is why time is so weird here, hours can feel like days or even years. Soulbound decides it all, how fast or slow time will pass. Okay?"

"So, the book's a time traveler? That makes no sense."

"Doesn't have to, it's magic."

"Okay, since you're me, or my soul, can you teach me

more about my powers and how to connect with my ego?"

"Yes, I can but you're not going to like it."

"Just tell me."

"You're going to have to die."

"Really?"

"No, idiot, why would that work? You'll have to figure it out on your own. You have to be worthy of its power and you won't get there if I give you the cheat sheet. Just know its test will not be a pleasant one."

"Okay. I get it. It's definitely a copout but I get it."

"There is no pleasing you."

"What else do I have to do to complete this part of the trial?"

"You already have. To complete Soulbound's first trial You have to reach me using the sensing and channeling abilities you gain during the trail. In part two we will do more advanced training that will help you with using your power to its fullest. Or, at least, as far as you can currently."

"When can we start?"

"Whenever you are ready."

"So, we can start now?"

"I'd say yes but you have other things to take care of for now."

"Sorry to break up the self-bonding time but you two will have to start that training another time."

"As for right now you will need to come with me. I have another exercise for you."

"Celeste, how did you get here and how long were you listening?"

"Long enough, Vestigium. Don't worry your secret's safe

with me."

"You heard that?"

"Well, well, well. I've been waiting for you to stop eavesdropping and join us, Celeste. Still calling yourself the witch of the wilds I'd imagine. I never understood why you hid that from me for all those years."

"I don't know what you are talking about, child, speak plainly."

"Don't play coy with me. I could let the other me know what and who you really are or maybe I'll let younger me figure it out himself."

"Celeste, what is he talking about?"

"I'll give you a hint. You and Celeste have a lot more in common than you think. I'm sure you've noticed how much she knows about us and the spells she uses."

"That's enough."

"Yes, ma'am, I shall respect my elder's wishes. But it may be too late. He's a smart kid. I know the thought has crossed his mind already."

"I said enough! We're leaving, Trace." *Swoosh.*

"Whoops, looks like I upset her. I am gonna pay for that later, you better go. I'll be here when you get back."

Chapter 8
Soul Man

"Go ahead and say it. I know you want to just come out and ask me."

"Say what exactly? Say that you're not a witch? Maybe you want me to ask what you really are? I could do that. But I'm not going to. Like I said before, I know a thing or two about keeping secrets. I concealed my identity from you and I had my reasons. I trust you have your reasons for not divulging your identity as well. My only question is that now that you are aware of who I am what will you do with that information?"

"You are Vestigium Rgis the crowned prince of Eden, the underworld world would flip on its ear if they knew you still lived. Demons and devils alike would erupt from hell to find you. They actually did it. "

"You make it sound like you're not surprised."

"I'm not, there are a lot of tells. Your powers and your strong feelings for the royal family and Vestigium. Now that I look at you, how did I not realize it before? And you even look so much like your mother and father."

"Well, that's usually how genetics work."

"And equally sarcastic, you're definitely a Rgis. Then does that mean your mother and sisters made it to safety? Well, are you going to say anything?"

"You never answered my question and before I answer any more of yours I will need you to do that. What are you going to do with the information you've learned?"

"What am I going to do with it? As I said, your secret is safe with me, I might hug you though. You have no idea how great it is to hear that the royal family still lives."

"I thought you didn't care for the royal family. Earlier you basically said they were shadows of their former glory."

"It is the opposite actually. I care deeply for them and wish they had paid better attention to the changing of the world. Once I thought they were all dead I had given up on hope. But a little birdy, or spider I should say, told me that there might be a chance they could still be out there. I thought she was crazy. I'm glad she wasn't. Listen, Vestigium."

"Trace."

"Excuse me?"

"My name is Trace not Vestigium. I am not my grandfather nor do I wish to be."

"But why, he was a great man? Vestigium was—"

"Exactly, he was. Not me. I know the legends better than anyone so spare me the story time."

"I am sorry. Wasn't aware that his name was such an issue for you?"

"Why are you sorry? Not like you picked the name or something. Can we just get back to the training and skip all the family stuff?"

"If that is what you want then yes. We can move on. Let's start with the progress you have made so far. Up to this point you have learned how to sense energy with two of your six senses; sight and hearing. You can hear and see the energy produced by a person to a certain degree. But we need you to be able to feel its presence around you. Once you can do that we will be ready to start the soul scrying. So for now we will work on the feeling portion. You will be sensing the energy a soul gives off. But this time there will be a twist. I will cast a spell that will blind and deafen you, then you will try to find me. You will be relying completely on using your energy alone."

"Is that the best place to start?"

"We only have so much time and this is the fastest way. Besides this will be the easy version, we'll stay in the cabin this time. You read the books, meditated with Thain and you faced yourself in the grimoire you are ready for this. Just focus your energy and your soul will lead you to us. *Oculi caecorum*!"

"I can't see. Okay, focus. Quiet your mind, you can do this. Focus."

"How can you focus on seeing when you won't stop talking?"

"How can I hear you?"

"Telepathy."

"Okay, I'll be quiet. Deep breath. I see something. Something green. A green floaty ball and next to it a pink one."

"What else do you see?"

"That's it. I thought that was the whole point of this."

"It is part of it. The other part is you trying to visualize the world around you to get to us. It will help you get the gist of what we will be doing in your inner world. So focus on sensing the world around you as it is. Fill the room with your energy so it covers every item and flaw in here."

"You could have told me that first, can I get my eyes back so I can look around?"

"No. You will have to do this with the memory you have of this area as you will be doing in your trance. You can't go back to the church that night so you can't see the room again. It'll be just like in the forest when you set the fires, your energy spread all over with the fires."

"I thought you said this would be easy."

"It is easy, you don't have to start from scratch like you will when we do this for real. Your goal is to reconstruct this room and get it as close as possible. Your energy will spread and will take care of the rest, that's step one. Step two, you will then have to walk through this room to get to the both of us."

"Not to be that guy but if I do this enough I'll eventually memorize it."

"You could do that but then you'd learn nothing and cheat only yourself."

"Okay, then."

"Oh and, Trace, please don't burn down my house by focusing too hard. This is supposed to be simple and relaxing. We will go hide and remember don't try too hard."

"Okay, I got this. Just let my energy flow and not set anything on fire. A blue aura starts to fill the darkness. Everything is a little fuzzy but I can make out the basics. I see the table, the chairs, and I see the green ball floating in the distance. Wait where did Celeste go?"

"I'm hiding, remember."

"From what it looks like Thain is hiding behind the curtain on the other side of the room. I just need to be careful to not run into the…" *Thump*

"Ouch! My shin. What was that?"

"It was a small table."

"Where did it come from?"

"I moved it in your way, you only didn't notice it because you were moving too fast."

"That's not fair."

"Doesn't have to be, it's my exercise."

"You are an evil woman."

"No, I'm a sweet old lady, besides, you're a Custodes you'll heal fast. Now try again."

"I need to slow down. I have all the time in the world. More energy is what I need."

"No, you don't, your energy output is fine, you just need to relax. Get out of your own head."

"This should be easy for you, Trace. You can do this. It's just like being in Soulbound. Make the world around me."

I try again this time not trying to overthink it. I can feel the energy flowing out of my body once more reaching out and spreading out across the room.

The blue aura coats the room and the green ball has transformed into a full Thain-shaped being. Whoa this is amazing I can see Thain. Like really see him."

"That is the goal Trace."

"I am Daredevil! This is awesome! Okay, where is Celeste? She's not in this room and she's not in her den. Where is she? Is it possible she's hiding her energy from me?"

"Maybe I am or maybe you just aren't looking in the right place. Expand your energy further."

"Okay. Whoa, are all of those other orbs other living

creatures?"

"Yes they are."

"That's super cool. So where are you? Hey! You said you were going to stay inside the cabin. Cheater."

"Did I cheat or did I teach you to expect the unexpected."

"No, you definitely just cheated."

"To each their own."

"Can I have my sight back?"

"No, at least, not yet. For the next few days this is how you will get around. Get used to using your energy filling in the blanks your other senses cannot. Once you do that you will be ready to start scrying."

"Honestly, this isn't that bad. I could totally do this for a few days."

"Good to hear. I'm glad you are comfortable with this. Why don't we go for a walk in the woods and see how well that goes?"

"Sure, sounds good!"

"Then get out here!"

I head out of the cabin door and Celeste jumps down from the roof.

"This is so cool. I can see so many things. I can see the birds in the trees, the ants on the ground. I can feel all of their energy. Is this what I've been missing out on? Thank you, Celeste. This might be my favorite ability that I've learned since I got here. Totally worth getting shot by all those arrows."

"This is nothing, Trace, what you see now is limited by reality. But when we go into your inner world the only limit is your imagination."

"Really?"

"Yeah. You construct the entire world the way you want it. If you want it to look like an active volcano, you are inside of Sakurajima. What you desire will exist in that world."

"That sounds pretty cool."

"It is."

"We should probably head back now."

"Yeah, we have gone a little ways away from the cabin. It didn't even seem like we walked that far. Guess I was too distracted by the energy sonar."

"Energy sonar?"

"Yeah! Where sonar uses sound waves to detect objects and surfaces this allows me to do the same just with energy."

"Hmph, energy sonar. I'm going to have to remember that for next time. Let's head back in."

Celeste wasn't joking about making me rely on my energy sonar. I spent every waking moment in a world of lights. It was truly a unique experience. I just wish I could share it with my brothers and sisters.

"It's so peaceful. I wish that everything could stay like this."

"That's how your inner world will draw you in, Trace. You'll get stuck on the feeling and never want to let go."

"Nah, I'm not that attached to my feelings or dreams."

"You say that now."

"As of late I've only had nightmares."

"Hopefully, once we go into your inner world we can put up some mental blocks as well so that stops."

"That would be great."

"I think that's enough training for today, Trace, go get

some rest for tomorrow we start scrying."

"Awesome!"

"Rise and shine, Trace its time to get started."

"I will never get used to hearing someone else's voice in my head."

"Okay, before we start I have to ask you this. Trace, knowing what you now know and learning all of the dangers of what we are about to do are you still willing to try it?"

"Yes, I am."

"Okay, did you want to call anyone to make your peace?"

"No! Have a little faith in me, I am not going to get stuck in dream limbo. Let's get this done already."

"In a hurry?"

"Yeah, kinda am, ready to purge this demon from me."

"Okay, have a seat next to me. I will start with the barriers and Thain will maintain them on this side. *Obice meam!* We are going to practice the soul scrying, similar to what we did before. I need you to close your eyes and focus on my voice. Now envision that night in the church, remember the feelings, the pain. The deeper the emotional connection the better. I will focus on keeping the barriers strong on this side."

I shut my eyes and open them to a world covered in a reddish black aura. Half formed towers, some melting and others crumbling to pieces.

"Celeste, what is this? Why is everything this weird color, feels like I'm in *Kill Bill* or something?"

"What you are seeing is your soul's energy projecting itself to recreate the church."

"So, my soul's aura is blood red? Seems kinda evil."

"It appears that way. The color of your soul has to do with

159

your nature. Many different beings have many different color auras. It may be like this because you still are having inner turmoil."

"You sure this isn't because of the demon?"

"No, this one is all you. The demon is currently trapped behind the barrier. You need to focus, Trace, we only have so much time. Okay. Imagine the church, imagine the smashed pews, the broken arm and the stake through the chest, feel the pain. This isn't working."

"Is that all you felt at that time, Trace? Do not hold back any of your emotions. You have to be honest with yourself or it won't work. What did you feel?"

"I felt anger, I felt alone, I felt…"

"You felt what?"

"I felt fear. I thought I was going to die, I thought my mother had abandoned me, I felt hatred for the demon and I felt weak for needing to be saved."

As I uttered the last word the poorly-formed towers slowly reconstructed themselves into a small city.

"That's good, Trace, keep trying to focus on those feelings. I'm right here with you. Go back to that night."

"Well, well, well. Very impressive, child. You've shattered the illusion," echoes throughout the world. Walls shoot up from the ground, this time more solid than the last. Flashes of the church crowd my mind. The broken confession booth, the collapsed altar, sprout into existence. Remember that night. The blood. All of the blood. *Smash! Crash! Snap!* My broken arm. The pews smashed and destroyed begin to appear.

"You're definitely not human? Why won't you break?"

The demon slowly walking toward me.

"You dead yet?"

Mors Ignis! Black flames erupting from my blade and the demon rising from the flames.

"That's it, Trace, you're doing it, the world is almost done stabilizing. You are almost there. How are you holding up?"

"I'm fine. I got this."

"Well done, child." *Clap clap clap.* "But this little game of ours is over." *Sshhluck! Booooom!* "*ALTA FRIGIDUS!*"

"Trace! Just hold on a little longer she's here, your mom is here."

"That's all I remember from that night, Celeste."

"That's all your mind remembers, time to go deeper. Let your soul fill in the blanks. Remember, let your energy flow to the world around you. Use the demon's memory if you have to. But be careful and make it quick. We don't want to let the demon gain any additional influence over you. I will have to weaken the barrier some. Find his soul. Sense the darkness spewing from it. Let it guide you through the past."

Booooom! ALTA FRIGIDUS!

"What the hell is that light?"

"Let go of my son, hellspawn!"

"What the hell are you? What is this power? Shit, after that last attack from the boy I don't have the strength to fight whatever she is. I doubt she'll let me walk out of here after what I did to her kid. Maybe I can take her soul instead? If what everyone said is true then the artifact I stole when I left hell could save my ass. But I'll need some time to prepare it. Everyone! Attack that woman she must not stop the ceremony." The parishioners charge without hesitation.

"I will obliterate you, demon! *Glacies duratus ossi draconem!*" Another flash of light and an avalanche of snow erupts from my mother's spear crushing some of the attackers. "There aren't enough of them to save you from me!"

"It's not possible! She can't be one of them! She can't be a custodes! They are all dead! I hope this thing works." The demon pulls a blackened bone out of his pocket. "Goddess Lilith, bless me with your power of corruption! And possess…" A black smoke begins to flow from both ends of the bone. The smoke flows toward my mother but it can't get through the light radiation from her. "How is this possible? Lilith's power is said to corrupt the souls of everything. But this woman is stopping it with ease. Her power is too much."

"Prepare for judgement, demon." Several ice spears appear around the demon.

"What can I do? There has to be another way. The boy! He's my only chance. He is weakened but still alive, the smoke should work on him. It'll corrupt him and he will fight for me. It's her son so she wouldn't fight back. Then I'll make my move."

The smoke changes course and heads to my body.

"Stay away from him, demon!" *Sshhluck! Sshhluck! Sshhluck!* My mother's ice spears skewer the demon and he falls to his knees.

"Damn it! It was all a lie that bone was useless." The demon's body starts to decay and is being absorbed by the smoke surrounding us. The smoke reaches me then vanishes into thin air as the demon completely fades from existence.

"That's it? That's what happened? What the hell was that bone?"

"Oh no, my child. That bone. It is Lilith's finger. But it seems that the demon didn't quite understand its purpose."

"That doesn't sound good."

"It isn't, my child. I am sorry to say, Trace, but there is nothing I can do for you."

"What? Why not?"

"That totem that he used was made by the queen of demons herself. It was made with her dark energy. It is very powerful and is used to corrupt one's soul. By allowing the user to implant their demonic essence into another being. Allowing them to feed on their soul and eventually turn them into a demon."

"So that's it. I'm as good as dead?"

"I didn't say that. I said that I wasn't able to help you. But I know someone that might be able to. There is a goddess that is known for her healing abilities and could purify the demon from your soul. She may also be able to restore the link between you and your ego."

"Where can I find this goddess? How do you know she'd be willing to help me?"

"The map Thain gave you should lead you to her. Why don't you pull it out?"

"Okay. Map, show me where I need to go." The map starts to reveal a location in the middle of nowhere. "Where the hell is that?"

"That is a desert."

"I figured that much out, Minerva."

"From the looks of it, it is somewhere in the middle east near Pakistan and India."

"You know I've always wanted to go to Punjab. I guess

this is as good of a time as any. Maybe I could go to Mumbai after this demon's gone."

"How do you plan on getting there? I don't think trains can take you that far."

"I, uh. I'll take a plane. Minerva, I need a flight."

"Already taken care of, the first flight leaves in four hours."

"Sounds good to me."

"You'd better get ready then, Trace. While you do I'll make you something special for the road. Who knows how long it will be before you have a home-cooked meal?"

"Who knows if this goddess can even help me? She might not be able to and then I'll just die and haunt Thain."

"Why? What did I do to you?"

I glare at Thain. "You know what you've done. I'm going to go pack now."

I have my sword, my bag, my Hun73r gear, emergency cash stash and identification.

"I think that's everything. You should call home. This may be one of the last times you get to talk to them until after the plane ride."

"You are right. Call home." *Riiiiiiiiing. Riiiiiiiiiiiiiinng. Riiiiiiiiiiiiiiinnnggg.*

"Hello, Trace!"

"Hiiiiii, Mom. I was just calling to check in. Some recent developments will have me heading out of the country."

"Really? Are you on a hunt?"

"You could say that."

"Do you need my help?"

"No. This is one of those things I have to do myself. Part

of the whole spiritual ego awakening journey."

"I see. I'm sure it'll be a piece of cake for you."

"I hope so."

"Hey, Mom! Whoops sorry I didn't know you were on the phone. I'll come back later."

"It's okay, Caeli, it's your brother. He is going on a hunt abroad."

"That sounds amazing. I wish I could go to different countries."

"I'm sure you'll go too far cooler places eventually, Caeli. Besides, a hot desert is not my idea of amazing."

"I take what I said back then. That sounds sweaty, arid and awful. I will stick to the air-conditioned bunker thank you very much."

"Ha ha ha ha. It won't be that bad its just a dry heat."

"I don't know how you do it, Trace."

"Do what?"

"No matter where you go or what you do you are never worried or afraid of the possibilities. I wouldn't be able to do half of the stuff you've done. You are definitely braver than me."

"I wouldn't call it brave. I just do what needs to be done. There's no point in trying to run from it, just face it head on. I know you can do it, Caeli, you're strong and have nothing to fear. Just take the leap."

"I'm working on that. But I don't think I am ready for my own first solo hunt."

"I know you're ready, you just have to believe in yourself. Go for it! I believe in you."

"Really! Do you mean that, Trace?"

"Of course, I do."

"Then maybe I'll give it a shot."

"Hey, Caeli, where'd you go?"

"Oh right! I was showing Leo how to use his energy to heal others. I should get back to him. Trace, good luck on your hunt. I miss you."

"Thank you, Caeli, I really appreciate it. Can you tell everyone I said hi and I miss them?"

"Of course, I can."

"Remember, Caeli, you are ready! You are a badass!"

"Thank you, Trace. I'll talk to you later. Bye."

"Thank you, Trace."

"What are you thanking me for, Mom?"

"For the pep talk. I have tried to talk with Caeli to get her to try small things on her own; she won't even think about it. It's hard to even get her to come with me. But just now she lit up when you said you believed in her. Hundreds of miles away and you can still inspire them in ways I could only dream of."

"It's not that big of a deal, Mom."

"It's your gift, Trace. You've always been able to inspire others to do better."

"I doubt that."

"Doubt it all you want, it's true."

"Sorry to butt in, Madam, but Trace has a plane to catch and we need to head out."

"Then I won't keep him any longer, Minerva. Keep an eye on him for me."

"And by that you mean make sure the power doesn't go to his already bulbous head?"

"Among other things."

"I'm right here, you know?"

"Will do, Madam. The babysitter protocol has been engaged."

"Babysitter protocol? Please tell me she's joking."

"She is, my son. There is no babysitter protocol that allows me to track all your moves, conversations and browser history."

"I can't tell if you're joking or not."

"I am."

"Okay then. I am going to go now. I miss you and I needed this. I'll talk to you later, Mom."

"I miss you too, Trace. Goodbye for now and stay safe." *Click.*

All right time to go. Let's go see Celeste then head out. Back to the kitchen I go.

"Celeste!"

"That was fast. Not much to pack?"

"No, I packed light. Which now that I think about it was probably not a good idea for where I'm going. But desert wasn't the plan."

"Good thing I have a few things ready for you to take with you to help with your journey. Put your bag on the table next to all of the other stuff and I'll get it packed."

"I don't think that will all fit in my bag."

"Trust me, Trace, it will fit." Celeste waves her hand and her staff appears. "Let's see what we can do with all of this." She waves the staff over the supplies and they all shrink then float into my bag.

"Impressive! I'm going to have to learn that one."

"Maybe I'll teach you the next time you stop by."

"Hopefully, there is a next time."

"I have faith that you will be fine, Trace. You are a Rgis, they are some of the strongest custodes to ever exist. Your journey is far from over."

"I appreciate the optimism and thank you."

"What for?"

"For everything; letting me stay here, the kindness, the training and saving me. I've learned so much over the last six weeks."

"It was nothing, child. Anything to make sure the next generation stands a fighting chance. The future is yours to shape but it is the old guard's job to guide you on your path. Don't forget to take Soulbound with you."

"Are you sure? It's a pretty powerful grimoire."

"I am very sure. Not like anyone else can use it now."

"What do you mean?"

"The title of the grimoire is more than just that. Soulbound is now permanently bound to you and no one else can access it without you. If you leave it here it would be a paperweight. Besides the other you said you weren't done with training. So you still need it."

"I guess you're right. Thanks."

"Trace if we don't leave now you will miss the check in for your flight."

"Thanks for the reminder, Minerva. Well, I guess this is goodbye then."

"It is but I'm sure we will meet again, my child. If I recall I owe you a hug."

"I do remember you saying something about that."

"I am gonna miss having you around. Reminded me that

there is still more to do."

"Can I hug too, Madam?"

"Why not. Get over here stone man."

"Hug!" *Crack.*

"Oh God, Thain, too tight. You're squeezing too tight."

"Jesus, Thain, are you trying to break our backs?"

"I'm sorry, Madam I don't know my own strength. I'm not used to showing affection."

"It's fine, just be gentler. We're people not trees."

"Yes, Madam. Shall I try again?"

"We don't have to." Thain's expression drooped, and a look of sadness washed over his face. "I mean we don't have to stop hugging is what I was going to say."

The smile returned to the rock man's face as he embraced us once more.

"I'm going to miss you, sir. Of all the homeless wolf people, I've met you were my favorite."

"I'm not a…" You know what I'm going to let it go. Take the compliment, Trace, the rock man means well. "Thank you, Thain, I really appreciate you and all your cold rockyness."

"Trace! We need to leave now."

"Okay, okay. Calm down. Thank you both I will stop by when I get this demon out of me. Goodbye you two."

"Goodbye, Sir Trace!" *Creak! Thump.*

"Oh! and Trace, Anahail, is the place you're looking for. It is a beautiful place with trees and mountains as far as the eye can see. There are a lot of Mythicon there so make sure you put your best foot forward remember you represent the custodes."

"But no pressure right? Next stop India."

169

"Technically we have to get to the airport first."

"Technically we have to get to the airport first. You know what I meant."

"Trace?"

"Yeah, Minerva?"

"I hope the demon swallows your soul and you spend the rest of your life in an unending abyss."

"Wow!"

"Too dark?"

"Yeah, a little."

"Sorry. To the airport?"

"Yeah, how about we do that."

Chapter 9
Mirage

"I'm so drained, I need a break. It's soooo hot. Why does a mystical valley have to be hidden in the hottest part of the Thar Desert? Whoever decides these things needs a fist to the face."

"Minerva, you're an A.I. you don't feel heat nor do you get tired."

"I do too, my CPU is practically melting. I don't know how you aren't even breaking a sweat."

"I'm well insulated. Besides it's not that hot."

"What do you mean it's not that hot? It's over one hundred and twenty degrees."

"Now how am I supposed to find this place that Celeste talked about?"

"Hey! Don't ignore me, mister."

"Minerva, please focus, we need to find this place as soon as possible. That way you can get out of the heat and I not have my soul feasted on by the devil."

"Okay fiiiinnnnnne. What does the paper say?"

"The parchment Thain gave me says Anahail should be right in front of me but all I see is desert. Something's not right here. I can't sense anything at all. Could the map be wrong? Minerva are you detecting anything?"

"Yes, my scans show small traces of supernatural energy similar to yours. But I cannot pinpoint its exact location."

"Cloaking spell maybe?"

"From what I can tell, yes, but it also has some sort of protection spell with it."

"So what am I supposed to do now?"

"If the spell was a normal cloaking spell you could just walk through it. But this definitely isn't a normal spell, maybe try disrupting it."

"That's not a bad idea. You said the energy is similar to mine right?"

"Yes, the ancient energy being emitted from the protection spell is similar to yours. Can you not sense that?"

"Look, I just learned how to sense things in general. I can't tell the difference between them yet."

"I still expect better of you."

"Then hold on to your pants because I have an idea. Celeste did say I can use my energy in numerous ways."

"So?"

"So I should be able to use it to disrupt a spell with energy similar to it right?"

"I suppose so, like an EMP?"

"Exactly like an EMP, but in this case it's a DMP, a disruptive magical pulse."

"It's worth a shot I guess."

"Okay, here we go. Focus your energy. Pull it all in to a point and let it go."

Hmmmmmmmmmmmmmmmm. Boooooooooooom!

A wall of energy surges from my body and expands over the area. Then a portal appears thirty feet in front of me.

"Impressive, that actually worked, and here I thought you were pulling that out of your ass."

"Yeah, right. It's like I'm some sort of child prodigy or something."

"Sarcasm detected."

"Great job. I was expecting a city not a portal."

"It makes sense, if a mystical valley was out in the open for anyone to access then someone could stumble upon it."

With the spell gone I could actually sense the power coming from it and it was getting bigger and bigger.

"There is a huge energy surge coming from that portal. You should probably take cover."

"Where? I'm in a desert."

"Trace, something is coming out of the portal in three... two... one."

A group of elves in cloaks with a spider on them came rushing out of the portal surrounding me with bows drawn. "Intruder! You have destroyed the barrier of the goddess, how have you done this? What is your purpose here?"

"Elves? Oh boy. Well, I can explain. I was sent here by a witch to find your goddess so she can help me."

"Demon! He is a messenger of the devils, here to finish what the others started. Kill him!"

"Hey, wait a minute. This a misunderstanding, I am not a demon." I drew my blade and stabbed it into the ground. "Ready. Aim. Fire." "*Ignis*!" A pillar of fire encapsulates me, burning the arrows to ash as they pass through the flames.

"The demon is using fire magic! Use the arrows goddess Farisah blessed to vanquish the demon."

"Trace, there's another energy source coming through the portal."

That didn't sound good. "Ready. Aim. Fir—"

"Hold your fire." A voice came from the direction of the portal.

"Lady Samara, what do you mean? We must kill the demon, it destroyed the barrier."

"That child is no demon. He is a Custodes and he is the one the goddess spoke of and I have been expecting him."

"It cannot be. Praise the goddess, the savior has arrived. Lower your weapons!" All of the elves lowered their bows.

"You can drop your wall, Vestigium, you are safe from harm."

"My apologies, Sir Vestigium, this has truly been a misunderstanding."

The elves shouted.

"What the hell is going on here and how does she know who I am?"

"She did say she's been expecting you. Maybe Celeste told her you were coming? Why did they call you a savior?"

"No clue, I've never saved anyone. If that were the case wouldn't they have been waiting outside of the portal when I got here?"

"Maybe she's psychic and is currently reading your mind?"

"If that was the case she wouldn't have called me Vestigium."

"Maybe she's confusing you for your grandfather?"

"So are you going to lower your wall of fire?"

"Why not, she stopped them from shooting at me again." I withdrew my blade from the sand and sheathed it. The flames started to shrink and die. As they did I saw a woman with long brown dreads to match her brown skin, a yellow dress with

174

sapphire scales along the shoulders, arms and bust with a necklace with an albino spider around her neck and a leather satchel on her hip.

"She's so beautiful!"

"Thank you, Vestigium, please come with me." The woman walked to the portal and made a come here gesture with her hand.

"Minerva, I think you were right she's a mind reader. How did she know what I was thinking?"

"Because you kinda yelled."

"Oh."

"Awwwkward."

"Shut up, Minerva." The elves broke their circle and headed toward the portal. They then began to vanish through the portal one at a time.

"You're next, are you coming?"

"Yes, ma'am!" I walked to the portal. "Sorry about the barrier."

"No, it is my fault I was late in welcoming you, and it needed to be repaired anyway. I'll fix it." She reached into the satchel and pulled out a white orchid and placed it in the palm of her hand. She then held it up and it started to glow and vanished into a white light that shot into the sky and created a barrier around us and the portal. "Done!"

"Impressive."

"With that taken care of let's get you to the goddess."

"Is there anything I should know about going through the portal? Any magic words? Do I need one of those spider amulets?"

"No, you just walk through and that's it."

"All right, through the portal I go." As I stepped through the gate a vision of blackened mountains and dying trees came in to focus.

"Welcome to Anahail, Vestigium. Though I wish it were under better circumstances."

"Whoa! What happened to this place? This is definitely not what Celeste described. I thought this place was supposed to be a lush valley not an apocalyptic wasteland. Where is everyone?"

"I regret to inform you the goddess is in no shape to help you. It is Farisah that needs your help, Vestigium."

"Is this what the elf was talking about when they said the demon's coming back to finish what they started? Samara, is there something I should know?"

"I will fill you in on the way to the temple. Let's get up to the rhizas, everyone, we are heading back. Aramis and Fenin Stay here and watch the portal and let me know if there are any other disturbances."

"Yes, m'lady."

"Join me on my rhiza, Vestigium, it's a short ride into town."

"Sure, lead the way."

We walked out of the scorched ditch and up to a group of horse like creatures made of roots woven together with a green glow leaking out between the branches. The elves and Samara all hopped on their mounts.

"Come on, I'll help you up."

"What are these? They definitely aren't like any horses I have seen? Minerva, can you scan them?"

"Already on it. There is nothing in the codex that speaks

of these creatures. But they seem to look and act like normal horses and the energy they are emitting is unlike anything I have encountered."

"I have so many questions."

"And I will answer them all in due time, we need to go." Samara reached her hand out to assist me onto the rhiza.

"I don't need the help, I can get on just fine, but thank you." I jumped onto the rhiza.

"Let us leave then. You may want to hold on to me."

One of the elves shouted something in an unfamiliar elven dialect followed by "onward and to the goddess." The rhiza took off at breakneck speed nearly knocking me off.

"Can we turn around? I think I left my spine back at the portal."

"I told you to hold on didn't I?" Samara shouted.

"Yeah, but you didn't say that these things had jet engines attached to them. What are these things and why are they so fast?"

"The Nyvx call them rhiza, they are an old and nearly extinct breed, with the only ones in the world remaining here in Anahail."

"Nyvx? What are they?"

"They are the elves, and just like the rhiza, they were nearly wiped out after the last war of the beast. There were a lot of species that were left without homes to return to after that, and the goddess Farisah welcomed them into Anahail. You could say that Anahail is the place for the lost, forgotten, weary and abandoned."

"Good, maybe Farisah could help me out with that too because I am definitely feeling a little lost."

"If that is the case then it sounds like you came to the perfect place. Everyone that comes here finds what they are looking for one way or another."

"And what did you find, if you don't mind me asking?"

"The goddess helped me find my purpose and gave me a family. Which is why you have to help her. If she dies then she won't be able to help anyone else and all the creatures that live here will have no place to go."

"Not like I can say no to that, how much longer to the temple?"

"It's on the other side of the dried-up lake."

"I was just going to ask about that too. What happened to this place? Why is everything dying?"

"The short version? We were attacked by an army of demons. We withstood their attacks for days on end. But most of our people are not warriors, the Nyvx, Duaka and I are the main fighting force. We got pulled to the front lines by the demons and they somehow poisoned the goddess and now everything is fading along with her life force. Farisah created Anahail and without her it will disappear."

"Demons attacked you guys too, Celeste said that a lot of creatures were getting bolder ever since Eden fell. But killing a goddess? That's a whole new level. They might have been planning this for a while. What are they up to?"

"I don't know and we'll worry about it later. For now we need to find a way to save Farisah."

"I'll try to help out any way I can."

"We're here, the temple is at the center of town, we can walk from here."

"Whoa."

"The demons burned down half of the town as a distraction. Farisah went to make sure everyone had been evacuated and sent the others to escort children and injured that were unable to fight back to the temple. Farisah held back the flames and the army with some of our own warriors. When I had returned to help Farisah with the fires, Farisah was poisoned and several of our people had been taken."

"That explains why this town looks like scorched earth. What exactly do you think I can do to help Farisah?"

"You are Custodes right? Farisah has told me many stories about your people and their ability to perform miracles that rival even hers. She told me that your grandfather Vestigium did the impossible and united the world and brought about the end of the war of the beast."

"I'm going to have to stop you right there, Samara, though we share a name. I am not my great grandfather and I cannot perform miracles."

"Nonsense, you are of the same bloodline so you must have the power to help Farisah."

"I have been trying to escape that man's shadow my entire life. I'm not him. Nothing like him. I don't have his power, abilities and I don't know how to save anyone."

"You don't have a choice, Vestigium, your great grandfather promised Farisah that if she ever needed help a Custodes would come to her aid and here you are. You have to help us, you are bound to us."

"That is not how that works. Yes guardians are bound by their promises but that is just it. OUR promises. Not another guardian's, I did not make the promise therefore I am not bound to it."

179

"Will you make him a liar, will you disgrace his honor?"

"You didn't let me finish. I already said that I would try to help you in any way I can. While I can't perform miracles I might be able to use my technology to see what's wrong with Farisah. I can't promise you I can fix her but I will promise to try my best."

"Then let's go. Farisah is waiting."

As we made our way to the temple I could see the people of Anahail reinforcing their defenses and searching through the burnt houses and rubble.

"You guys are still on edge, are you expecting another attack?"

"It is a possibility but who knows at this point? They have constructed a fortress on the other side of the valley but it has been deserted since the last attack. I feel that this is only the beginning of something far more ominous."

"I see. Can I ask you another question?"

"Go ahead."

"So is there anything else I should know before I meet this goddess of yours? Is there a specific way she prefers to be addressed? I've never met a deity before. Is it similar to speaking with royals?"

"I'd imagine not, most of them prefer gifts, or to be put above all others. Farisah is not like that; she enjoys being around her people. Before all of this, this place was a paradise, Farisah would walk around the village speaking to everyone, she is eloquent, gentle and beautiful. She would heal the wounded, bless the crops, sing, dance and teach so many things to the children of the vale as well as show them how to connect with the nature around them and how to harness its energy to create new things."

"Sounds like Farisah is a very kind and hands on god. The complete opposite of any of the ones I've read about."

"She believes that one should not simply be worshipped for what they are. They must earn that along with the love and respect of their followers. A god that does not help their people is like a painting, pretty to look at but not much else."

"I can agree with that."

"Here it is, the temple of goddess Farisah." We approached a building covered in what seemed to be sapphires that had symbols of an albino spider all around it.

"How did it manage to stay unharmed during the attack?"

"During the attack, Farisah created a barrier around this temple so the people that retreated to safety would be protected. If only I had been there, I could have helped her."

"Or you could have been hurt or possibly taken just like the others. You shouldn't beat yourself up over that. You cannot change the past."

"Your words are kind but it doesn't help me feel any better, if I could I would trade my life for Farisah to get better."

"She must really be something else for you to want to do that."

"She is and once you meet her you may feel the same way. Through the doors up there." As Samara says that, the doors open to the temple and a group of elven and satyr-like children rush past me to speak with Samara.

"Lady Samara, we heard that the savior is here to help Farisah."

"Yeah, where's the savior they need to get started healing the goddess?"

"Hey, who's that kid, m'lady he's dressed funny?"

"He kinda looks like you, m'lady is he a human like you?"

"Where did he come from?"

"Calm down, everyone, this is Vestigium and he is the savior the goddess spoke of."

"No way, he's a kid like us, how can he help?"

"Farisah said the savior was a strong warrior, not a little shrimp."

"Ouch."

"These kids don't pull their punches do they?"

"Shut up, Minerva."

"Who's he talking to?"

"I think he's crazy."

"That is enough, children, he is here to help us and you will treat him with respect."

"Yes, Samara."

"How is the goddess doing?"

"She was resting for most of the day and since she can't move we sat with her to keep her company."

"That is very sweet of all of you. I bet you guys could use a break from the sitting, why don't all of you go gather some orchids for the goddess to help her feel better?"

"Anything for the goddess!"

"Onward, we quest for flowers!"

The group of children ran toward the town and the yelling and screaming about flowers slowly faded in the distance. They seemed excitable. "My apologies, Vestigium, they are not used to seeing new people."

"No big deal, they kinda remind me of my siblings."

"That is right, the goddess did say you left your family to

find your own path."

"That journey is kind of on hold until I don't have a demon riding shotgun in my soul."

"Once the goddess is better she may have the answers you seek."

"All the more reason we should get to the helping."

"This way, we're almost there. Farisah is just through the door."

I approached the door and it slowly opened. A voice sneaked though the crack in the door, "Please come in, my child. I have been waiting." I pushed the door open the rest of the way.

A giant albino spider awaited me on the other side of the door. "Ummm, that's a giant spider."

"That isn't just any spider, it is the goddess Farisah and you will show her the respect she deserves."

"I mean no disrespect. I just honestly didn't expect a spider when you described her earlier."

"It is okay, Samara, I take no offense. Allow me to formally introduce myself. I am Farisah the goddess of nature and illusions and the protector of Anahail."

"I am Trace King and it is an honor to meet you."

"I see, you do not prefer the mantle of your great grandfather."

"Not particularly seeing as I've been in his shadow my entire life."

"Wait why didn't you say you didn't like being called that? I've been calling you Vestigium this entire time."

"My honest answer?"

"Yes, please."

"You're hot. So, you can pretty much call me whatever you like."

"If you don't like your name then I will not call you that, especially if it only brings up mixed feelings. Your name is part of your heritage, I apologize for my assumption"

"It's really not the biggest deal and nothing to apologize for, I have been called way worse. Anyway, how about we take a look at you? Minerva can you scan Farisah? I need to know her condition."

"Right away! My scans show that Farisah's body is shutting down slowly. I would need a blood sample for further diagnosis."

"How are you feeling, Farisah?"

"I have seen better days to be honest and I have hope that you can help me, my young friend."

"I'll try my best."

"Excuse me, Lady Farisah, may I take a blood sample to run some tests to see what kind of poison this is?"

"Does it need to be fresh? I don't want to cause her any more pain than necessary."

"Minerva?"

"Technically no. While a fresh sample would provide more information on how she is being affected by the poison it is not needed."

"It would give us more information on how Farisah's body is handling the poison if it comes directly from her. However, it is not necessary to provide the information about the poison itself."

"It is okay, Trace, please take what you need."

"I promise this will only hurt for a second." I held my

Hun73r gear up to one of Farisah's legs and a small needle came out and poked her.

"Cross checking known poisons with venom of all known beast and poisons from around the world. This may take a few minutes."

"Done."

"That's it?"

"Yeah, that's it."

"I hardly even felt it."

"That's the point, the sample gathering function of the Hun73r is meant to be noninvasive and as painless as possible. Minerva is searching for possible matches of what poison is in you, it shouldn't take long."

"That was easy."

"Yeah, technology has come pretty far when it comes to diagnosing some things."

"Is that what brings you here, Trace? I know you didn't come here solely to help dying ancient one, what ails you?"

"I've sorta been poisoned by a demon myself."

"So you seek my knowledge to help you with that." *Cough. Cough. Cough.*

"Lady Farisah, are you okay? M'lady allow me to sooth your pain." Samara pulled out another orchid and began chanting. The orchid began to glow and white light surrounded Farisah, the coughing subsided and the light slowly dissipated.

"Thank you, dear Samara, you have become quite the healer. Must have had a great teacher."

"You are my teacher, m'lady, and I only wish that I could help you more."

"Step closer, my child, so I may get a good look at you,

with my illness my vision has begun to fade as of late."

"Yes, ma'am, I can do that."

"That is much better, you are the spitting image of Vestigium Rgis, it is amazing how much you are like him."

"I highly doubt that, at my age, my grandfather would have already healed you and slain all of the demons."

"I very much doubt that, dear boy, your grandfather wasn't always the legend we know today. He had his fair share of struggles similar to yourself. He also came for my help once."

"Really? What for?"

"He needed knowledge and my healing magic."

"Why?"

"Scan completed."

"Hold that thought, Lady Farisah, Minerva finished the scan. Minerva, you can switch from headset to speaker so everyone can hear you."

"Okay. The cocktail used to poison Farisah was a combination of both venom from a basilisk, devil's snare and Parthenium. From what I can tell this was to both weaken her severely but also prolong her death. By the looks of her vitals and the progression of the symptoms Farisah has a little over Sixty hours to live."

"Farisah only has two and a half days left to live, this can't be true. How do we cure her?"

"It would take the tears of a phoenix to heal me. There hasn't been a sighting of a phoenix in nearly a thousand years."

"And being short on time we'd need a miracle to find one."

"Then we will make a miracle happen. Farisah cannot die,

you have to help her."

"Okay, okay. Farisah you know a lot about other mythical creatures right?"

"Yes I do."

"So phoenixes are old right? Like ancient creatures, sorta like you."

"Yes, they are."

"Then wouldn't that mean their energy is similar to yours?"

"I would suppose so."

"Minerva?"

"Yes, Trace."

"I have another idea. You know how you said the barrier and cloaking spell had similar energy to mine?"

"Yes."

"So, can you—"

"Scan for all ancient energies in the world excluding exact matches to you, Samara and Farisah?"

"Yes, that."

"Already on it."

"I knew there was a reason I kept you around."

"How long will this scan take?"

"Scan time unknown."

"It kinda depends on how many ancient creatures are still around and honestly this may not even work."

"Let's just say it does, how do we narrow down which creatures are which? And what do we do if the phoenix is too far away?"

"That is a good question."

"Phoenix's have a unique energy around them. Being as

they have been touched by both life and death there would be a swell of dark and light energy around them. When they resurrect it has been known to create energy vortexes in their wake."

"That should narrow it down, you hear that, Minerva?"

"Yes, modifying algorithms to fit the new parameters."

"It will take seven days to complete the scan."

"Better than time unknown."

"Still too long, we don't have that much time."

"Okay. Let me think. Minerva search for all of the ingredients and where they originate."

"Why would I do that?"

"Because maybe all of the ingredients came from the same place and that can narrow the search area down. Start with the basilisk and the last sighting. The last one was sighted by a researcher that said they saw a small serpent being kept as a pet by a sultan near Uttarakhand. The researcher said that the sultan may have used the venom to poison the rest of his family to get access to the proverbial crown. He describes similar symptoms to that of Farisah."

"And the other two ingredients?"

"The other two plants are commonly found in various parts of the middle east and Asia."

"That narrows down the search area a lot."

"How long will that scan take?"

"With all of the additional information it will take twelve hours."

"Is there anything else you can do?"

"I'm sorry, Samara, but no. We are searching for a needle in a haystack."

"Don't worry, Samara, I have faith that everything will work out as planned. We cannot rush this process."

"She's right you know. Besides it would take us time to get ready for the trip anyway. So spend the time prepping and resting for the journey ahead, who knows where it might lead. Not like we have much of a choice."

"He's right, Samara, you've been running nonstop so take this time to gather yourself. I can tell you're exhausted, you're having to concentrate harder and have had to use more orchids than usual to boost your power. If you don't rest you will collapse and be powerless to help others."

"Okay, I'll take a break, I do have to admit I feel my own strength fading and that barrier spell took a lot more out of me than usual."

"Precisely, you go rest. No one would blame you if you took the night off."

"But what about you? Who will stay with you?"

"I'm sure I can find someone to keep me company for one night. Go and try to relax."

"Yes, Farisah, and I will let the others know what our plan is."

"Before we go can I ask you one more question and maybe a favor, Lady Farisah."

"Yes, my child."

"Can you tell me more about why Vestigium came here?"

"Ah yes, Vestigium came here to find himself, just as you are now and that is all I will say currently."

"What? Thats not fair."

"If I tell why he came here it could interfere with the journey you are on now. Just know he wasn't always perfect and he didn't always have all that power."

"That is the biggest copout I've ever heard so far. Did you really just 'your journey is your own' and 'knowing too much can have adverse effects on your future? What's next 'The power was inside me all along?'"

"What did you really expect? I'm an ancient spider god where do you think the clichés started?"

"You know what? Fair enough."

"As for the favor I know it probably isn't the best time to ask this of you but are you able to purify the demon from my soul?"

"Hmm. That is an interesting question. I may know of a way but in my weakened state my power would not be enough."

"Can you at least tell me how much time I possibly have left?"

"No, my senses have also dulled over the last few days. So that is also beyond my capabilities."

"While I don't like it, I do appreciate the information you have shared with me."

"But if you get the chance try talking to the Nyvx, they might be able to help you in some way. They have travelled the world for generations and have battled demons before. They may know of something to slow the process."

"I'll do that thank you."

"Anytime, Trace, now go so I can rest and you two can go unwind. The road ahead will be a dangerous one for the both of you."

"Farewell, m'lady."

"Yeah, See you tomorrow bright and early."

"Goodbye, children."

"Vestigium. Sorry I meant Trace, please follow me and I'll show you where you will be sleeping."

"What about a place to eat, because I've been living off trail mix for about a week."

"Let's get your gear put up first then we'll get to the food."

"Lead the way."

We went back outside into town toward the side that still had houses standing. The other half of town was virtually untouched.

"What stopped the fires from reaching this far?"

"We did. Myself and the others used our magic together to create a wall to hold the line, so Farisah could focus her energy elsewhere. But it didn't really help much."

"I wouldn't say that. I'm sure the creatures that live here appreciate having their homes and other places to go. It's a light at the end of the tunnel."

"It won't matter if Farisah doesn't recover."

"She will. I will do everything in my power to help her as I said before. We're just waiting for Minerva to finish her scan and I'll be the first one through the portal."

"Thank you, Trace. I do appreciate your kindness and your help."

"Anytime."

While walking through the streets we passed tree forts and stone houses and a small pond. Some of the creatures were trying to salvage what they could. We made our way to this tree-house covered in flowers and vines. "Up the ladder, the door should be open." I climbed up the ladder and was met with a red wooden door with a lotus carved into it. I opened the door to a slightly familiar sight.

"Ah another person that loves the natural leafy nature everything look."

"What's wrong with that?"

"Nothing at all. Where's the ceiling? Do you guys not believe in roofs?"

"We like to be able to see the stars and it helps us stay closer to nature."

"What happens when it rains?"

"You see that stalk with the bud on top of it in the center of the room? Whenever it starts to rain it blooms and creates a leaf umbrella. Pretty much everyone's place looks somewhat like this in some form."

"Y'know that's honestly about what I expected in this Shangri-La-like place. There's a certain woman you'd get along with."

"She sounds like she has good taste in furniture. I know it's not much but there is a hammock you can use to sleep and you can put your bag anywhere. I'm going to get cleaned up, I suggest you do the same."

"Sure, you wouldn't happen to have a shower would you?"

"Sorta, the bathing area is back down the ladder to the left, it's that pond we passed on the way here."

"Wait really? Okay, very retro I guess. I'll be back in ten to fifteen minutes." I made my way to the door.

"Where are you going?"

"The pond to rinse off, I haven't showered in days and I have sand in every nook and cranny."

"I was joking, silly. We're not savages, we use magic in

place of the technology." She laughed. "I have a bath here. You see the curtain against the wall on your right? Open it."

I walked over to the curtain of flowers and slid them aside and a bathroom with a massive lotus in it appeared. The lotus opened up. As it did so, it filled with a blue liquid. I ran my hand through the liquid, it was water and it was surprisingly hot. No technology whatsoever, yet you could still have a hot bath, running water and power. Why didn't we use magic like this back home? It would have made finding a power source for the Hun73r system much easier.

"You can put your clothes into the basket and I'll clean them for you later. There's a towel on the branch next to the light." I took my clothes off and climbed in. "Don't forget we have to go meet with some of the other guards after."

"Okay, I'll try to hurry up so you have time to bat—"

"Move over, there's plenty of room for both of us in there."

"Samara?"

"Yeah?"

"What are you doing?"

"Joining you. Nyvx and the Duaka all bathe together at least once a week and it's a bonding experience also it'll be faster this way. Do you and your tribe not do this?"

"Um. As a baby maybe but not usually at my age."

"Then how do you bond with them?"

"By watching movies, hanging out, training together simple stuff like spending time together."

"You would be closer if you'd bathe together."

"I doubt that highly. I don't think any of us want to be that close to each other."

"If this is not what you are used to I can leave."

"It's fine. I'm just gonna face this way."

"Great idea we should wash our backs first. I'll do you then you can do me."

"Oh boy."

"Shut it Minerva. So, Samara, clearly you've been here a long time seeing as you share the customs of the people here. How long have you been here?"

"I've been here since I was five, so a little over twelve years."

"Do you mind if I ask how exactly did you end up here? And how did a human become the shaman to a goddess?"

"It's really simple, Farisah saved me."

"Saved you? Are you talking spiritually or literally?"

"Both I guess. If it weren't for her and Nök I would probably be dead or worse."

"I'm going to need you to elaborate more."

"When I was a kid my family was very poor. There were five of us, my mother and father, then my two brothers and I. There was never a lot to go around. My parents were farmers but with the drought that recently plagued our farm our land couldn't produce anything of value. Every night we prayed to the goddess for a blessing to help our family. No miracle ever came.

"But one night a stranger came offering to help us. He told my parents if they planted a seed in our field the crops would grow. My father being ever suspicious asked the man what did he want in return. 'Well, Samir, this seed will cost you a fourth of your crops. If it doesn't work I won't take a single thing from you." My father agreed to the deal. He planted the seed and the next morning an entire field full of crops sprouted up. More than we could ever pick. Almost as if by magic. I was looking out the window when the man approached my father. He said he had come back for his share of the crops. And my father said, "Of course, Sir! I don't know who or what you are but thank you. You have saved us. The gods must have sent you to help us, you are an angel."

"'It was nothing,' he said, 'that isn't even a fraction of what I can do for you.'

"What do you mean, kind sir? I could change yours and your family's lives with the snap of my finger. You'd never have to worry about food or money ever again. You'd be treated like a king."

"Surely you jest, sir that would never happen."

"Have I not proven I can make miracles happen?"

"If you want me to believe that you can make anything happen then make this drought on our land end." *Snap! Drip drop. Drip drip drop. Drip drip drip drip drop.*

"'Done! Any other request?'

"'By the goddess how is this possible?'

"'I have the power to grant you anything your heart desires. If you want to leave this meager existence behind just say the word. I'm sure we could make a deal."

"What would it cost us? What would it cost you?

"Huuum. One of your three children."

"'One of my children? Surely you aren't serious?'

"'Oh I am very serious, my friend and rest assured the child you pick will be well taken care of. If you want everything you desire it will only cost you one of them.'

"'I can't do that, sir, my children they are my own flesh

195

and blood.'

"'You can always have more.'

"'No and that is my final answer.'

"'This is a once in a lifetime offer. Why don't you talk it over with your wife and I'll come back in a day or two. Have your answer for me by then.'

The man gathered his crops and left our farm. My father came in and spoke with my mother about what the man said. Over the next day my parents argued in their room nonstop about the man's offer. My mother was willing to give all three of us up but my father always said no. Until she said she would leave him if he didn't take the offer. She said, 'We don't deserve to live like this. We deserve better. Besides the man said that whichever one goes with him will be taken care of. It is a win-win. You have to choose one, that's it. It is a necessary task for us to have everything we've dreamed of."

"Is this what we have come to?' My mother stormed out of the house and my father closed the bedroom door and the house fell silent.

"The next morning there was a knock on the door. *knock knock.* My mother answered the door it was the man again. 'Good morning, kind sir, please come in.'

"'No, Ana, he won't be staying long.'

"'Does that mean you have made your decision?'

"'Yes, I have. Let's speak outside,' my father said. 'After you.' My father and the man left our house and spoke in the field for a few minutes. They were too far away for me to make out what they were saying. The man and my father shook hands then he departed from our farm and my father returned to the house. My father came to my brothers and I, and said everything was going to be okay.

"Later that night, my father asked if I wanted to go for a walk with him. 'Would you please join me, I'd hate to go alone on such a beautiful night like this.'

"'Of course, Father, where are we going?'

"'For a walk outside of town, my dear.' I had never been that far before so I jumped at the chance. My father and I headed out of town stopping at a small pond so we could gaze up at the stars and the moon. 'It's not often that we get to relax and enjoy life, Samara. So it is best we do it whenever possible.'

"'Yes, Father.'

"'The lord blessed us with you, our special little girl. You are a good girl, Samara, always doing what you're told and helping out wherever you can.'

"'Thank you, Father.'

"'No thank you, my child. Will you help your father one more time?'

"'Of course I will, Father!'

"'I'm here for my vessel.' The man from before approached us from the darkness. But this time he wasn't alone. Two dog like creatures were at his side.

"'Father what is happening, why is that man here?'

"'You said you wanted to help me right? I need you to go with the man, Samara.'

"'No, Father I won't, I don't want to go with him. I want to stay with you.'

"'Don't be so selfish, you useless girl, go with him so we can have everything we ever wanted. Take her away!'

"'No, Father I won't!' The man reached for me and I ran

away as fast as I could. 'Help me! Someone! Anyone! I need help!'

"Whistle! Woof woof! Woof Woof! I kept running. I could hear the beast closing in on me and finally I felt a sharp pain in my leg. The hound had latched on to my leg and it had no intention of letting go. 'Help! Please help me. Goddess Farisah help me!' *Sob,* I cried out and no one answered.

"'There's no point in screaming, child, no one will hear you. You don't matter. You belong to me now.'

"'You said she wouldn't be hurt.'

"'I did but she ran.' I reached for my father's cloak.

"'Please help me! Help! Papa please help me it hurts. I'm sorry. Please help me.' *Sob.*

"'It is okay, Samara, you've done nothing wrong. Now let go.'

"'Sir what about what you promised?'

"'I said you'd have everything your heart desired and you shall. Return home and your new life will be waiting.'

"'Thank you, kind sir. It was a pleasure doing business with you. I just realized I never got your name.'

"'How silly of me, my name is Balthazar.'

"'Well, Balthazar thank you again for everything.'

"'No, Samir thank you.' My father walked away disappearing into the night.

"'Papa please don't leave me! Please come back. I'll be good I promise!'

"'See, child, you were nothing but a means to an end. Your family didn't care about you. You were a leech on their lives. They will be far happier with you gone.' Balthazar snapped his fingers and shackles appeared on my feet and wrist. 'Time to go, child.'

"'I won't go with you.'

"'You don't have a choice.' He attached the shackles to the dogs. *Whistle* The dogs pulled me forward.

"'No! I won't! Help! Help me! Someone? Farisah!' With my leg bleeding and injured there wasn't much I could do other than scream for help. We walked for hours until I collapsed in the desert sands from exhaustion.

"'Get up, child! We aren't even halfway there.'

"'I can't do it.'

"'Fine! Mayhem and Chaos, our friend doesn't want to walk. Drag her!' *Woof Woof!*

"They drug me until my legs bled from rubbing against the hot sand. 'Let's stop here! I need a break.'

"'You better still be alive girl! I've got plans for that body of yours. After I break your spirit of course.'

"'Farisah help me!'

"'Still going on with that, huh? Look, kid, there is no god or goddesses. They are all gone even if they were still around they wouldn't care about you. You're nothing but desert trash. So stop wasting your breath.'

"'Farisah will save me! Farisah will come for me.'

"'Ha ha ha ha. You won't be saying that for much longer.' *Cling cling thud.* 'Go find yourselves some food you two.' *Woof woof.* The two hounds ran off towards a sand dune. *Bark bark bark. Thump yelp*!

"'What was that sound? Chaos and Mayhem return to me!' Nothing. No barks, just silence. 'Listen to your master return to me now!' *Whoosh thud.* One of the hound carcasses landed in between Balthazar and me. 'What the hell is this?

199

Someone is going to pay for this!' *Whoosh thud.* The second hound landed at Balthazar's feet. 'Enough! Balthazar snapped his finger and the dune exploded into a ball of black flames. 'That should take care of whatever that was.'

"'Not even close. Demon filth.' *Whoosh!* A large shadow fell from the sky on top of Balthazar. *Booooooom!* A cloud of sand dispersed around the impact. 'I hate monsters like you!' *Bash!* 'All you ever do is take and take.' *Bof!* With each strike the cloud of sand would raise and the pit they were in would grow deeper and wider. 'I will teach you a lesson.' *Bam!* 'You demons are nothing but cowards.' *Whack!* 'Picking on a defenseless child.' *Wham.* The sandpit slowly became a canyon pulling me down in it as well. As I tumbled into the hole I could hear the punches and kicks getting harder and harder. Once I reached the bottom I could see this large imposing creature pummeling Balthazar. 'Back to hell with you!' The creature raised its hoof above Balthazar's head and was about to stomp on it. Then Balthazar turned into a cloud of black smoke and disappeared. 'Dammit he got away. He won't escape next time.'

"The creature turned to face me and said, 'Are you okay, Samara?' This very large muscular creature with a goat nose, legs and horns knelt down to me. 'My name is Nök and I'm here to help you. The goddess sent me to bring you home. You are safe now.' Nök reached into his pocket and pulled out a white orchid and handed it to me. 'This should help with your wounds.' Once the orchid touched my hands it began to glow and my wounds began healing. 'Let's get you out of here, Farisah has been waiting to meet you for a long time.'

"After that Nök brought me to Anahail and to Farisah. She

blessed me with an amazing power and new abilities. She taught me how to use magic to heal people and become one with nature. Over the years Nök has been like an older brother to me, he looked after me. He even built this very treehouse for me."

"That explains why the doors in here are so much wider than a human person."

"Yeah, Nök is pretty big even for a Duaka. I would introduce you to him but he was one of the ones that went missing in the attack."

"I'm sorry to hear that. Maybe we'll find him while we look for the goddess's cure."

"I just hope he's okay. Wherever they took him I will hunt them down and take him back."

"Then we should probably get to the others and let them know what the plan is. So, we can get to saving everyone. Farisah doesn't have a lot of time and neither do I."

"Right! Onward!" *Splash.* "Bath time is over!"

"Hey, Samara?"

"Yes, Trace?"

"You might want to put some clothes on before you head out."

"Yes, clothing would be nice."

"Let's get a move on, the others should still be at the camp near the center of town."

"Lead the way."

Chapter 10
Ego

"Samara is here, everyone!"

"What news do you have about the goddess?"

"Gather around everyone, we have something we need to say. This man here has discovered what is wrong with our goddess. Those foul demons poisoned her with basilisk venom. Do not fret there is a cure! It is the tears of a phoenix."

"Are you telling me this child told you all of this? How do we know if he's telling the truth? Even if he is, how do we get phoenix tears? A phoenix hasn't been sighted in a very long time they might not even exist any more."

"Have faith, my friend!"

"We have faith in Farisah and you, not some puny kid."

"This kid has a name and it's Trace. You see this device on my wrist? It can locate energy signatures among several other things. If there are phoenixes left this will find them."

"And he's not just any kid, he's the guardian the goddess spoke of. He will save us all."

"No way. That shrimp? I barely sense any energy coming off of him. I've met guardians before, this kid ain't one of them. He's just a human playing pretend."

"Ouch! That was just mean and uncalled for. I am not that short. 5'8" is a respectable height for someone my age."

"And what is that, seven or eight?"

"No, I'm fourteen if you must know. And I am a guardian you pointy eared tree stump."

"Ha ha ha ha, tree stump. He got you, Anrael. Ha ha ha ha."

"Shut up, Tor, it wasn't that funny."

"It totally was though. Besides, from what I hear this kid is no joke. From what the other scouts say he stopped a barrage of their arrows with ease and that was after he broke through the barrier. Don't judge him because of his stature or looks. He may be the real deal so treat him as such."

"Tor is right, Anrael. Trace is here to help and deserves your respect. If it wasn't for him we would have no clue on how to save Farisah. Even further how to obtain what we need to cure her."

"My apologies, Lady Samara."

"Don't apologize to me, apologize to Trace."

"Do I have to?"

"Yes, Anrael you do."

"All right. Sorry, half pint. I shouldn't have judged you. If Samara is vouching for you I guess you're all right."

"Good. Now we can get back to it. Once Trace's wrist locator finds a phoenix we will use a portal to get it and save the goddess."

"Sounds easy enough, a simple smash and grab."

"In theory, yeah, but we have one issue. The demons."

"What do you mean?"

"If the demons poisoned her then they know the cure for it. They might already be waiting for us wherever this phoenix is. Or it could be a trap to get us to leave this place unguarded."

"Which is why I want you guys to be prepared for

anything and gather what troops we have left because we only have four days. We have to fortify our defenses and gather the resources we can over the next day and a half. We need everyone ready for anything."

"The demons can attack at any time and it can last minutes, Hours or days. Start gathering everything we need and move it to the goddess's temple."

"When that is done we will select a small group to go with us on our mission for the tears. We will need ten to fifteen people to volunteer. We may only have one chance at this so make sure you only get the best of the best. Tell the troops and spread the word about what needs to be done. We can still save Farisah and protect this place. I will use all of my power to get this done. Tonight rest and recuperate, in the morning we prepare for what the demons may have for us."

We spent the next four hours by the fire talking and getting acquainted with the rest of the troops. Since both the Duaka and the Nyvx are magical beings I had asked if any of them knew of a way to keep a demon from taking over your soul. They said that they had never seen a case like mine because usually the demon would have taken over by now. No one could even tell me how much longer my body could hold out against the demon inside of me. Celeste didn't give me a time frame. And the goddess didn't know either. Celeste just said that once my ego stops fighting, the demon will take over. And I need Farisah to get better so she can heal me too. Once again my life is in the hands of another and I am very sure it won't be the last. In the morning Minerva should have something for us to go off of. Until then some much needed sleep.

BEEEP BEEEEP BEEEEEP. BEEEP BEEEEP BEEEEEP.

"Scanning complete. WAKE UP!"

"Jeez, Minerva do you have to be so loud?"

"Oh, I'm sorry, I thought you wanted to save a goddess thereby saving yourself. But I can just let you sleep a little longer if you like. Let her die and take Anahail with her."

"I get it! I know what's at stake, smart ass. Samara! Minerva is done scanning. Okay, Minerva show us what you got."

"There are several energy sources all over the world that match ancient ones like yours and Farisah."

"You said that already."

"I wasn't done yet. There are several in the area but there is only one that fits the suggestions that Farisah made. There have been reports of miracles in a town called Raaja Aaraam Karate Hain or Kings Rest. From what I gathered on this town it is ruled by a duke and duchess with their eight kids. The town itself seems to have popped up overnight twelve years ago. Recently they have had people come from all over to be blessed by them. There was a very staticky video streamed on one of the sermons held in the town that shows the resurrecting of a dead child."

"That does sound exactly like what we're looking for, Minerva. I will admit you have done a great job."

"That can't be right. Is she sure that is the town there?"

"Minerva may be sarcastic and sometimes annoying but she's never wrong. Why? Do you know the place?"

"I don't just know it, it was my home."

"You don't think that—"

"Stop interrupting me because I am still not done yet but

205

thank you. As much as I'd hate to say it, you were right. There were also a few other dark energies as well located somewhere in the town. So this might be a trap or the rarity of this power could be luring all manner of monsters and men to it. I tried to pull some images of the town for an image search but all photos of Kings Rest are blurry at best."

"Then I will tell the others and we can leave now!"

"We can't leave yet, we haven't finished prepping."

"We can worry about that later."

"No we really can't. What about the defenses? What about all the injured people? There is no way they have all moved to the temple yet. We can't rush into this headfirst, Samara."

"We have the location so we need to strike before they know we're coming."

"You mean before we are ready. They might already know we're coming like, I said before."

"They probably planned for someone to figure out what they poisoned the goddess with. The symptoms and ingredients were unique enough that you or I could have eventually figured it out on our own without a computer. Not only that, they were all found in the same general area. Think about it, Samara, out of all the locations in the world, the place we need to go is your hometown. It's not a coincidence. Someone is trying to get your attention. As a wise squid man once said, 'It's a trap!' and we are going to need to plan our attack now that we know where we are going. You know this place, Samara, so we can use that knowledge."

"I don't care what it is, Trace. If it means saving Farisah then I will do whatever it takes. Even give my life."

"Samara, I get it but you need to relax. We still have three and a half days to work with. And we'll need at least another day or two to prepare for what could be an ambush. What would Farisah say if she saw you acting this way?"

"She would say that I need to stop letting my anger become my master, let my mind and heart guide my actions."

"Right, so think about this before you go running off and get yourself killed, and then you won't be able to help anyone. You're not expendable. Your life matters just as much as Farisah's. Be rational about this. Now let's go fill everyone in and help with the preparations, and think up a plan and who would be the best for defending Anahail. And who would be the best for the recovery mission?"

"Okay, Trace, I am okay. Everyone should be taking stuff over to the temple."

"Then let's go give them a hand."

Samara and I made our way back through the town but this time instead of empty streets we saw people heading toward the temple with their belongings and weapons. As we made it to the temple we were met with a wall made of woven roots and a deep trench with spikes at the bottom. A narrow pathway leading up to a door in the center of the wall opened to the populous. "What happened here? and what is this line?"

"I assume the Nyvx used their root magic to construct the walls and the Duaka used their strength to dig the trench and make the spikes."

"Are you sure that these roots will be strong enough? Why not just have the Duaka make the wall?"

"These roots are made by Nyvx magic so they are far stronger than stone."

"I find that really hard to believe."

"She's right, Trace. All of my scans show that the density of the roots are nearly twice that of steel."

"While that is impressive, what about fire? The demons already scorched half of the town with fire before, can they not just do it again with this wall?"

"Trace, look around what do you see? What did you see on the way here? What were most of the buildings made of?"

"Hmmm. Now that I think about it most of the buildings that were burned down were made of stone."

"Correct. Most of the town's buildings and the Duaka's homes are made of stone and wood from the trees around Anahail. But the Nyvx tree houses are made of roots. The very roots you see here. In the fire the tree houses took minimum damage to the outer walls. It would take days for them to burn down."

"Seriously?"

"Yes seriously."

"What happens if they throw something over the wall?"

"Try it and find out."

"Really?"

"Yes no harm will come to the people on the other side."

"Okay. *Ignis!*" I conjured a smaller fireball in my hand and threw it a few feet above the wall. *Boooom!* "A barrier? I should have known."

"You should have sensed it too, dummy."

"The goddess's temple has a natural barrier surrounding it but it can only take so much damage before it falls. The root walls are additional reinforcement to draw fire away from them. Shall we head inside?"

"Yes, we shall."

We cut through the line and made our way into the first inner wall. On the inside there was another trench and root walls with archer perches. The second wall was still being constructed but had a similar design to the other walls and several towers with vines leading over the trenches to the other towers for the archers to take shots at the demons and retreat with ease.

"How did they build all of this in eight hours?"

"The Nyvx and Duaka are fast and hard workers. They could build an entire town in a week and a half."

"With the progress, they have made here I don't doubt that."

In the distance, I hear a familiar voice shouting at us. "Samara! Everyone, Samara and Trace are here."

"Everyone, we have more news! The device has located the phoenix!"

"I can't believe it the boy actually found the phoenix."

"Yes, Trace did, but the downside is it is most likely a trap. The bird is in my hometown that seems to be flooded with dark energy according to the scan. We have a few days to come up with the best plan possible with the knowledge I have of the town. Anrael, how's the defenses coming?"

"We are slowly getting there. The Nyvx are going to make several barricades and sniper perches with our arbor magic. While Tor and the Duaka are making trenches and pitfalls around bases. We are also making trebuchets and ballista's to assist the Duakas with their range attack challenges. We should have it all done in the next day or so."

"That's great and all but what about the close quarters? Sure the Duaka can beat the demons into submission but their fists alone can't kill them."

"This isn't our first demon fight, kid, we have a plan for that as well. Come with me and I will show you what we've done so far. I'll have our blacksmith explain what she's done. Kanali is on the other end of the compound." As we walked through the outside of the temple I saw some of the troops crafting more arrows with their magic, and more trebuchets being constructed and the Duaka taking them to the other side of the temple.

As we approached the forge, a fire bellowed from it and Anrael yelled, "Kanali! Kanali step away from the forge and come explain to our small guardian friend what you have been up to."

As the fire started to die down a small pale dwarven woman with fire red hair running down her back wearing a smock and gloves stepped from behind the forge. "Oh my god, you're a—?"

"A female. Yes I am." Kanali interrupted with her thick Scottish accent. "I am tired of you people judgin' my abilities because I'm a woman. My weapons and armor are just as tough as the men's. And I'll 'ave you know mine are some of the best in the world."

"Of that, I have no doubt."

"What? What did you say, tiny?"

"I don't doubt your abilities, I haven't actually seen them in action. So, I don't really have much to say about them one way or another. What I actually was going to say is that you're a dwarf. I didn't know there were other races in Anahail other than the Nyvx and Duaka."

"Oh. Well, of course, there are other races here. Anahail

is open to all wanderers and lost souls. Specially, the ones tryin' to escape the stigma of their people and make a name for themselves. The Nyvx and Duaka are just the majority of the population."

"Hmm. Didn't know that. Then I guess I was bound to end up here eventually and my name's Trace, not tiny."

"Okay, Trace, I'm Kanali. What is it you came here for, laddie?"

"The weapons you're making."

"Oh right. Tor did say I'd be havin' visitors askin' 'bout them. So what I've started doing is meltin' down the weapons of the fallen Nyvx and started constructing weapons made from the same ebony ores."

"You mean like the wood?"

"No not like the wood. They just share the same name. Ebony is magical metal harvested by dwarves deep in the earth. It has special properties and as much as I'd hate to destroy such beautiful craftsmanship it's a necessary evil. I've been makin' spiked knuckles and boots since the Duaka like to punch and kick stuff."

"That's very interesting I've never heard of ebony as a metal or much about the dwarven people other than your skill with crafting and repairing arms. Minerva can you add that information to the codex?"

"Already done."

"Y'know I've never had the chance to meet a guardian in the flesh. I've been told that their weapons are truly unique. Do you think I could take a look at that sword of yours?"

"Sure, I guess." I unsheathed my blade to hand it over to Kanali. She reached for it with an excited look on her face.

211

"Let me grab my goggles so I can get a better look at these." When I handed her my blade Kanali immediately sank to the ground.

"What the hell lad? What's that thing made of and why is it so heavy?"

"Heavy? What are you talking about? My sword is light as a feather." I grabbed the sword and held it up for her to look at. "Well, isn't that curious. Handling it like it were nuthin." Kanali then inspected the weapon for a moment or so and the smile began to droop. "Is this it? This is one of the legendary weapons I've heard so much about. It's unrefined and unfinished."

"What do you mean?"

"This blade of yours is nowhere near the caliber of what has been described. I wouldn't use it to cut me steak let alone an enemy."

"Hey, watch it, dwarf, that's part of my soul you are talking about."

"That's the scary part of it. I'm sorry to tell you this, kid, but this blade of yours won't last much longer with all of the cracks in it and it looks to be on the verge of breaking."

"I didn't know a guardian's weapon could break."

"They don't, lad. From all the stories that have been passed about them their weapons are said to be near indestructible."

"Can you fix it?"

"No, Trace, I cannot. As you said before the weapon is part of your soul. Even if I could fix it I wouldn't know where to start."

"So my blade is going to break. Do you know when?"

"It's hard to tell, the cracks in the weapon are weird and fractures are stemming from the hilt."

"From the hilt, how is that possible? I've never even hit anyone with the hilt and I didn't think I was squeezing it that hard."

"The fractures are not from physical damage. If I had to guess I'd say it's from the energy you've been channeling into it."

"So I did this to my own sword?"

"Yes and no. Like I said it is unrefined. This weapon was not meant to withstand that kind of power. Since it wasn't able to release the excess energy you put into it, it started cracking. It's amazing it has lasted you this long."

"Trace you're a guardian can't you just summon another one?"

"Not that I know of? I didn't summon this first one."

"I'd get rid of it."

"Anrael!"

"What, Samara? You heard her, his sword is junk and he needs to ditch it. I'm sure Kanali could craft him something better." I couldn't believe what I was hearing. My sword was on its last leg and it was my fault. How could I have let this happen and how didn't I notice this? I'm a terrible guardian.

"No, she can't. No one can. This blade is a part of me and cannot be replaced. And it's not junk. It has cut down dozens of enemies and will continue to do so."

"Listen, laddie, I understand that you and your blade 'ave a connection. If you want to continue to use this blade that's your choice but I would refrain from channeling any magic

213

into it. It still has its mystical properties and will be useful in your fight against the demons. But at least allow me to make you something else for you to channel your energy into."

"Do what you want. I won't use it."

"Look lad—"

"He'll take it," Samara interrupted.

"I'll 'ave it ready for you before you all leave on your mission."

"Thank you, Kanali."

"Anytime, Samara."

"I'm not going to use it, Samara."

"Let's just talk about that later, Trace. So, Anrael what about the food and injured people?"

"That would be Tor's department but I don't know where he is."

"I heard he's in the temple gettin' the others settled."

"Then let us go see him."

"You two go on without me. I'll go gather the troops and meet you by the temple so we can go over that plan of yours."

Back to the temple we went. Now with more depressing things on my mind than the first time. In the temple hall there were dozens of people walking around with food and bandages.

"Don't worry about it Trace, maybe Farisah can tell you how to fix it."

"How can I not, Samara. If I lose my sword than I might as well just give up completely. I'll be useless."

"No, you won't be, Trace. You're plenty powerful and you've already helped us so much. It would have taken us forever to figure out what was wrong with the goddess and you figured it out in minutes."

"That was Minerva. Not me."

"Doesn't matter, if you had not come here Farisah would have died. But now we have a chance to save her. Because of you we got some of what we had lost after the attack."

"And what's that?"

"You gave us hope."

"Hope isn't a weapon and it can't kill demons."

"That's not true. Hope is one of the strongest weapons there is. It can change the tides of battle and give people the strength to carry on. It is the light at the end of the tunnel. If it wasn't for hope I would have died in that desert long before Nök rescued me. Look around you, Trace, these people here have had a fire lit under them and that's because of you. Because of you they are working harder than ever before. They have all shaken off the darkness that was plaguing them just to help make your plan a reality. This is because of you."

"Ugh. You sound like my mother and I don't need that right now."

"She sounds like a very caring woman."

"She is. But she's also crazy like you. She thinks I'm some type of beacon of hope too."

"If we both are saying it then it must be true."

"Or you're just as crazy as she is."

"Hey, you two, over here," a voice shouted from the crowd of people.

"Tor!"

"Good to see you guys decided to join us."

"Well we wanted to have some news to share before the next time we saw you."

"Is that right?"

"Yeah it's about the phoenix. Trace's device found one."

"That's great to hear. I knew you'd come through, kid. Actually, I have some good news for you guys too."

"What's yours about?"

"As you can see we have accomplished a lot defense wise over the last few hours. Since everyone has pulled all of their resources the whole moving people to safety has actually gone a lot smoother than we thought. The children have been helping escort the injured and making sure they have what they need. We will be done in another ten to fifteen hours."

"That's good to hear. Has anyone spoken with the goddess?"

"Yes, I have been checking on Farisah off and on throughout the morning. She seems to have more energy today; she managed to bless the swords, shields and a few hundred arrows."

"Really?"

"Yeah. With another attack pending Farisah wanted to help in any way she could."

"Every little bit helps."

"With the arrows and other weapons we may actually have the upper hand in this battle against the demons."

"So, you two, tell me where's this phoenix located?"

"We can't tell you everything yet, we have to wait for the others. So we can go over the plan as well. But what we can say is that it is in a town not too far from here and it may or may not be infested with demons."

'Sounds like fun to me. We get to strike back at them on their home turf this time. Who's all going so far?"

"Don't know the full details of that yet but I do know that you, Trace and Anrael will be coming with the recovery party."

"We probably don't need much more than that. The four of us would be a wrecking crew."

"I like your confidence, Tor, but I'm pretty sure we need more than that."

"Ha ha ha ha. My little friend, I am a Duaka, some of the strongest creatures on the planet. We have the goddess's shaman and one of the best Nyvx archers ever. And we have you, a guardian. You are a walking talking immortal killing machine that has enough power to wipe out demons with a single blow. Anyone else will be overkill."

"You have way too much faith in my abilities, Tor. I am none of that. And I have never killed a demon."

"Have you fought one?"

"Yeah. One."

"Have you killed any monsters?"

"A few."

"Can you heal from wounds that will kill most beings?"

"I guess I can."

"Do you have a blade that can kill anything?"

"Sorta if it doesn't—"

"Close enough!" Tor interrupted. "The two of us on our worst day are still walking tanks with the ability to shatter mountains."

"Maybe you can. I max out at half a ton."

"Wow, Trace, you're really strong."

"Not really. That's like half of a beetle or a mini cooper."

"I don't know what species that last one is but those sound like heavy bugs."

"Samara, they're not bugs they're cars."

"Oh. Well, cars are still heavy too."

"Samara, you have lived a very sheltered life haven't you?"

"No, I've been outside most of my life."

"Oh no."

"Joking! I'm joking. I know what sheltered means."

"Good. I was almost disappointed."

"Tor, Samara, Trace! Anrael is looking for you guys. She's outside with the rest of the troops."

"Thanks, Milon. We should probably head outside then. Don't want to keep everyone waiting."

"Back through the crowd of people?"

"Back through the crowd of people."

"Make way everyone, demon wrecking crew coming through. One side, people, important business," Tor shouted.

The people looked at Tor and separated. "After you."

"I wish I had that power."

"When you're an eight foot tall half man, half goat and half giant, people know when to get out of your way."

"I didn't know that halves came in thirds."

"Very funny. At least I know what my halves are."

"Touche."

Tor, Samara and I made our way back out of the temple. From the top of the stair we saw a large grouping of Duaka and Nyvx by a fire and a large table. "I'm guessing that's the group we're looking for."

As we headed over to the fire we saw Anrael waving everyone over. "All right, everyone the others have arrived, stand at attention." The Nyvx and Duaka turned to face us, and their eyes followed as we made our way to the table then turned their attention back to Anrael.

"Trace and Samara you said you had some information on the location of the phoenix."

"Yes, everyone, Trace has found a phoenix."

"Yeeeaaaaaahhh. We can save the goddess."

"Hold on, guys, it's more to it than that. The place we have to go is probably filled with demons and it is possibly a trap for Samara. So we will have to fight for our prize and keep an eye on her."

"Would it not be simpler for us to leave Samara here? That way she's safe and able to help the people here?"

"While it would be the best for Samara to stay here because they obviously want her to come with us, they would probably figure out that we know something and possibly run. We will have to give them what they want. So here's the plan. In the cover of night, Samara, Tor, Anrael and I will make our way through the town with a few archers in tow."

"I don't want to be there any longer than we have to be. We will be like lightning. A single flash and we're gone."

"I agree with Anrael we need to move as fast as we can. Besides, with my size there aren't many places to hide."

"The jolly green giant is right. Everyone bring it in. Minerva can you show us the map again?"

"Right away, Trace. Displaying map."

"So from here we just head north through the town. The manor has three entrances, one on the south, west and north sides of the building. That means we either split up to find the phoenix as fast as possible. Or we stick together and clear the place out by going room to room."

"It would be a bad idea to completely split up knowing that we could be walking into an ambush. But we can do two groups with one going from the south entrance and the other from the west. That way if one group gets stopped we have another force able to come from behind and ambush the ambushers."

"That could work but if we all get caught up in a fight they could just take the phoenix and leave."

"They wouldn't do that; they want us to go there and get that bird. They want to keep us in the town so the bird will stay there."

"Anrael is right, Samara, like we said before, this whole thing is probably a distraction to go after the goddess anyway so we need to get in, get out and back to Anahail. So let's break into the two groups, one for infiltration and the other for misdirection. Me and Samara will take five archers to act as our support while we search for the phoenix. Tor and Anrael will take the rest of the archers and act as the distracting force. Once we get what we need we regroup at the north entrance and use a portal to extract."

"Trace, are you sure we will only need five?"

"Samara, the both of us are pretty powerful on our own and so are the Nyvx. We will be using the full force of our power to take out threats immediately to avoid further detection. The whole point of our group is to move fast and eliminate everything in our way, any more people than that and it will slow us down or attract more attention."

"Right, I understand."

"Everyone clear on what we need to do?"

"Yeah." In unison.

"What about us? Can we come with you guys?" A Duaka with blonde and green hair and two more with a grey beards stepped up from the crowd.

"Sorry, Reinor, Lenka, and Danik but we already have Tor and we will have to move fast. You'll probably be best suited to protecting the goddess."

"Come on, Anrael. we can help you guys. I'm fast and I'm as strong as Tor, same goes for Danik and Lenka. You might need more muscle than that and archers may not cut it."

"What do you guys think?"

"They are pretty strong but they hasn't had much experience in real combat."

"But they did do a good job fending off the demons in the first attack."

"He is right, we may need additional muscle. It isn't really fair to expect Tor to do all of the heavy lifting."

"All right, fine, you guys are coming with us,. Danik you will be on the distraction team with Tor. Reinor and Lenka will join Samara and Trace on the infiltration team."

"Sounds good."

"Everyone clear now?"

"Then let's get that bird," Tor shouted.

"Everyone that's going will meet back here when the defense preparation is done. Samara will open the portal for us and we will head to King's Rest. Minerva, how much time do we have left?"

"You have fourty-four hours remaining before the venom overwhelms Farisah's body."

"Okay, everyone go finish your preparation and say your goodbyes, be back here tomorrow at sundown." Tor, Anrael

221

and all of the troops dispersed. Some went to help finish the wall, weapons and escorts. While others went to speak with their families and try to receive blessings from the goddess.

"How do you think tomorrow will go, Trace?"

"Honestly? I don't know. With me not really being able to use my sword my firepower will be limited."

"Kanali will have a weapon for you to use so don't worry about that."

"Samara, I already told you I am not using whatever that dwarf makes me."

"Why not?"

"What kind of guardian relies on any other weapon than their own? It's the principle of it."

"Are you saying that guardians have never used another weapon but their own?"

"No. Most guardians are trained in many forms of armed and unarmed combat. They have used any means or weapons necessary to get the job done."

"Then why can't you?"

"Because it's not the same. They used other weapons by choice not because theirs was broken. Or not able to perform its duty."

"So, it's a pride thing?"

"No, it's a me being a terrible guardian as always, thing."

"Like I said, pride. Trace, we need you at your best and if you can't use your actual weapon, the one Kanali builds will be a close second. So please think about it. That is all I can ask."

"I'll think about it but I won't make any promises. Enough standing around, we should actually help out a little so we can finish preparations sooner."

"Maybe you should go see Farisah at some point about your sword? Maybe she knows how to fix it?"

"Doubt it. I have never heard of a guardian's weapon breaking. And I can't ask my mom because then she'll know I'm a failure too."

"You're not a failure, Trace, everyone has their struggles that test their resolve. This one must be yours."

"Maybe I could try to contact Celeste. Do you think Farisah can do that?"

"Under normal circumstances she could communicate through scrying but in her current condition I would say no."

"Did you say communicate through scrying?"

"Yes, I did."

"Why didn't Celeste mention that while we were training? I can totally do that."

"Then give it a shot."

"I will. Later. As for now we need to help the people. I'm going to go help with the ballista's."

"I'll go tend to the injured then." Samara and I separated to help the others complete the task at hand. I could feel it in the air, war was coming to Anahail. Here's hoping that everyone was ready for it.

Chapter 11
Hell Fire

"What to do first? Maybe I could help with the heavy lifting and defense building." After all this time and combat it was time to put my engineering classes to work. "With myself and Minerva we should have been able to come up with some modifications. Like an auto-loading magazine for the ballista's so they can continuously fire. Maybe we could make some holy water bombs for the trebuchets to launch at the demons. Oooh, some explosive bolts would do nicely. Maybe I could get the Nyvx to infuse their magic in the bolts and barrels to ensnare the demons. Decisions, decisions." I headed over to the smithy to gather the supplies needed. I'll be honest making things again like me and my mom used to was just the distraction I needed. While I was working I had Minerva create some plans to show everyone so they could better understand what we were trying to do. I had two small teams working on the bombs while I worked on building the magazines for the ballista's. The others continued to build the rest of the walls and artillery late into the night and early into the morning.

"All right everyone, it is now three a.m.," Tor shouted. "We have a little over thirteen hours left to finish the last parts of the weapons. If you can continue to work go right ahead but remember to take breaks, replenish your energy and to work in shifts. As for the warriors that will be joining us on our mission, and defending this temple along with the people in it. It is quitting time for you. Go get a long rest, you are going to need it. You all have your orders. We all are depending on you. The goddess is depending on you. The last time the demons attacked we weren't ready but this time we will be, just in case they do show up while we are gone. Back to work, everyone. And may the goddess bless you in her divine light!"

Samara came and found me working on the finishing touches for the weapons. "Whatcha working on?"

"I'm still trying to infuse some of my own energy into some of the projectiles so they explode the enemy into a blaze of glory. But they keep blowing up in my face instead."

"Well, finish up. You heard Tor, every fighter needs to get rest for tomorrow. You've been working nonstop for the last ten hours."

"That means you too, Ms. Healer."

"I know let's go."

"Just let me finish this last one and we can leave. Alllllllmooosstttt." *BOOOOOOMM!* "Come on why is this so hard?"

"Maybe you just need to step away from it. I don't know about you but I am exhausted. I barely have the energy to walk home."

"Same and I can't wait to get back so I can contact Celeste. Minerva, what time is it in Maryland?"

"It is six fifteen p.m."

"Great, it's still early there. I hope I still have enough energy to try scrying."

"Then let's hurry home."

As we walked home we passed several now empty houses.

"It's quiet."

"You mean exactly how it's been for the last few days?"

"Yes. This quiet is something I am not used to. I miss the laughter, and the joy on the faces of the children. I miss the old Anahail."

"We'll get it back, Samara, by any means necessary."

"I hope so."

We make it back to Samara's tree house. She makes her way to the bath and I to the hammock. "Are you not going to join me? I'm sure you are just as dirty if not more so than I."

"Uh, maybe later. I'm going to try to reach Celeste first. By the way, Samara, how does one communicate through scrying? I have only ever used it to see past events."

Splash! "It's really simple, Trace. You see that crystal ball on the table in the coroner."

"Yeah?"

"Grab it but be careful not to drop it. The crystal ball amplifies your scrying abilities and should let you reach Celeste. So once you have it you just focus on the person you want to talk to and start scrying."

"Yeah, you see I am a novice when it comes to scrying is that all I need to do?"

"Yes, if it helps think of their location."

"Okay. I'll give it a shot."

I grabbed the crystal ball and peered deep into the center. I thought back to the cabin in the woods and pictured Celeste. I called out for Celeste. "Celeste! Celeste can you hear me?"

"Sir Trace, is that you?"

"Sir? Celeste doesn't call me—"

"Sir, it's me. It is Thain," Thain interrupts.

"God why? Thain I need to speak to Celeste."

"The madam? She's right here, Sir, what message do you have for her so I might relay it?"

"Who am I talking to? It's the young sir, madam."

"I need to speak with Celeste directly, Thain!"

"Then why are you talking to me?"

"I'm bad at scrying that's why."

"Are you sure. Madam? I don't think that is necessary. Well. You do know best. I will pass your message along. Sir Trace, Madam Celeste said to hold on a second she is grabbing her crystal ball—"

"Hello, Trace is that you?" Celeste interrupts as Thain's voice trails off.

"Yes, Celeste it is me."

"What can I help you with, dear boy?"

"I had a question about guardian weapons, more so my weapon in particular. I spoke with a dwarf that examined my sword with some magical goggles. She said that my sword has several fractures along the blade starting from the hilt."

"That sounds odd."

"That's not even the worst part. She also said that if I continued to channel energy into my weapon it would shatter and break."

"Impossible! A guardian's weapon can never break."

"That's exactly what I said. But if she is telling the truth would you know of a way to fix this? The blacksmith also said that my weapon was unfinished and unrefined if that helps."

"Well, I did mention to you before that because your blade was not summoned the normal way that there could be some unknown effects. From what you have told me your blade is

227

being crushed under your own energy."

"Is there any way to stop it or repair it?"

"My best guess. You'll have to summon your weapon properly."

"But you said that I can't do that because of the demon currently fighting with my ego."

"Correct, there is no way for you to establish that link with what's currently going on in your soul. So I would advise that you do not channel any energy into your weapon and try to minimize the general usage of it to prevent further damage."

"You said minimize, so I can still use it in battle?"

"Trace, heed my words. If your weapon breaks you may never be able to connect with your ego ever again. Use your blade if you truly must but only as a last resort for the time being. Do you understand?"

"Yes, ma'am I do."

"I'm sorry I couldn't have more pleasant news for you child."

"It's not a big deal, Celeste I already knew how this conversation would play out anyway."

"Don't sound so down, Trace. You still can use your powers without the blade."

"Yeah on a very small scale compared to with my sword."

"That's only because you have not trained enough in that form of casting. Everything takes time. You still have Soulbound so use it for some extra training, maybe the other you can give you a better peptalk."

"Maybe I will give that a shot. It couldn't hurt."

"That's the spirit, Trace. Never give up, and keep pushing forward like a true guardian."

"Thank you, Celeste I appreciate the help."

"I am sorry I could not help more. Goodbye for now, Trace and good luck."

"Thank you and goodbye. Tell Thain I said bye as well."

"Will do. Hey, masonry man! Trace said bye. No I will not ask him that for you. No, he's busy training and he doesn't have time for your silly questions. Ugh, Trace, Thain has a question for you before you go."

"Okay."

"He said, have you found your wolf self? Whatever that means. He said to find it you have to look deep within yourself."

"What is he talking about?"

"I dunno, Trace, he's lost it. Have a good night!"

"You too."

I came back out of my trance to see Samara less than two inches away from my face. "Ah." *Thud.* "Samara what are you doing and why are you naked."

"Observing your trance state. I have never seen such focus and eyes twitching. You must have been focusing really hard. Did you get any good news?"

"I got some news. But first would you please put some clothes on!"

"I guess I can. I don't really understand your issue with the human body, Trace, it's very similar to yours."

"I don't have issues with it other than it being very distracting when trying to have serious conversations."

"Whatever, give me a second." Samara waved her hand and a white nightgown appeared on her. "Happy?" "Yeah. Back to what I was saying. Celeste confirmed what Kanali said. She told me that if my weapon did break it could spell the end of my guardian career and to only use my sword as necessary." "Celeste also said that I should try to train with Soulbound so I can get more used to casting without a conduit."

"What is this Soulbound you speak of? It sounds mysteriously ominous."

"I will agree to the mysterious part but it is a good idea."

"But you really don't have time for that do you?"

"Sure I do. Soulbound doesn't operate at the same flow of time as the real world. Hours here are more like days there. So if I go in there for the next few hours I could get a lot done."

Zzzzzzzzz.

"Samara? Saaamara? She did say she was exhausted. I guess I could carry her to her bed. *Umph.* Up we go." I walked over to Samara's bed and laid her down and tucked her in. "Get some rest, tomorrow is going to be a long day. Now back to the grimoire." I grabbed my backpack and scrounged through it for Soulbound. "Where the hell is it? This is the last time I let someone else pack my bag for me. Come on where is it?" I continued to feel around and felt a solid book-like item. "Found it." I pulled the book out and laid it on the floor. "Going in." *Swoosh. Thud.*

"Welcome back, other me. I was starting to think you forgot about me."

"Nope just traveling the world, getting sand in my crevices. Also possibly destroying my sword along the way."

"Oh, so the same old same."

"Yeah, pretty much. Trouble seems to follow me wherever I go."

"Just for the record, little me, that never changes."

"Good to know."

"What can I do for you?"

"I need your help. My sword is breaking because I suck and can't use it any more. But I don't know what to do without my weapon. I've always fought with it and if I can't use it at all I might as well just sit on the sidelines. My fire is weaker and smaller without my weapon. Even if I use Kanali's weapon I still won't be of any use to anyone. I don't know what to do."

"Well, the first thing you need to do is take a deep breath and calm down. Second, you're not weaker without your sword, you just lack control over your power."

"Wait what?"

"It isn't anything to be ashamed of considering you just learned how to cast without your weapon not too long ago. Others have taken a lot longer to accomplish less. So now we have to work on getting you combat ready and show you how having control can make a world of difference. Tell me, Ves, in all the times you've trained with your sword have you ever given thought to how much power you're actually using?"

"No not really I just channeled my energy into my sword and it worked."

"And what about the last time you were here with me. When you were setting fires with your power did you think how much you were using?"

"Um. No I was not. I just poured my energy into the trees until they caught fire."

"Exactly. You weren't thinking about how much power was needed, you just wanted a result. You think your flames are small without your sword but that is only because you weren't regulating your energy on your own, your sword was. If it helps, think of your sword simply as a conduit for your power. The only reason it made you seem more powerful is because of the energy you stored in it."

"Are you saying my sword is practically useless then?"

"Not at all, a guardian's weapon serves two purposes, one is to be a manifestation of that power and the second is to help keep them in control of said power."

"So if I understand you right. My sword is a conduit but it is also a generator at the same time."

"To simplify it? Sorta but no. Your weapon does have power on its own but it does need you to activate it, just like how it did for you when your powers first manifested."

"So, the sword is like a car now?"

"No, it's not like a car. While you and your sword may seem like separate entities you are one and the same. The power you have, it has. It is forged from your power and soul. It is you, in a way."

"Okay, one last time just to make sure I have this right. You are saying my sword and my powers share a symbiotic relationship and that the sword is just my soul's way of making sure I don't lose control of said power?"

"Yeah let's go with that."

"So how do I get more control of my power?"

"Coming here is one of the ways to gain control. Throughout your combat experiences your weapon has in some ways become a crutch for your lack of control. But here in Soulbound you don't have your sword. No fancy gadgets. Just you. You are the only thing currently standing in your way. Sorry, that's not exactly true. The battle of your ego and

232

the demon that's trying to possess you is also in your way but one battle at a time. Come with me, we only have a few days so let's go to the range shall we?" As the other me said that the world changed to an arena with multiple targets at multiple ranges in every direction. "Welcome to the arena!"

"Wow! It looks exactly like the forest we were just in. Now with some training dummies."

"You are a hard one to impress. Does it matter if the place changed that much?"

"Not really."

"Good. Now pay attention, Ves. Here in this place I will go over how to better utilize your energy. Making you more effective with your 'fire' power. No pun intended. What I need from you is to simply make fire."

"I can do that. *Ignis!*" A small fire appeared in my left hand.

"Perfect! Now I want you to make that fire a little bigger. Just add a small amount of energy to it."

"Okay. Small amou—" *Boooosh!* A giant fire exploded from my hand and sent flames flying all over the training grounds.

"I said a small amount of energy, not a tsunami."

"I did do a small amount. At least I thought I did, I just did what I always do when I use my sword."

"Jesus christ, Ves! This is why your sword is cracking."

"Sorry."

"Don't be, that was kinda impressive. I mean Smokey the bear would be pissed but that was a lot of fire. That does show me that you definitely have the energy to spare. Which is good because this is going to take a while. Let's try it again."

"Ignis!"

"Just a small amount of energy. Let the fire grow."

"Okay. I got it." *Boooosh!*

"Looks like you don't got it. Ha ha ha ha."

"That's not funny."

"Oh but it is. One has to remember to take time to enjoy the little things in life. Like laughing at your younger self making the same mistakes you once did."

"Wait! You've had to do this before?"

"Yeah, a long time ago. I learned the same way you are now."

"I know I'm not supposed to ask questions about the future and all but how long does it take for me to learn this control thing?"

"Without giving you the exact answer? It'll take a lot more than two or three tries."

"Will I be able to control my power well enough to battle the demons after this?"

"Yeah, sure. Totally."

"Why did you say it like that?"

"Say what, like what?"

"The way you said that had a weird inflection in it."

"Oh, did it? Sorry I didn't mean for it to. Let's just get back to the lesson. More fire!"

"Fine. Ignis!" More flames and more explosions. One after the other the fireball would form then erupt into chaos.

"Okay it's time for a break now."

"What? I was just starting to get it."

"Ves, it's been three days. Take a break."

"What? Three days! How much time has passed in the real

234

world then?"

"I'd say about three or four hours."

"That's it?"

"Yeah, Soulbound is trying to give you as much time as possible but I will have to limit you to two more days."

"Why? The last time I was here I spent nearly two weeks running and dodging arrows."

"True but in that case you were repeatedly taking breaks via ejection from the book as well as you weren't expending anywhere near the amount of energy you are now. As much as I would like to keep training to the last minute, this place puts a strain on you. It's part of the cost of being here. You are pushing yourself harder for longer periods of time allowing for you to progress faster than normal. However, to you it only feels like an hour or two."

"I can keep going longer than two more days."

"I'm sure you feel like you can but your body needs to rest or you will collapse. I feel like there is a basic rule for something like this, oh wait there is. Rule number three of combat; know your limits. And I am telling you your limit is two more days."

"Yeah, those rules didn't work out for me the last time."

"No one said that they were absolute. Ves, can I be honest with you?"

"Yeah, I guess."

"Those rules aren't real rules, they are mostly guidelines. Should you keep them in mind while in combat, yes, but sometimes you need to improvise. At some point you'll have to figure it out on your own. A lot of these guidelines conflict with the others. One of the other rules after knowing your limits is don't be afraid to push yourself beyond your limits to achieve victory. It's useful combat wisdom but try not to let it bog you down. Take a break and we'll get back to training after that."

"If I have to."

"You do."

"So, older me, I have a question for you. And don't worry it doesn't have to do with the battle ahead. Clearly, I survive so I'm not that concerned."

"Are you sure about that?"

"Yeah. You're proof that I survive."

"Not necessarily. Yes I am an older version of you but I may not be the you that you are. I could be the you from another dimension."

"There are other dimensions?"

"Yes. I mean no. I mean what was your question."

"I was just curious if I would ever return home? To Eden."

"Isn't that your goal?"

"Well, yeah but that doesn't mean it will happen."

"The answer to that question is yes. You will return home one day but by then you won't recognize it. In the time it takes you to get there Eden and its people won't recognize you either."

Ten minutes passed as I sat gazing up at the sky. I started to think that in just a few hours I would be waging an assault to get a mystical bird to save a goddess. "Not a kid any more, I guess I had to grow up eventually."

"What are you talking about over there?"

"Oh nothing, just staring at the sky has me wondering and I have another question."

"Always another question with you. Shoot."

"Do I even become a true guardian?"

"What do you mean? You are a real guardian."

"I mean do I ever become someone? Will people recognize me for my own skills, powers and deeds or will I stay in my family's shadow?"

"You already are someone, Ves, and there never was a shadow for you to hide in. You are your own person and you will do many great things between now and my time. In the future people come to you for advice and help. To them you are Vestigium Rgis the savior that surpasses the legend."

"Really? I mean that sounds hard to believe. I'm not strong enough to be anyone's savior."

"Yeah, really. Maybe or maybe not only time will tell."

"I have one more final question."

"It better not be about the future."

"No, it's not."

"Really?"

"Okay maybe a little. It's about our family."

"Okay?"

"Are they happy in your time? Do they ever resent me for leaving them?"

"That's two questions. But I will answer them both. Yes they are happy and no they never resent you for leaving. They didn't lie to you when they said they understood your leaving. They knew you wouldn't have left them for no reason."

"That's good to hear. One more question."

"I swear if it's about the future again."

"Nope. I just wanted to get back to training again and was wondering if the break is over?"

"What's it been, fifteen minutes? And you're already wanting to jump back in."

"No rest for the wicked. And after what you told me I can't sit around here waiting. I can't surpass my grandfather if all I do is rest. I have to take action to be that person that helps people, the one they can depend on."

"Fine then let's get back to work."

"Yeah! Ignis!" A large flame exploded out of my left hand.

"Whoa, calm down there, mini-me, I get you're excited but try not to burn the forest down."

"Sorry."

"Just relax. Let me tell you something that works for me when I channel my energy. Think of your power like a sink or a faucet. Just like you would control how much water comes out, do the same for your energy."

"That sounds dumb."

"I know it does but try it. Imagine you are a sink."

"I'm not going to do that. I am not a sink, faucet, fire hydrant, water hose or any other water spewing appliance."

"Why not?"

"Like I said, it sounds dumb."

"Why does it matter what it sounds like? It's simple and gets the point across. Do you or do you not want my help?"

"I do."

"Then do as I say because it works."

"Ugh. Fine."

"Now create more fire."

"*Ignis!* I am a faucet."

"Now try adding your energy."

I closed my eyes and envisioned myself turning on the

sink, slowly I turned the knob, letting my energy flow bit by bit. "Is this even working? I don't really feel like my energy is flowing enough."

"Open your eyes and see for yourself." I opened my eyes and the small flame had grown into a mighty blaze.

"I did it! I really did it. I can't believe the faucet thing worked."

"Told you it would. I'm a little bit of an expert when it comes to us."

"This is awesome!"

"Yeah, now throw it at that target to your left." I hurled the fireball at the dummy and it burst into flames.

"I never thought I'd be able to have this kind of power without my sword."

"You'd be surprised at what you are truly capable of. We still have a day and a half so let's do it a few more times. And let's try moving around a little bit."

"Y'know I have always wanted to try something but never could because I always had my sword in the other hand. *Ignis!*" A fire spawned in each of my hands.

"Impressive!" The fire in my right hand started to fluctuate.

"No. I want you to grow." I started to focus my energy on my right hand and the left flame started to fluctuate. "No not you too."

"Listen, Ves, you just learned how to control your energy in one focal point. I think two separate places might be a bit too much for right now."

"Do you doubt me? I'll just concentrate on both flames." I focused my energy on the left flame and it started growing again. Both flames slowly grew bigger and bigger. "See I got this." *Boooooom!*

"Did I tell you or did I tell you? "

"I was so close though."

"One at a time for now. You will get to two fireballs and so much more later."

"Fine. I'll stay at one. *Ignis!*"

The rest of my time in Soulbound was me making fireball after fireball until I could do it on command. For the first time in a while I was starting to feel like I had real power and it was all my own. The training sessions with myself really helped me grow as both a person and a guardian. Not to mention I got to see a glimpse at my future self. I hoped that I really did become the person he said I would. Because honestly I thought I sounded pretty damn awesome.

"Okay, little me, I think that's enough for now. You have learned all I can show you for now and completed part two of Soulbound's trial."

"This was part of the test? How? It didn't take nearly as long as the first one."

"Not every test is about being a challenge. The point of them is to help you get stronger and to develop the skills you'll need. It's about learning who you are as a person and a guardian. Accepting your weaknesses and learning from your failures will show you where you need to improve. Why do you think I'm here?"

"I just figure that Soulbound knew that I probably wouldn't have listened to someone else about being a water fountain."

"I said sink and let it go already. But seriously from me,

the older you, and I know I've said something like it before. I am proud of you. You've grown a lot in such a short time and more is still to come."

"Thanks! You've taught me a few things that I'll never forget."

"Well, I hope not because it's all the basic fundamentals of your job."

"Hey! I'm trying to have a touching moment okay. Thank you for the help. I hope I can continue to make you proud."

"I have no doubt that you will. I'll catch you later, little me."

"Yeah, I'll see you sooner or later."

"I'd wager sooner, definitely sooner. See ya." *Swoosh.*

"Back to reality. Minerva, what time is it?"

"It is eight a.m., and you were in your trance for five hours. You have T minus eight hours before the infiltration mission, And twenty-nine hours before the goddesses demise. I suggest you get some rest."

"You don't have to tell me twice but I'm still wearing the same clothes from earlier. I think I'm going to take a quick shower first." I run to the bath to clean up then head to bed. "Minerva, set an alarm for five hours."

"Alarm set."

"As your strength grows, I grow. Infecting your soul with my darkness. Soon your soul will be mine!"

"*Beep. Beep. Beeeep.* WAKE UP! WAKE UP! WAKE UP!" Minerva interrupts.

"I'm up. Do you always have to yell?"

"It worked the last time and you were tossing and turning again I suspected that you were having a bad dream, so I

241

figured it's the best way to wake you up."

"You really don't have to yell, But thank you and yeah I was having a dream about the demon again. From the sounds of it I might not have much time left."

"Then you better get to saving the goddess then. Your life depends on it."

"Yeah I should probably go talk to Kanali about that weapon she's making for me. I should probably let Samara know I'm heading out. Hey, Samara?" I called out for her but no one answered. I looked around the room and Samara was nowhere in sight. "I guess she already left." I grabbed my gear and headed back to the goddess's temple.

As I approached the closed gate and walls around the temple I could see that the towers and the rest of the traps were completed. A Nyvx was standing at the tower near the gate door. They shouted down to me. "Ah, the guardian has finally arrived. We thought you were going to sleep through the infiltration. Come on in, Samara and the others are getting geared up and finishing their preparations. OPEN THE GATE!" The massive door made of woven roots separated to show the inner walls and temple. Unlike yesterday the artillery and the troops were far more organized. The Ballista's were positioned on the walls and the trebuchets were lined up behind the inner wall.

"These guys are truly amazing. They have created a fortress in such a short time."

I walked through the camps and headed to the forge. "Hey, Kanali! Are you there?"

"Yes, I'm 'ere. I'm guessing that you're 'ere for the weapon? You're kinda early."

"I figured that I should get some practice with the weapon before I head into a life and death battle with it."

"Fair enough. You're in luck I finished it a little while ago. Let me go get it." Kanali disappeared back into her weapons hut. Clinking and clanking could be heard as she came back out of the hut with an object wrapped in cloth in her hands. "Jus so y'know I slaved over the forge all night. I wish I 'ad more time to work on it and make it perfect for you but as it stands this will 'ave to do. I hope you like it." She handed me the cloth-wrapped item. "Well, what 're you waitin for? Take the cloth off." I removed the cloth to reveal a long black slender curved cylinder with golden glyphs engraved in it. "What do you ya think?"

"It's very, uh… fancy."

"And what else?"

"Um, it is very cylindrical."

"And?"

"And… uh… I… uh."

"You don't know what it is do ya?"

"Not a clue. It looks like a hilt."

"That is more than just some hilt. It is a conduit, lad. Similar to your sword but with two differences. One, the material it's made of is strong and won't break from you channeling your energy into it. Second, this hilt can essentially become any weapon you want it to be. You want a sword, it's a sword, you want a shield or a spear and that is what it becomes. You jus' 'ave to pour your energy into it and shape it. Give it a shot."

"Okay, here goes nothing. *Ignis!*" I took the hilt in hand and focused my energy into it, and fire shot out of it.

"That's it, lad now shape it into your weapon of choice."

"How do I do that?"

"It's your energy, tell it what to do."

"Right. I want a sword." I focused my energy to try to shape the sword to match my real one. The flames slowly morphed into the mirror image of my sword. "That's really cool, it kind of reminds me of a flamethrower."

"Tis more than that. Once you have the shape you want, reduce the energy you put into it and the blade will harden."

"Really?"

As the blade finished forming I stopped channeling my energy into it and it hardened and became an actual blade. "That's amazing."

"It is. And no matter how many times the blade breaks you can reforge it by focusing your energy back into it. As long as you 'ave the hilt you 'ave a weapon."

"This is awesome! Thank you, Kanali and I apologize for my behavior yesterday."

"Don't worry about it, lad I understand. I may not be a guardian but I do understand 'aving a connection with your weapon. I 'ave made many weapons in my time, they're a part of me, like me children. It's always been hard handin' them over for others to use because I don't trust them not to break 'em or not care for them properly. Which is why I usually reforge weapons instead of makin' new ones. But you. You understand what it is to have a weapon be a part of you. So I trust that you will take good care of this weapon."

"I definitely will, and thank you again."

"No problem, lad, now run along. You've got some practicing to do right?"

"That I do."

"Oh, wait, before you go, if you want the weapon to revert to its original state there's a button on the bottom hilt that will disperse the energy you stored in it, and return it to its natural state. Jus' don't press the button while you're channeling energy."

"Why?"

"Cause it will shoot the raw energy out of the blade like a laser. If I 'ad more time I would have made a better safeguard for you but what can you do? Don't go aimin' it at any of your friends if you do happen to do that."

"Good to know." I pressed the button on the bottom of the hilt. *Hiiiissssss.* Steam flowed from the blade as it vanished into nothing. "Cool. I better go get some training with this so I don't make a complete fool of myself. "

"Oh, wait, one more thing. 'ere's a holster for the weapon. It should clip on your belt."

"Thanks. I'm going to go practice."

I made my way through the goddess's fortress and, on my way over to the training ground, I stopped by the command area to talk with the others. I saw only Tor by the war table. "Hi there, Tor how's the prepping going?"

"Ah, Trace you've finally joined us. The prepping goes well! Samara, Anrael and I were actually taking a bet on when you'd show up. Since you were up late training. Even though you were told to get some rest."

"Is that right? So, Tor, who won?"

"I did of course! Samara thought you'd be here sooner and Anrael thought you'd sleep through the whole thing. I went for the middle."

245

"Trust me, with my nightmares, there is no sleeping through anything. Do you guys need my help with prepping?"

"Nah. We got this, everyone else is off getting last minute things. You should probably do the same."

"Actually, I was going to get some practice using this weapon Kanali made for me. Wanna come with?"

"Me train with a guardian? Seriously?"

"I mean if you don't want to that's—"

"Of course, I am all about it," Tor interrupted. "Some light sparring will loosen the muscles before the main event."

"Good, let's get to it then."

Tor and I make our way to the makeshift training area outside of the fortress. "Open the gate! Me and Trace are gonna box a bit."

"What? You versus the kid? Tor, go easy on him."

"He's not just a kid, he's a guardian he might even beat me."

"Doubt it. He's so small. OPEN THE GATE!"

"So, Trace, Samara said you went to train in some book? How does that work?"

"You mean the grimoire? It's basically a training ground constructed by the magical properties of the book. It uses your soul—"

"No, not that!" Tor interrupted. "The training. What kind of training did you do in there?"

"Oh. I, uh, I learned how to better control my energy."

"Through combat?"

"No. Actually I really haven't had the chance to use any of my training in combat other than for evasion."

"Evasion? You're a guardian, you don't run away, you

246

fight and you win. People run from you."

"Well, I was running from myself so technically you're right. I had to go back to learn a few of the basics."

"Fundamentals are important. You definitely sound more sure of yourself today. I guess that means your training bore fruit?"

"It did."

"Then let's see what you got!" We walked about fifty feet away from the wall into the burnt wasteland of Anahail. "This should be far enough, Trace. Show me what you've got."

"All right! Let's do this!" I pulled the hilt from the holster. "Ignis!" The hilt absorbed my energy and manifested a ten-foot tall plume of fire. "Whoa way too much energy, I need to reel it in. I'll reduce my energy." The flame shrunk down to a more manageable size then hardened into a slender blade. "Let's see what this thing can do."

I ran at Tor head on but he didn't move a muscle. *Whistle.* I stopped dead in my tracks. "What's wrong? You were about to charge me right?"

"I was, then I sensed the energy coming from the ground in front of you and decided otherwise."

"Impressive. You caught on to my trap pretty quick. I should have expected that from a guardian. No matter I'll just bury you in rubble." Tor planted his feet firmly in the ground and put his hands in front of him. *Whistle.* The ground began to shake and I could feel the waves of energy pulsing through it. "Here it comes, Trace. Don't just stand there you should move."

"Not yet."

"Move!"

"Not yet."

"Trace, move!"

"Okay." I jumped in the air right as several stone spikes shot out of the ground.

"You saw that one coming too, huh? I better step my game up." As I fell back to ground a pit opened up beneath me. "Looks like I win."

"Shit!"

"Trace, if you don't do something you're going in the pit."

"I know, Minerva. Come on think." I looked at the hilt and an idea struck me. I pointed the blade down and focused my energy in the hilt. The blade became a flame once more. "Ignis!" I focused a large amount of energy into the hilt and pressed the button on its bottom. *BOOOOOM!* A large explosion of fire erupted from the hilt, downward to the bottom of the pit. My descent started to slow as I got closer to the bottom. "That wasn't enough. I guess I need to try it again. *Ignis!*" *BOOOOOM!* The force from the second blast propelled me out of the pit and at Tor. "You haven't won yet! My turn." As I flew through the air toward Tor, I focused my energy into the hilt once more. "*Ignis!*" The flames shifted into the form of a giant war hammer. "Brace for impact in three... two... one..." Tor stomped his foot and a cloud of dirt shot up from the ground. *Thud! Whistle.* With the dirt cloud still too thick to see I could feel that my attack did find its target.

"That was a close one, Trace. If that had actually hit me I would have been in trouble." Once the cloud fully cleared I saw a rock statue with Tor's likeness crumbled to pieces. "That was pretty clever. Using your fire to propel you out of the pit."

"Where is that coming from? Why does it sound so muffled."

"It shouldn't be that hard to find me. Let me give you hand." *Whistle.* A hand reached up from the dirt and grabbed my weapon. "Nice toy. Mind if I borrow it?" The hand disappeared back into the dirt.

"Oh, come on! The whole point of us sparring was for me to get used to the weapon."

"Yeah, but what happens when you get disarmed?" *Whistle.* Tor shot out of the ground and propelled himself toward me on a boulder with my weapon in hand. "I'm gonna borrow your trick. I hope you don't mind."

"Trace, you may want to move. Tor is traveling at very high speed and if you combine that with his weight it is the equivalent of being hit with a freight train."

"Fine by me but now you can't dodge. *Ignis!*"

I pointed my left palm forward and sent a torrent of flames at Tor. "You're right I can't dodge but I don't need to." Tor grabbed the boulder from underneath him and transformed it into a giant shield, blocking the flames. "That flame isn't nearly strong enough to stop me," Tor shouted as he continued to fly at me.

"Is that right? Let me turn up the heat then. I know older me said not to try to cast with two hands but if I don't push myself I won't get stronger. Here goes nothing." I raised my right hand and aimed at Tor. "*Ignis!*" Another wave of fire shot from my palms and into Tor's shield. The power of the flames against Tor's shield completely stopped his momentum. "See, Minerva, nothing to worry about."

"You stopped him but it did cost you a moderate amount

249

of energy and is causing energy fluctuations within you. If you wish to win this battle you might want to take him out quickly."

"I feel fine. Let's give it a little more umph." *BOOOOM!* The waves of fire combusted and sent both Tor and I flying in separate directions. "Ouch. I didn't expect that to happen."

"I warned you, didn't I. But you never listen."

Tor got up and walked over to me and put his hand out. "Ha ha ha ha. That was awesome, kid. Let me help you up. Those last two attacks caught me completely off guard. I don't know what Samara and Anrael were worried about. You held your own just fine and without your weapon. And you never once went for your sword. She told me that you were down on yourself because of what Kanali told you. But I didn't sense a single shred of doubt or despair within you. Here's your hilt back."

"I was told not to use my sword unless it was an emergency and this wasn't an emergency."

"Either way. You did good. Glad you're on our side."

"I should say the same to you. We should probably head back in. Before people wonder where we went."

"Oh, I am very sure everyone knows where we're at."

"What makes you say that Tor—"

"That was amazing, you two!" One of the Nyvx shouted from the wall. *Cheering.* Several people were along the walls towers and bridges applauding.

"That was awesome."

"Well done! The weapon performed perfectly as I designed it."

"Enough showboating, you two, get back in here!"

250

shouted Anrael.

"We're coming, calm down." The gates opened back up and at the entrance was Samara waiting for us. With a disapproving look on her face.

"That was truly impressive, you two, but remember we only have a few hours before we leave. I hope you didn't expend too much of your energy in your horseplay."

"Samara, we were just having a little fun. Trace needed some help training. We still have plenty of power left so don't worry about that little warm up. Right, Trace?"

"Yeah, I'm fine, got plenty of energy left in the tank."

"Good. But I still suggest you two go rest so you can conserve your energy."

"I'm fine, I don't need to conserve anything." Samara gave Tor a very stern look. "I mean yeah, actually, I could go for a nice sit down, maybe a water break. Let's go, Trace. I bet you're probably hungry."

"Yeah, come to think of it, I haven't eaten anything in like twelve hours."

"Well, let's go get you something to eat. Far away from here and any furrowed brows. We should go to Kai's hut, it should be open by now. He should have something delicious cooked up."

Tor and I walked over to one of the huts near the entrance of the Temple and looked around. "Where was Kai's place again?"

"Was it a left or a right at the entrance?"

"Y'know, Tor, we could ask someone."

"No, I know where I'm going. Follow me. It's to the right." Tor and I spent the next hour and a half looking for

Kai's hut with no success.

"Tor, where's this hut? We've gone around this temple multiple times."

"Um, I don't know. I thought it was out here somewhere."

"I just need some food, don't care what it is. We only have like an hour and a half before we leave."

"Fine. There are some other places to get food inside the temple."

"Great!" Tor and I headed into the temple. We saw numerous places with all kinds of food to eat.

"Ah, Tor I've been waiting for you to stop by." Someone shouted from the hut closest to the temple door.

"Kai, is that you? I thought you said you were going to build your place outside."

A humanoid cat with white fur and a scar over their right eye waves us over. "I thought about it but realized that if an invasion were to happen everything would probably get destroyed in the commotion. Besides it's way cooler inside the goddess's temple. What can I get you guys?"

"Meat! I need meat."

"What my small friend here said and some fruit for me please."

"Then you are in luck. I found an elk whilst I was roaming around outside of town. I also have some of your favorites Tor, palm berries and bolba apples."

"You're the best, Kai. By the way, this is the kid I was telling you about."

"This is the guardian that is going to save the goddess? Well in that case eat as much as you like. The goddess needs you to be strong and full."

"I'm going to try my best to save her."

"Don't try, just do. There are a lot of people depending on you and the others. The lives of all the people and creatures in the realm are at stake."

"That's enough, Kai, I think he gets it. Right, Trace?"

"Yeah, I do, and there is far more at stake than just Anahail."

"What do you mean?" Kai and Tor say.

"If we fail I'm as good as dead and if I die I won't be able to keep my promise."

"I thought if you failed you'd be possessed," said Tor.

"I thought it was becoming a demonic harbinger of death and destruction that unleashes the apocalypse upon us," said Kai.

"That's pretty dark, Kai. Why in the hell would you say that?" said Tor.

"Ooops! Did I say that out loud?"

"Yes! Yes you did," Tor and I said.

"My bad. Sometimes I say things in my head and they fall right out my mouth."

"Only to replace it with your paw…"

"Anrael! What brings you here?"

"The small one and Tor."

"Is it time already?"

"Fifteen minutes until the portal is opened, so finish up here."

"Aye, aye, Captain Mom! Thanks for the reminder."

"Shut up, Tor. If you weren't always late to everything I would stop having to remind you."

"I'm never late. I arrive exactly when I mean to."

"Ugh. Fifteen minutes!" Anrael said as she stormed out of the Temple.

"Do you always have to piss her off, Tor?" Kai chuckled.

"No, just Monday through Sunday."

"Um, isn't that every day?"

"Minerva, I'm pretty sure that was the point."

"Oh. I mean I knew that. I was just making sure you were paying attention."

"Sure you…"

"Less talking, more eating," Minerva interrupted.

"Your watch is right, Trace, we should hurry so we can gear up," Tor said as he raised his plate of berries and dropped them in his mouth.

"So, it's a race? Fine!" I began shoving food in my mouth hand over fist.

"Why does everyone always have to make a mess at my place? You two are lucky you…"

"Done!" Tor and I interrupted and said loudly.

"Whoa, Kai, sorry about the mess I'd stay and clean up but you know, duty calls. C'mon, Trace, we gotta go get ready," Tor said while picking me up by my collar.

"Not a problem, Tor, the mess will be here waiting for you to return."

Tor, with me in tow, hightailed it out of the temple to our gear.

A booming voice was heard from outside the tent as I put my gear on. "Five minutes! Everyone, the Portal will be opening in five minutes! Unless you are keeping watch on the walls, head into the Temple for safety. No one is to remain outside once the portal opens. As for the infiltration team, meet at the base of the temple stairs when you are ready!"

"Was that Samara?"

"Yeah, that's one of her spells. She can amplify her voice over most of the city if necessary," said Tor.

"Maybe she could tone it down a little. She's gonna make me deaf."

"It wasn't that loud, Trace, stop being a drama queen."

"How would you know, Minerva, not like you have ears?"

"I have audio input ports. How else could I hear all of your whining?"

"I wish I could mute you, my life would be infinitely better."

"And by better you mean deader?"

"Don't go patting yourself on the back too hard. The only thing you do is nag me into action. You're like an older sibling that thinks they know it all."

"Two minutes! We have two minutes until the portal opens!"

"Trace, you ready?"

"Yeah, born ready, Tor, let's go!"

"All right, all of the civilians have been moved inside the Temple! Everyone line up!"

"I'll open the portal. Everyone, defend the goddess until we return. The rest of you into the portal! For the goddess and for Anahail!"

"For Anahail!" *Whoosh!*

"For Anahail!" *Whoosh!*

"For Anahail!" *Whoosh!*

"Where is everyone? I can't sense anyone. Why is it so dark here?"

"Trace, didn't you say that your scanner detected a lot of dark energy here?"

"Yeah, there is supposed to be."

"Is it possible your scanner was wrong?"

"Minerva is never wrong when it comes to detecting energy. They could be cloaking themselves. They did know we were coming after all."

"From what I can tell there are still small traces of dark energy lingering in some of the houses up ahead."

"You heard Minerva, everyone stay on your guard and move forward. Let's get to the manor so we can get the bird and get out of here. Anrael and Tor you know what we need to do. Trace, with me. We're going straight up the middle."

"Right! And if you encounter the enemy, call for backup. Minerva keep me posted on all energy traces in the area."

"Continuous scan already active." Time to move out. As we made our way into the town. There was nothing, no noise, lights, not even the sound of wind passing between the buildings.

We finally made it to a large open area with two thrones. In those thrones sat the duke and duchess of Kings Rest. As we stepped into the village the buildings started to shift and morph into these demonic structures. With spires shooting out to the sky. With eyes and fingers protruding from the faces of the buildings. The Duke and Ductches had vanished. "Quite the illusion."

"Looks ominous."

"I guess it would draw the attention of passersby if a hell mound was visible to all."

"Love the whole this, the end, struggle is futile, look. Very um… What's the word?"

"Draconian?"

"Creepy?"

"Gothic?"

"Ugly! Yes, that's the word I was looking for. A complete and total eye sore. Pun intended."

"You can share your exterior design tips with them after we get what we came for," interrupted Anrael. "Tor, Trace. Focus you two. Enough standing around."

We all went our separate ways and started heading through the town. We saw a T-intersection surrounded by houses ahead. "Which way do we…"

"Anrael was right, this place is creepy. It feels so empty, and those eyes don't help the feeling of being watched. Sniff… sniff… sniff… sniff… Ugh, what's that smell?"

"Yeah it smells like rotten eggs and death."

"Um, Trace?"

"Yes, Minerva?"

"You remember when you said to keep an eye on energy levels?"

"Yeeeaah?"

"There's a swell of energy coming from the houses ahead."

"You heard her, prepare for an ambush."

"Arrowhead formation! Trace, you and the archers will hang back behind the muscle."

"Behind the muscle? I am the muscle!"

"Ha ha ha ha. Oh really, kid?"

A wave of energy traveled through the ground and met the beast, it split up into two separate energies. "It's not just one enemy. There was a second hiding with the other!"

"Hmm. They think if they split up it will change things. Lenka you take one I'll take the other."

"On it Rin!" They both stomped their hoofs in unison. The wave met both creatures again and the two energies halted. "See, easy as stumpin' berries in a troth."

The ground started to rumble again and the two energies split into four. "Um, guys? It split into four separate energies. I think we have a…"

"Monsters!" We heard shouted in the distance.

"Hydra?" All of the energies emerged from the ground. Four fifteen foot scaly creatures with golden beaks and slender bodies and claws shot out from the ground!

"Earth wall,!" The two Duaka stomped in unison and walls of earth started to form around us. *Woooosh. Whoooosh. Whoooosh.* A blanket of arrows fell from the sky and struckk each of the hydras. Then the bodies crashed into the rock walls. At the moment of impact their bodies split again and the creatures dug back underground. Multiple flakey husks were left above ground.

"They split again! They actually are hydras. I thought they dies out in the war of beast"

"Hydra sprout multiple heads not bodies. Minerva! Do you know what these things are?"

"Thinking… Thinking… Thinking… Um. Not a clue."

"No clue! What do you mean no clue?"

"This entity has never been encountered before or at least the information has never been entered into the database."

"That's just great. Can you start analyzing it?"

"Sure! But I will need more time and I will need you to

get a better view of it for the scans."

"Consider it done! Well at least it'll be done the next time they surface." The ground started to rumble again. "Here comes another wave." The serpent like creatures dug under the wall and lunged out of the ground at us.

"They circumvented the wall."

"Clever girl," said in an Australian accent.

"Minerva, now is not the time for movie references!"

"Sorry, couldn't resist. Maybe try dodging."

"No duh!" We all dodged out of the way of the four massive creatures.

"No one attack until we figure out a solution to stop their multiplying. Just dodge while Minerva analyzes them."

"Maybe we should hold our fire! Keep an eye out for the other creatures. Until we know how to deal with this," one of the archers shouted.

"We really don't have time for this. Minerva, how long will it take to analyze them?"

"A visual analysis could take a few minutes. But a genetic analysis could take a matter of seconds. But for that I would need a sample of its DNA."

"Well, there's the skin it's been shedding. Will that work?"

"Yes! That should be enough to start breaking down what that creature is."

"All right, let's get that skin. Hey, Reinor, mind making a door for me to grab the shedding?"

"One doorway coming up." He walked up to the wall and touched it and a small door appeared. "Go for it. Keep an eye for those things."

"I will." I made my way through the ten foot thick wall of

stone and glanced out the opening. "I can't really sense any movement under us."

"Maybe they left?"

"Yeah, that's it, Minerva, they left."

"Just being optimistic."

"Let's just get that skin." I spotted the freshly-shedded skin laying at the foot of the wall. "Okay, Minerva, time to get you your sample." I reached out for the skin and the scales started to stand on edge. Almost as if it was still alive and could sense my presence. I put my wrist out for a scan. A teal light started to scan the length of the carcass.

"This is peculiar."

"What is?"

"From what the scan says this creature has some similarities with dragons."

"Why is that peculiar? Don't most serpents and reptiles stem from dragons and wyverns?"

"Somewhat yes. But these scales seem a little weirdly underdeveloped. And until I get a closer look into the creature's DNA. My preliminary guess would be that whatever this is, its skin continues to grow after it is shed, unlike dragons."

"What makes you think that?"

"Take a closer look at the scales, Trace." I went to grab the scales to take a closer look and the scales came to life and wrapped around my arm.

"Crap, what is it doing?" *Crunch!* "Ow, my arm, it's breaking my arm. Let go." *Crunch!* "It's getting tighter. Shit. Think, Trace. I got it. I'll burn it off. IGNIS!" The skin released my arm then split in half and fell to the ground. "That was a close one. No more touching weird dead skins."

"See, the skin is clearly still alive."

"That's putting it lightly. And now my arm is covered in whatever was on that skin."

"Analyzing. Seems that it is possibly a lubricant to help the skin slide off the creature. Wait… There are small traces of venom on the tips of those scales."

"Why is the world spinning?"

"Oh no, not again." *Thud!*

"Trace! Hold on don't pass ooooouuu…" As I faded in and out of consciousness. Everything started to hit the fan.

"They're everywhere! (Echoes)." I felt the ground start to rumble.

"Someone grab the kid! (Echoes)." The rumbling grew stronger.

"Sir! The creatures are preventing us from reaching him. We need to move, or we're going to be surrounded."

"Is this really how this ends? Is this how I die? I guess it's better than becoming a deeemmoo…"

"Trace wake up! Trace can you hear my voice! Wake up!" That voice, it sounds like Samara's. "Trace! WAKE UP!"

"Gasp! My head feels like it's about to explode." *Ching clank.* "Samara, where are we? Why am I in chains?"

"You're awake! Trace I need you to focus. Those creatures from earlier overwhelmed us and grabbed me then brought me to this place. Minerva filled me in and said something similar happened to you too."

"What is this place?"

"I don't know but we need to figure a way out. The others could be in danger. Can you get out of your chains?"

"I can try. Ignis!" Nothing happened. "Weird. Why didn't that work? I just need to focus more. IGNIS! IGNIS! IGNIS!" Nothing. Not even a spark.

"Is that normal?"

"No it's not. I may not have a lot of spells but that one has never failed me."

"What about brute force? Guardians are stronger than normal people right?"

"It's worth a shot. Okay. C'mon hmph! Ugh! Hmph! Ugh! Nothing. I'm stuck. What about you? Can you use any of your powers?"

"No, it's as I feared, something is blocking our powers."

"Could it be a field?"

"I don't think so. While you were unconscious, I scanned the area, there are no fields or spells at work here. Or at least none that can be scanned. Odds are that this may have something to do with those things that attacked us. Which, I did find some interesting things out from the sample I managed to get."

"And?"

"Whatever that thing is, it is ancient. Like older than dragons ancient. Like primordial ooze ancient. Like, like…"

"We get it. Get to your point," Trace and Samara interrupted.

"So what I could see in that DNA is that this creature even predates the new gods and most of the creatures roaming the world today. If I were to guess, these beings are from purgatory. It is said that the beings from purgatory were put there after the beast war because they were very dangerous to all that walked the earth. Mortal and immortal."

"Hold on a sec. I need to roll over to try to get up. Ugh. Enuh. Minerva, I need you to test my blood for the venom and see if it matches that of the venom in Farisah."

"Will do but… What would make you think it's the same thing?"

"They may not be, it's just a hunch. But like you said these creatures are primordial and all reptiles may come from their family tree. So maybe it wasn't basilisk venom that poisoned the goddess but this thing."

"If it did, does that mean the phoenix can't help us?"

"Not necessarily. A phoenix's magic is very potent and can bring people back from the dead. So it still should work."

"Analysis done… From what's left of the venom in your body I can gather that the venoms are a match."

"This just got interesting and what do ya mean what's left of it?"

"The venom in your body has somehow burnt away. Maybe the dose wasn't as high as Farisah? And what do you mean by interesting?"

"If those things are from purgatory then how did they get here? And why not send them to just wipe out Anahail in one go? I thought there might be more to this. This is definitely bigger than just going after one goddess."

"Do you think someone might be targeting immortals?"

"I don't kno…" The north wall turned from solid metal to sand and crumbled. And it revealed a throne room covered in gold, statues and gems. "What is this place?"

"Samara, you have returned home. It's been so long. I can't believe that someone managed to find a use for you. After Balthazar was forced to flee without you he returned for your brothers. We were lucky he was still willing to deal after what you did to him. It was a hard decision to make but your mother and I deserved better. With the wealth we gained power, respect and we even had more useful children. The thing is, child, some very powerful people have promised us more power and more money for you. Seeing as you've been blessed by a god. You've finally managed to pay us back after all. All we have to do is keep you here until the demon arrives and he'll take you off of our hands. Then he'll wipe out those mongrels you call friends. And we'll be on easy street for the rest of our soon to be immortal lives."

"You're monsters the both of you. Selling off your children to a demon for riches. What you have done is unforgivable. I will make sure you pay for your crimes."

"Will you now? Big words from a child. You are cattle to be done with as we please. You know nothing, are nothing and will always be nothing. You are meant to serve not to speak. Let us show you. Get the sacrificial altar ready to summon Balthazar."

"Trash!"

"What? Did that little vagabond just say something to us? Let's hear it, boy. Speak!"

"You're trash! Both of you! How could you trade your family, your own flesh and blood for wealth? You deserve nothing because you are low lives. You both are a waste of space. Selfish assholes!"

"What an insolent child? How dare you speak to us this way, you peasant? I will end you. Ooh or better yet I will have our dear Samara end you."

"I'd never hurt him and there's nothing you can do to

264

change that."

"I can and will. Open the portal!" *Wooosh!* "Prepare for a reunion, child." The room started to shake. And flames erupted from the portal. Demons started pouring out of the flaming maw. Out stepped a slender man with a black cloak with flame pauldrons and horns stemming from the sides of his temple. With a scar from the tip of the brow to the bottom of his chin and an eyepatch on the left side of his face.

"Well, well, well. Everything has gone according to plan. The two of you have truly proven to be my best assets."

"Thank you, sir. It is truly an honor to work alongside you. We got her here and we used those things you provided. And that fake phoenix you provided lured them in like a charm."

"As planned. Now where were we? Ah yes the blessed child. Little Samara, you will finally be mine."

"Another scumbag demon. Just great."

"Quite audacious of you, child. Who is this one? I only asked for the girl."

"It's one of her friends, those lizard things brought him with her. I don't know why. But, sir, may we ask a favor? Since you don't need him why don't we have a little fun with him? He has spoken out of turn and now must pay for it don't you agree?"

"Yes, what do you have in mind?"

"Well, a little possession could be fun and it'll teach both him and Samara a lesson."

"I'm listening. "

"Have her kill him."

"Oh, you two are vindictive. But I like it. She should suffer for what she's done. And after we kill the impudent one we'll make her kill the rest of her friends. Now, child, get up!"

"I refuse."

"I'm not asking." Balthazar grabbed her by throat and breathed black smoke into Samara's mouth. "That should be enough."

"Let her go, you demonic pollup."

"Ha ha ha, defiant to the end I see. You've got a strong spirit, kid. Too bad you hitched your horse to this one. You might have lived longer. Now rise, child."

Samara's body started to contort against her will. "Please don't! Please don't make me do this." Samara walked over to me and grabbed cracked blade from my sheath. "Please, I'm begging you, he has nothing to do with what happened back then."

"And now he will be the first of many that will die at your hands. Now take that sword and drive it into his heart!"

"Please don't do this! Trace I'm so sorry." With tears in her eyes.

"Don't worry, Samara, everything will be okay. You can't kill me. I'll be fine."

"I'm sorry I can't stop myself," she said as she drove my blade into my chest. The world went black.

"So this is how it really ends. Stabbed with my own blade. A world of eternal darkness. I feel no pain, nothing. I was told death was cold. There's not even a bright light. Wait, wait a minute. I know this place. It's that world that Celeste and Thain brought me to that night. But how did I end up here? No spell was cast."

"That's because you came here willingly."

"Willing? Don't think dying is... the... same... Who the

hell just said that?"

"I did, child."

"Who is I? I don't know anyone named I."

"Always the smart ass. I am Flare and I am your ego. I am part of your soul, I am the source of your powers."

"If that's true then where in the hell have you been all this time?"

"I've been with you the entire time. Trying to help you but you could only hear my call when you were under great duress. But since we have been united in this way you can hear me."

"This is so confusing. So are you saying you've been watching me the whole time? Then does that mean you've been roommates with a demon?"

"Not willingly, for a while now I've been keeping that thing at bay. But my power, or what I've been able to use of it, has been all but depleted. And soon he will take over completely. I need your help. I need you to accept my power child."

"Is it that simple?"

"No, it's not. Because of the impurities caused by the demon the process will be painful. But if you can survive the pain you'll have access to untold power."

"So succeed and be awesome or fail and die? Got it! How do we do this?"

"Do you see that edge over there?"

"Edge what edge?" As soon as I say that a cliff edge presented itself.

"You need to jump."

"Jump? Jump where?"

"Just do it. Trust me. Jump!"

"You know you could just be the demon pretending to be something else."

"I could be or I could be what I say I am and trying to save your life."

"Fine, here goes nothing." I jumped off the cliff and an immediate warmth started to build in my chest. A flame started to appear at the bottom of the pit. The flame grew brighter. The closer I got I began to make out a cage with bars. As I reached the bottom the gravity started to lighten up. And I slowly descended to my feet. The flames started to dissipate as I walked closer to the cage.

"Finally, we meet face to face, child. Come closer so I can get a good look at you." I walked to the bars of the cage to try to see the creature. A black mist filled the inside of the cage. The only thing I could make out was these piercing red eyes. Like embers in the night. "You've grown quite a bit since your last visit to this place. You should be able to handle some of my power. Do you see the chain that surrounds my cage?"

"Yes?"

"I need you to break them and free me."

"Well, that definitely sounds wrong. You are caged for a reason. I don't know if that would be wise. How did you end up in there? With your possible demon eyes and now chained cage."

"The demon put these chains on my cage to stifle my power so it could take my power and yours. The longer you take the weaker I will get. You'll have to trust me. Break the chain!"

"Fine, but promise you won't eat me."

"Ew, why would I eat you?"

"Well, if you could be a demon that eats supple teens. I want you to promise you won't eat me."

"I promise I won't eat you. Happy?"

"I promise not to eat your supple young body."

"I am not saying that."

"You want to be let out don't you?"

"This is a matter of life and death."

"Exactly! Say it."

"Fine! I won't eat your supple young body! You are a weird kid."

"Ha, I can't believe you said that. Creepy. Let's get this over with." I reached for the chains.

"Wait!"

"What am I waiting for?"

"The moment you try to break those chains you will be in excruciating pain until all the impurities are gone from your body and our link restored. Or die."

"That all?"

"Um? Yeah that's all."

"All right, let 'er rip."

"Don't do it child. It is a trap. It's the demon trying to get you to release it."

"Where is that voice coming from?"

A small fox pup limped out of the shadow. "Don't do it, that is the demon. Look at its eyes. Look how it hides in that miasma. It's trying to lure you in. If you break that chain you will die and the demon will take your soul. He will reincarnate!"

"Hmm, is that true?"

"Oh darn, you've got me red handed. I was hoping you

would just touch the chains and release me so I could be free to terrorize the world… Is that evil enough for you?"

"Terribly so. I'm opening the cage."

"No!" The fox's voice deepens. "You can't free her! She is the devil. She will destroy everything."

"She will, will she. Sounds good to me."

I grabbed the chain and pulled with all my might. And the moment I pulled the chains my blood started to boil. And the pain I once felt all those months ago came flooding back. *Booosh!* My body became consumed by the blood-colored flames. "MY GOD. THIS HURTS SO MUCH!"

"You have to keep it up. Once the impurities are gone the burning will stop and the chains will shatter."

"EASY FOR YOU TO SAY! IT FEELS LIKE MY SOUL IS BURNING."

"Well, in so many words it is."

"Is ahhhhh. Why does it hurt so much." *Chink. Crack.*

"You're doing it! Just hold on, it's working." Seconds turned into minutes and minutes to hours. Who knew how long I held on to that damned chain. But it felt like an eternity. As the time passed the flames had changed to a bright white flame and the pain had started to fade. *Crack, crack, chink, clunk.* "I know you've been through a lot but just a little longer. We're almost there. Break the chain!"

Dazed and exhausted I muttered to myself, "One last push. I can do this!" *Snap, clunk, ching, clang.* The chain shattered and fell to the ground. The cage door hadn't even opened yet and I could feel this massive wave of energy wash over me. "What is this feeling? Is this my true power?"

"Well, what are you waiting for? Open the door."

"Excuse me but this is kind of a big deal you know." I reached for the door.

"Your hands are shaking. Are you scared?"

"Sorry, but no. I'm shaking with excitement. Because one way or another once I open this door, my life will be changed forever."

"Then do it already! Open it! Set me free." I grabbed the cage door and flung it open. And out stepped a giant red wolf with multiple tails. Flare put her paw to my chest and said, "Let us burn our enemies with our purifying flames!" A surge of power flowed into me and flames covered my body as I started to rise out of the pit. And like a missile I shot straight toward a light and the fox from earlier appeared and blocked the entrance.

"You're not limping any more. Congrats."

"You insolent child. What have you done? My plans ruined, I will destroy you. You will not escape. I will not be defeated." The small fox transformed into a two-headed hell hound. "I will devour your soul." *Awooooohh!*

A wave of fire pushed the demon away. "Nice try, Fido," Flare said, appearing next to me in her massive multi-tailed wolf form. "The kids with me, so that means no devouring him, his soul or any other part of him. I'll protect him and those he cares about and destroy his enemies. And right now, the enemy I see is you, tiny. Vestigium, go ahead and go save your friends. Leave this leech to me."

"You sure? It would be easier if we fought him together. This thing has been draining me of my power for quite some time. I would like to repay him. You have the other demon to worry about. Be careful out there, with me fighting him in here

271

I won't be able to regulate your power. It will fluctuate a lot. You'll have to manage on your own."

"Understood! Send him back to the hell hole he crawled out of!"

"You dont have to tell me twice."

With him out of the way I raced up to the light. "Ugh, it's so bright." With a bright flash I awakened on my side still in chains. I heard two unfamiliar voices as I came to.

"So, what do we do with this body?"

"I don't know? Maybe we can eat it. I don't think master Balthazar would care."

"Okay, I'll take the arms. You take the legs. And we split the torso and head. Deal?"

"Deal! Legs are my favorite!"

"Trace, you're alive! I thought you were dead it's! Awful…"

"Minerva, shh."

"Hey! He's not dead!"

"Not yet he's not. I'm not missing a meal because he's too dumb to stay not living."

"Well, there goes the element of surprise. Let's get these chains off. Ignis!" *Boooooom!* Flames erupted from my body melting the chains and scorching everything in the room.

"Whoa! I did not mean to do that."

"Um… where did that come from?"

I think I finally let my ego go to my head to say the least.

"What's the situation, where is everyone?"

"Oh, right. After that demon guy made Samara stab you, He made her kill another Duaka name Nök. Btw you still have a sword in your chest. You should probably take care of that.

"Right!" I grabbed the hilt of the blade and slowly pulled it out.

"Hmmm."

"Hmmm? Why Hmmm?"

"This doesn't hurt like I thought it would. It doesn't even hurt at all."

"Really? Maybe because there's already a hole there, pulling it out is painless?"

"I don't think that is how any of this works, Minerva. As I pulled the blade out, it started to crack more. After a few seconds, the entire blade came out. And fell to the ground and the cracks that started to spread all the way through the blade. My sword erupted with energy and then shattered."

"Well, that's not good."

"No duh, Minerva!" I'd have to worry about the sword later. I could use the hilt for the time being.

"Hey Trace?"

"Yeah Minerva?"

"I know it was really cool and all but what are your plans for patching up the wound in your chest?" Before I could answer the wound started to burn and close by itself.

"Problem solved!"

"Wow, that was some stabbing. Most people die when they are mortally wounded. But you've gotten stronger. You should get stabbed more often."

"I don't know how to take that, Minerva."

"Take it as you having my approval to be stabbed as much as you like."

"Thank you? I guess."

"You're welcome, back to the situation at hand. You need

to help Samara and the others! While you were dying on the ground. In a puddle of your own blood. In the fetal position, like a baby."

"I get it, Minerva."

"Right. Shortly after you died the others made their way to the palace to get the bird and rescue you guys. But then the demon guy sent a bunch of demons and the now possessed Samara after Tor and the others!"

"Anything else?"

"Oh yeah, that demon guy made Samara turn her parents into those two demons you charbroiled."

"Serves them right."

"Agreed! Enough talking. Get to saving the others."

"Which way did they go?"

"They went do the corridor on the right fifteen minutes ago."

"Fifteen minutes!" I shouted as I stood and sprinted to the door. "How long was I out for?"

"I don't know about thirty-five minutes give or take."

"I really have some catching up to do." As I ran through the palace bodies both friend and foe littered the ground. "What if I'm too late. I hope there are still people to save."

"Focus Trace. Just focus on the battle ahead of you. Focus on saving Samara from that demon." *Whistle.* "Something's coming from below.

"Jump!"

"It's those things again. Minerva did you ever figure out a way to beat these things?"

"Not really, I got distracted by the whole kidnapping and

killing of you. But I suggest you avoid them." *Whistle.* As I landed another one came out of the wall.

"I don't have enough time to dodge. Ignis!" *Boooooom!* The entire hallway filled with fire.

"I don't sense those creatures any more. Must have fled." I kept running through the palace.

"I have to be getting close."

"Why not try locating them with your energy?"

"There's too much demonic energy around us to single them out."

"Must I do everything for you? I'll scan for you, just keep an eye out for more of those things. Keep running straight."

"All these hallways look alike." *Whistle.* "More of those things. We really should come up with a name for them." Four more of the creatures shot out of the ground, walls and ceiling. "Why are these things so attracted to me?"

"Who knows? Maybe it's your magnetic personality."

"Hahaha. Very funny. Ignis!" *Boooooom!*

"I've got it!"

"Got what?"

"The name. The name for the creatures, let's call them molgrons."

"That's a dumb name."

"You're a dumb name!"

"That makes no sense."

"Doesn't have to!"

"I found them! Take the hallway to the right."

"Can you tell if everyone's alive?"

"Not really. The other energies are fading fast though. You might want to hurry."

"I'm running as fast as I can."

Whistle. "More molgrons!"

"See, its pretty catchy."

"No it's not, I'm just tired of calling them creatures."

"They keep multiplying. There's eight of them!"

"No more than what we've had to deal with before."

"That was with a small army with us. And let's not forget you got kidnapped last time."

"Ignis!" *BOOOOOOOOOOOOMMM!*

"The explosions are getting better. You keep that up and you'll blow this place to smithereens."

"It's not my fault. I'm not used to this much power. It's kind of hard to control."

"Well, get control. I wasn't joking about you destroying this place. This building can't take much more of your mini-nukes."

"I'm working on it!"

"Take the next left. And they should be straight ahead." As I rounded the corner I was met with fifty molgrons poking out of the walls.

"Well shoot! Looks like they're blocking the door."

"Thanks, Captain Obvious. Have you figured out how to get rid of these things yet?"

"I have not. But I have noticed something weird about the ones that you fought earlier."

"Which is?"

"Their split rate is a lot slower than before. Five seconds slower than the ones before them as well as the scales becoming more immature and them shrinking in size."

"And how does that help me?"

"I was thinking about why that could be happening? I mean look at the molgrons in front of you. There is quite a bit of variance in size. Is it because of how much they have multiplied? Is there only so many times they can multiply?"

"Or do they shrink based on how far they are from the original?"

"Maybe. That also could mean there is an original to begin with. We could try to find it and destroy it and maybe that would get rid of all the rest of them."

"We could do that, but we really don't have time for that now. We have to save the others from Balthazar. So, we'll deal with them after, now we need to get through them."

"Okay but remember to calm it down with the explosions. Consider using that hilt you got."

"Oh yeah, I forgot about that." I drew the hilt and yelled out. "Ignis!" Flames shot out both ends of the hilt. "That's pretty cool. I feel like that guy from that Star Wars. With the red light sword."

"Stop posturing and take them out."

"On it." I dashed through them slicing and dicing my way to the door, leaving scorched corpses in my wake. "Minerva, if you're right that should buy us some time. Let's get through that door." I charged the door at full speed. Knocking it off its hinges. Bang! The door fell flat on the ground. "Whoops. Guess I don't know my own strength." As the dust cleared from the door I looked over the balcony to the courtyard. "There they are! They're pushing them back!"

"Get down there and help them." With a demon horde setting upon them. The Anahail troops didn't stand much of a chance. "At least, we have the element of surp…"

"Death to all demons!" I yelled as I jumped from the balcony. "We have to get to the others. Or, at least, draw the demons to us." I aimed my palm at the group of demons yelling. "IGNIS!" A massive fireball released from my hand. It didn't reach them before exploding. "What happened?"

"From the looks of it, your lack of control of your power is destabilizing the structure of your attacks. My recommendation would be close range attacks until you get better control over your power."

"Fine! Mini-nukes it is. Look out below!" *Thud!* As I landed in the middle of the demons.

"It's a kid. Kill it!"

"Like to see you try. IGNIS!" *BOOOOOOM!* Leaving a small crater and ash around me, the flames still lingered.

"Better! But now they're all looking at us." I drew my hilt again and readied myself for battle.

"This should be fun. Bring it on you unholy sacks of crap."

"HE KILLED JON! That little bastard."

"Not Jon, that guy told the best jokes."

"Kill him!" They all said in unison." The demons charged me.

"All according to plan."

"Okay. What's next in this master plan of yours?"

"Disintegrate as many as possible. Mors Ignis!" The demons reel back in terror.

"Oh no. This one is going to be a big one!" *Pfffftttt!*

"Uh, was that supposed to happen?"

"No that's not supposed to happen, Minerva."

"Looks like he's out of tricks, boys. Get 'em!"

"I've got plenty left for you. IGNIS!" *BOOOOOOM!*

"Trace, you need to calm down with overusing your power. I'm seeing a huge drop in your energy after that last attack."

"Huh huh huh, I don't know what you're, huh huh huh, talking about. I'm fine."

"Sure, you are that's why you're wheezing like an out of shape soccer player. Start conserving your energy or this fight will be over before it begins."

"If I can't rely on ignis then the hilt will have to do." The demons started surrounding me and attacking. I cut through them like a knife through butter. Wave after wave of demonic entities swarming and swiping at me. "Minerva I need a better plan than this. Their numbers aren't thinning."

"That's because the thing that summoned them is still alive. You want it to stop, take out the head demon in charge."

"So get to Balthazar and kill him. Got it!"

"Easier said than done I'm afraid."

"What makes you say that? I have plenty left in the tank."

"Not what I meant. I forgot to mention something that happened while you were off in La la land."

"And that is?"

"Hmmm I thought Samara killed you. Let's try to make death stick this time."

"That voice sounds like…"

"Oh, do you like my new body? I must say having a host that has been blessed by a god feels delightful. I feel so powerful. So. So… holy, if you will."

"You bastard, give Samara her body back!"

"I don't think so, runt. With this body my potential will be unlimited. With my power and the goddess's people will fear me once more."

"What am I supposed to do now? I don't have anything to force a demon out of a person. And I'm not fighting Samara. I need some time to think. What about the others? They are on the other side of all the demons. I still need to check on them first, but how to get to them?"

"You're in quite the predicament aren't you?"

"Flare, is that you?"

"Who else would it be? Do you have other voices in your head?"

"Oh, great another smart ass."

"Maybe it's karma."

"What do you want, Flare? Shouldn't you be fighting the remnants of that demon?"

"I am but I could sense the other demon from before again."

"Does that mean you have a plan?"

"Yeah, but you'll need to hold him off until I deal with our other problem."

"How am I supposed to do that with him in my friend's body?"

"I don't know, you're supposed to be the smart one. Figure it out!"

"Wait, Flare. Flare? Really!"

"Maybe you should try to reach the others? They managed to hold out this long."

"Worth a shot. But I'll need a diversion first. Let's make this one as big as possible. IGNIS!" *BOOOOOOOOOOOOM.* The fiery explosion sent dozens of demons flying.

"MY EYES! Its like looking at the sun."

Using the flames as cover I made a run for it. I darted across the courtyard, weaving between demons and devils alike, until I made it to a wall of stone. "Hey! It's me, Trace. Let me in." Nothing. Not a single sound. "I know you guys are in there I can sense you." As soon as I finished my sentence a pair of hands reached out of the ground and pulled me down. "Whoooaaahh." *Thud.* "Ow! I fell on my hilt."

"Trace! You're alive! Our scouts reported your untimely demise. Glad to see that was untrue. Let me help you up."

"Tor? Where am I?" I made it to my feet and looked around the room. Tunnels going in every direction.

"We're under the palace. We should be safe here."

"Not for long. I found you pretty easy."

"No, you found what we left behind. Follow me."

Tor led me down one of the passageways. As we walked we talked about what had happened over the last hour or so. He explained how they had used an item that absorbs energy as a decoy. "We usually would use that item for an S.O.S. but it came in handy thanks to Anrael's quick thinking."

We came to what looked like a storage room filled with what was left of the troops . "You're alive! There's still hope then," Anrael shouted. "Glad you all are safe."

"You too."

"Hey, Anrael I was right, it was Trace setting off those explosions we were feeling earlier. This one here was crazy enough to attack a demon hoard head on by himself."

"I thought you guys were in danger. Minerva said the energy she detected was fading so I had to act fast."

"You've got guts, kid! I don't know many others that

would charge headlong into battle for people they hardly know."

"I'm a Custodes! Protecting people and fighting monsters is what we do."

"With all the damage you did up there you've definitely earned your title. But enough of the pats on the back. Now that you're here we can set our save Samara plan into action."

"You guys have a plan? Awesome!"

"You may not think so after we tell you what it is. So the plan is to capture and bind Samara and purge the demon with these glyphs." Tor presented a rock with a sigil on it.

"Okay, so what's the problem?"

"Well, it will take some time to make the sigils. They have to be created at the same time."

"Oh."

"Thats not even the worst part. Once these sigils are created it will only weaken the demon. It will be up to a team to get up close and personal and use this purification powder made by the goddess to purge the demon."

"Wait, we had demon purging powder and you're just telling me about it now?"

"The demon within you is bound to your soul. This powder is to force a demon that is using someone as a puppet out."

"Okay, so what's the bad part?"

"The powder only purges the demon. Not kill it. The group that purges it will be stuck in there with the demon. The sigils will bind all creatures in it until all the dark energy dissipates. So the group has to both fight the demons and protect Samara."

"Great! Awesome! Please tell me that's our plan B or C."

"Unfortunately, no. That's all we have."

"Oh boy. How many men do we have?"

"Eight!"

"That's it? What happened to the other half." At that moment something started nawing at me."

"What about the group that was with me? I don't see Reinor or the others anywhere. Are they out scouting or something?"

Everyone's heads sink down in despair. "We didn't make it in time to save them. They got overrun while trying to save you from being taken."

My heart sank when I heard that more lives had been lost to save my own. "No! Not again! I can't let anyone else die for my failures! This can't keep happening!"

Soon the sorrow that had filled my heart was replaced with anger and hatred. "Trace, you need to calm down. Your energy levels are spiking and raising the temperature with it."

"This has to end! Grrrrr."

Distorted: "Trace!"

"I'm going to tear those demons to pieces. Rip them limb from limb. Grrrr! Destroy them! Destroy them all! I'll make them pay! They'll all pay!"

"Trace! Trace! Trace get a grip!" *BOOOOOOOOOOOM!* A giant explosion was heard from one of the passageways.

"Find the rats and bring them to me! Dead or alive!"

I felt my blood boil as the demons flooded into the tunnel. "You all know the plan. Move out! Trace let's go!"

"Grrrr. Destroy, destroy, death to all of them.

283

Awooooohh!" I ran head on into the hoard ripping and tearing my way through them. They didn't stand a chance against my rage and flames.

"Trace get ahold of yourself! TRACE! Are you even listening? Answer me!"

"Grrrrr."

"Everyone run, that thing is coming!" the demons shouted.

"No one said they had a shifter with them. Where did that thing come from?"

"It's actually killing our men. What manner of monster is it."

"Don't know and don't care. We need to get out of these tunnels. It sounds like that beast is gaining on us. Run for your lives!"

"Keep an eye on the walls and ceiling. If you see it call it out."

"Ahhwooooohh."

"That thing can breathe fire too."

"How is its flame burning us? We're demons. We bathe in the pits of hell. How is this possible?"

"Oh god, it's running on all fours now. Get out of the tunnel. There's the exit!"

"Ahhwoooohh."

"Nooooo…"

"Keep moving, guys. Trace cleared the way for us! Who knew the kid had it in 'im."

"Tor, I don't think he's in control. Did you see his eyes when he ran off? Those eyes were filled with rage."

"Are yours not? Our comrades died at the hands of these

devils. I'm just as angry as him, we all should be! Besides he's on our side. Now let's go! We've got a demon to destroy!"

"I hope he stays that way. We should be close to the exit."

"Where are demon? I smell them. No see them. Destroy them! Ripp 'em to pieces!"

"They're above, you raging wolf thing… Where are you going?"

"Above."

"Now you listen to me. Look out. that exit is not big enough for you to fit through."

BOOOOOOOOOOOOOOOOOM!

"We're back at the courtyard?"

"Demons death, demon die, demon I eat your eye."

"Oh now you're a poet?"

"What in the actual hell is that thing?"

"Looks like a twisted hell hound to me."

"Why is it looking at us that way? Why is it opening its mouth?"

"It's breathing fire!"

"Ahhwooooohh!"

"Well, well, well. What do we have here? I thought all that commotion from the tunnels was my demons. Seems it was you. May I ask what you have done with my men?"

"Death, die, claw eyes. You next."

"Trace, wait you can't attack the demon now. He's still in Samara's body."

"The elf is correct. You wouldn't want to harm your precious friend now would you?"

"Die, die, die!"

"Oh no, he's degraded to one syllable words. This is not

going to end well. Hey! Tor and Anrael, if you don't want this mindless beast to kill Samara, you might want to distract him!"

"Damnit, he's charging Samara. We have to do something, Tor."

"I'm on it! We just need to distract him until Balthazar is out of her body. I have a plan, we need to pin him in place. Or at least make it hard for him to move. Try to trap his feet." Tor stomped the ground, turning the ground underneath me into a sand pit. While Anrael shot an arrow into the pit causing roots and vines to sprout upwards and wrap around me.

"He's trapped for now."

"Thanks for taking care of that thing for me. But now who's going to stop me from killing the rest of you?" Balthazar vanished without a trace.

"Where did he go?"

"Tor, behind you?"

"Die, you foul beast!" Balthazar appeared behind Tor with a dagger in hand.

As he went to stab him, Tor said, "I think I won't." Tor span around and grabbed Balthazar's hand. "Did you forget? I may be big but I'm fast. Now, Anrael!"

Anrael let loose one of her arrows from earlier, trapping Balthazar in place. "I'm a demon you moronic elf, branches and brambles cannot hold me. Besides I'm in a chosen vessel, you can't hurt me."

"I'm just buying time."

"Buying time you say, ha ha ha. While I could break out of this you have me intrigued. What could you possibly have planned?"

"You'll see soon enough. In ten more minutes."

"I can spare you for that much longer. It gives me time to think of ways to torture you."

"Rooooooaaarrr!"

"Sounds like your friend is having fun. So I have to ask, since the two of you attacked it. Who do you think he'll attack first once he's free? I hope that raging bull is a part of your grand plan. Maybe I'll let him tear your friends to shreds and make you watch. I have no problem waiting the ten minutes. You better hope those restraints hold him for that long."

"I hope you don't plan on talking for the rest of the ten minutes. I might have to off myself before then."

"You wound me. I have the voice of an angel."

"No, you have my friend's voice and her body."

"You mean my body? Because you know it's now my body for as long as I see fit."

"Shut up already! You devil scum."

"Ho oh ho. Taking a page out of that kid's book are we? Must have struck a nerve. Just so you know, your dear Samara feels, sees and hears everything. So when I make her fillet you alive she'll see it and hear it all."

"Anrael, report on the plan and the kid?"

"Well, the restraints are barely holding, as for the rest of the plan, I'd say we're right on schedule. Five!"

"Good, then finish it."

"Five more minutes, eh? Good starting to get bored."

Anrael notched an arrow. This one different from the last. She fired it into the sky and a bright flash went off. Seconds later five other flashes go off. "Oooh, I get a show too. You creatures sure know how to entertain."

A red glyph appeared in the sky and one on the ground,

both in the shape of the star. And walls of light sprouted up to the sky. "Sorry to tell you, Balthazar, but this will be over way sooner than five minutes." Tor took the bag of powder out of his bag and dumped it on Samara. Then Anrael did the same.

"Liberate ei daemonium de constringantur vincula vestra consummationem. Give us back our friend, demon." Tor and Anrael shouted. A flash of light then nothing.

"Is that all? You wasted my time and now I will end yo…" Retching. "What is this?" Black smoke started to flow from Samara's mouth. "What have you done?" Retching. "You've poisoned me."

"Yeah, I did."

"I will obliterate you. You stupid goat man! I can not be stopped! That powder means nothing!" Balthazar broke free of his restraints and stabbed Tor in the stomach.

"Tor! No!"

"I'd worry about yourself, elf." Balthazar appeared behind Anrael and grabbed her by the throat.

"Anrael! You monster, let her go. Your fight is with me!" Tor punched the ground causing it to shake.

"Exactly, and killing your comrades is how I win."

"Kill us all you want you bastard. You're still stuck in here."

"We shall see." Balthazar slowly choked the life out of Anrael. The others started attacking Balthazar but with a wave of his hand their bodies became bloody and mangled. "This new power of mine is amazing. Where have you been all my life!"

"You killed them! All of my friends! My family! You're a monster! A demon!" With each word Tor struck the ground.

288

"Even if we all die I won't let you have Samara!"

"Not like you could stop me." Balthazar turned into smoke and re-entered Samara's body.

"Ahhwoooohhh!"

"Yes, Tor, I am killing everyone you care about and from here I will head to Anahail and kill everyone there as well. But first I'll deal with this one here."

"Destrrrrrooyyy demon!" *Rooooooaaarrr* a torrent of white flames flewtoward Balthazar and Anrael. *Boooooom!* "IT BURNS WORST THAN HELLFIRE!" Balthazar shrieked. As the smoke cleared you could see Tor standing in front of Anrael.

"We're okay? How are we okay? Why did you do that you idiot? Why would you save me?"

"Samara would never forgive me if I let you die."

"Samara!" With the last remaining smoke clearing Samara and Balthazar were standing there.

"What was that flame? My powers, where have they gone. What have you done foul beast. Give them back!"

"You used me to hurt my friends, my family. You will suffer for what you did!" Samara approached Balthazar and held her hand to his face and a light flashed, then Balthazar turned into stone. "You will never harm anyone else again."

"Samara, you're okay!"

"Tor! Are you okay? How's your wound?"

"My wound?" Tor checks his stomach. "It's gone. How?"

"What about everyone else?"

"Balthazar shredded them." The rest of the soldiers get back up checking themselves for wounds.

"All of their injuries are gone too?"

"What happened? For a second I thought we had joined our ancestors. Then a warm feelings ran over me."

"Could it have been that white flame? But where did it come from?"

"Well, the only fire-breathing beast I know of in the area is…"

"Grrrrrr. Ahhwooooohh!" *Thump. Thump. Thump.*

"Trace! Shit I forgot about him. Whoa there, boy! No need to do anything crazy."

"Grrrrrrr."

"Yeah, we only trapped you because you were out of control."

"That wolf is Trace?" *Thump. Thump.*

"And I wouldn't get too close. He has a penchant for burning things to ash." Grrrrr. Thump. Thump. "Destroy*!* DEEEEEESSSSSTTTRRROOOYYY"

"Oh no, what are we supposed to do now?"

"I don't know Tor, but he's our friend we can't hurt him."

"Tell that to him Samara."

"Everyone try to restrain him!" Anrael shouted.

The Nyvx loosed their arrows to pin me down but the flames surrounding me instantly burnt them to ash. "He burnt them so fast."

"Let me give it a shot Tor stomped his hoof to created wall of hands to hold me in place." AHHHWWWOOOOOOHHH. With one howl and the hand disintegrated.

"Okay does anyone else have any other plans? Samara?"

"Not really, I'm kind of low on energy. And from the feel of it, he's only getting stronger. Trace! Listen to me! You need to come back to us." AHHHWWWOOOOOOHHH "That's not working. And he's getting closer.

"Initiating babysitter protocol. Deploying sleeping agent." *Hiiiiisssssssss*

Thud!

"He passed out?"

"That's a good thing. There's no way we could have taken him down."

"My question is how do we get him back to Anahail?" *Hssssssss.*

"Steam is starting to come off his body. And he's shrinking and transforming back to normal."

"Well, that answers your question, Anrael."

"What about the phoenix we came for? Did you locate it?"

"There was no phoenix. It was all a setup to get me to come here."

"So what are we going to do about Farisah?"

"I don't know, maybe the flames that healed us can heal the goddess."

"So, the goddess's life is in the hands of a kid that can't control his anger?"

"Knock it off. That kid did just save our asses. So anything is possible."

"Didn't think I'd hear that from you, Anrael."

"Glad to see you changed your tune."

"Let's just get out of here."

"What about all those demons that were let out? Surely Trace didn't kill them all?"

"Some of them fled once the portals opened. Not to mention that lizard snake thing."

"That's an issue for another day. For now we head home.

Samara can you please open a portal? I'll grab Trace."

"Give me a minute to recuperate Tor." We don't exactly have all the time in the world." All right I'll try it now, everyone , together. Back to Anahail."

Multiple portals opening can be heard around the town. *Swoooosh!*

Epilogue
Happily Ever After

Woooosh!

"We've made it home. Tor, make sure you take Trace to the recovery area. We'll need him up and ready to go as soon as possible. Anrael and I will check on the others. And make sure they got home safe."

"Will do! I'll check on the goddess after. Meet me there?"

"As soon as we can."

"See you there."

"Mr. Tor, do you believe Trace can help your goddess?"

"I have to, talking box, he's our only hope. Besides, he purged a demon out of Samaraand brought multiple people back from the brink of death. Clearly he has extraordinary power. Now let's hope he can recreate it."

"I'm sure he can. I just hope it doesn't require that transformation again."

"We can only hope. Well, here we are. Healer! This boy needs your strongest potion."

"What did you just say? My strongest potion? That boy can't handle my strongest potion. I suggest you go to one of the other healers."

"I'm not asking! It's life and death. He may not wake fast enough. Now give me your strongest potion!"

"There is no point in giving him my strongest potion because it would simply kill him! It would be wise to just let him heal naturally."

"Potion seller, I am telling you the goddess and all of Anahail are relying on your potions now give it to me!"

"Do you truly believe he can handle it? These potions are not meant to be taken lightly. If you are wrong he will die and the hopes of everyone will perish with him."

"I have faith and you should too."

"Fine, take this red vial. It's the same potion I used to speed up the goddess's healing. It only slowed the venom killing her. It should fully heal him, but if his body can't handle it his cells will rapidly reproduce like cancer, aging the body, then killing him."

"Scanning the vial. Analyzing… From what I gather Trace has a seventy five percent chance of surviving what is in that bottle."

"See those are great odds. All right, kid, bottoms up!"

Glug glug glug.

"Whoops, I forgot to move the decimal point. One second… Ooooouuu."

"What do you mean, Ooooouuu?"

"Um, the survival rate wasn't seventy five percent it was 7.5 percent…"

"Oh god! I've killed the goddess's only chance of survival! What do we do? Healer!"

"Don't look at me, I warned you. The potion hut is now closed come back another time."

"Hey. Hey wait. Stop shoving us out."

Slam!

"That old bastard kicked us out. What are we going to do, talking box?"

"Um... Shutting down... Critical update needed... Shutting down in three... two... one... Zzzzz..."

"Crap. Let's just take him to Farisah and maybe she can make sure he lives. Farisah! Farisah! Outta the way! Goddess I need your help!"

"Tor, you're back already! Glad to see you're okay. I had a vision of you and the others falling to the demons. Whaa..."

Tor interrupted, "Yes, ma'am we're fine I'll explain later! Trace drank a potion from the healer and now he might die. What do we do?"

"Lay him at my feet, Tor, so I can take a look at him. It seems that he is..."

Tor interrupted again, "He is what? Going to live? Die? Live and die?"

"Tor! Calm down. Trace will be fine. The potion you gave him is just speeding up his recovery. His body is already metabolizing the potion without an issue. He just needs some rest."

"Really?"

"Really, Tor, now let the boy rest."

"Yes, ma'am."

"Now. I think you should explain what has happened since you left."

Tor told Farisah about the events that unfolded at Kings Rest. The molgrons, the demons, the healing flames, the loss of some of the warriors. Some of the details the goddess did not seem so surprised by. "A healing flame you say? Was it the phoenix? Did you manage to bring it back with you?"

"Goddess, that's just it, there was no phoenix. The healing flame actually came from the boy. He had lost control of himself and became this beast. He breathed a flame that purged the demon out of Samara and healed everyone else. He is the answer."

"So, you did find the phoenix. I told you, Tor, Trace would be the one to save us."

"Farisah, he wasn't able to control his power. So, who's to say that he can heal you."

"I have faith in him."

"Goddess! Anrael and Samara have returned with the others!" The children shouted. "Mister Tor! You're already here!"

"Tor! I thought you were taking Trace to the healing tent to rest?"

"I did but there was a small mishap,I went directly to the healer and got one of his potions."

"Why would take him there? Those potions are dangerous."

"The wrist box said it was a seventy five percent chance of survival but she lied."

"I did not! I just miscalculated."

"I thought you were updating!"

"I was, I finished as Farisah was talking."

"Focus you two. Will Trace be okay?"

"He just needs rest, my child."

"Thank you, Goddess. Tor filled me in on everything that happened. Will you be okay? You went through a lot."

"You all did."

"I'll be fine once I know you and Trace are okay."

"Everything is fine. We both need rest, see to it that Trace gets plenty of it."

"Yes, m'lady. Tor, can you help me get Trace back to my place so he can recover in peace?"

"I can do that!"

"Then let's go. Goddess, we shall return after we get Trace settled."

"There is no need. You all should rest. The only thing we can do is wait."

"Yes, m'lady. I will see you in the morning."

"Hey, Samara, the goddess said something earlier. When we first started talking she seemed surprised to see me and hear that so many of us made it back. Like she expected something different. She also said that we found the phoenix. What do you think she meant by all of that?"

"I think she meant Trace is the phoenix in a way and maybe fate has a different plan for us."

"Maybe. Maybe she had a vision?"

"That is always a possibility. Tor, lay Trace down on the bed there. Let us go pray for our fallen."

"Reinor and his men would be proud to know their sacrifice was not in vain."

Step... step... step.

"What did I tell you? I said not to lose control! And what did you do?"

"I know and I'm sorry, Flare. I couldn't help it. After hearing that more lives had been lost because of me. I got angry."

"Obviously. It's my fault. I should have warned you. Trace, you're unique. Unlike most Custodes your power is greatly amplified by your emotions. When you lose control of your emotions, you'll lose control of your powers. You got lucky that I was finishing off that demon if it weren't for that babysitter protocol your friends would be barbecue."

"What was that white flame by the way? I've never seen or felt anything quite like it."

"That flame is known as the ortu phoenice. It is a flame of mine that can purify all it touches of ailments. However there is a limit to what it can heal as some of the damage is reflected up its user in the process. It shouldn't be used to try to bring back the dead."

"Can I use it to heal, Farisah?"

"Of that I am certain. But it will take a lot of power to do so."

"Will you grant me this ability to save her."

"Trace, I am your ego you needn't ask. My power is yours, so long as you don't lose control again."

"I'll try not to."

"Then step forward and I shall teach you this technique. To learn this technique, you must clear your thoughts of any negativity. Your only thoughts must be to help another. As you focus on that your flames will change from their normal color to a white purifying flame like this."

A ball of white fire appeared in Flare's paw. "Wow, that's amazing."

"You try."

I spent what felt like days trying to figure out that

technique.

"Farisah doesn't have much time left. A matter of days, can't you just do what you did before?"

"Calm down, Trace, you don't need to master the technique to heal her. I haven't mastered it and I created it. When I used that flame through you it was when our power was at its peak and our minds in unison. I don't think I could do that again if I tried."

"What if I can't figure this out in time?"

"I wouldn't worry about that. This world is your inner sanctum. Much like earlier, when you freed me, time passes differently here. So you have plenty of time to train. So clear your mind of all of your worries."

"Okay, clear my mind and focus on the flame. Don't think about all the bad that will happen if I fail. Don't think about the deaths."

"Trace! Stop it! You're overthinking this."

"Well, I've been at this for weeks and still haven't figured it out. Can I get some help?"

"Hold out your hand."

"Okay, what now?"

"Just give me a second." A small white flame appeared in her paw again. Then she handed me the flame. The flame flickered a bit but stayed lit. "Feel the energy emanating from the flame. Add your energy to it and make it grow. How about we start there?"

"Why didn't we? I've been at this for what feels like a month. With no progress. Other than making my normal flames bigger and not explody."

"I would consider that progress, Mr. Mini-nuke."

"Not the right kind of progress."

"You sure about that? Can't have you blowing the goddess up while you try to heal her."

"I, uh. Point taken. We should get back to work."

Multiple failures and weeks later. We finally did it. "Well, well, Trace you've managed to not only increase the size of your flame but you also managed to create it all on your own. I'm impressed with how fast you've grasped this technique."

"Thank you for the help. Now it's time to save a god. Oh, uh, Flare how do I get back here if I want to train or talk with you?"

"Meditation if you want to train. Otherwise as long as you're listening we'll always be able to talk."

"Then I guess I'll see you soon."

Gasp! Cough. Cough. Cough.

"Where am I?"

"You're in Samara's place! You should hurry, the goddess doesn't have much time left."

"What do you mean? How long was I out?"

"A day and a half."

"What? How could I sleep that long? I need to get to Farisah!"

I ran out of the tree house and made my way to the temple. On my way to the temple I noticed a mound covered in flowers with a tablet of stone behind it. "Am I too late?" quickly ran through my mind. "Come on don't let me be too late. The walls of the temple are in sight. But the gates are raised and the towers are unmanned. I guess I'm going over." I jumped and pointed my palms at the ground. "Ignis!" *Boom!* With that blast I cleared the gates. As I made my way over the second gate I saw the area around the temple was empty. But the temple door was wide open. *Thud!* I landed at the temple steps and sprinted inside, still not a single soul in sight. Where was everyone? I ran through the halls of the temple until I got to Farisah's door. *Thud!* I barged through the door to see all of the villagers laying around their goddess.

"Trace, you made it!"

"Yes, Samara, am I too late? I saw the memorial stone."

"No, Trace you made it just in time. Everyone make way! Give him some room." I walked over to Farisah I could feel her energy fading away.

"Can I do this?"

"You're thinking too much. You've trained for this. You can do it. Believe in yourself."

"Thanks, Flare."

"Is everything okay, Trace?"

"Oh, uh, yes, Samara. Just concentrating." I held my hand out and focused my energy. Ortu phoenice! A white flame brimming with a purifying light flowed from my hands. Okay. Now comes the easy part. The flames surround Farisah's body making her body glow with the same bright light.

"Trace, it's working! Everyone, look, he's healing the goddess."

Ow, ow, ow. This does not feel good. Just need to hold out a little longer.

"Trace, your nose is bleeding are you okay? Maybe you should stop for a second."

"Nope, I'm good. I got this. Never felt better." Is this the pain she's been in the entire time? Just a little longer. I say to myself. The flames glow brighter and brighter. Little more. *Cough. Cough.*

"Trace, stop this you're coughing up blood."

"I've got this trust me. I can take it. I'm almost done."

The light grew even brighter filling up the room like a flashbang. "I did it!" *Thud.*

"Trace! Are you okay?"

"I'm fine, Samara. I just used a lot of energy is all." As the light started to fade a silhouette of a woman walked out of the flames.

"Farisah! The goddess is okay! Trace saved her!"

"Goddess! You're okay."

"Trace, don't try to move so much you're hurt."

"I'm fine, Samara, I think I can stand just fine."

"Everyone, can you give us a moment? Samara, Tor, and Anrael you should stay. Trace, if it wasn't for you I would have faded from existence. I must thank you for what you have done not just for me but all of the residents of Anahail. I must apologize as well. I deceived you. I told you I could help you if you helped me."

"I wouldn't say deceived. Because trying to help you did help me in the end. The demon has been purged from my soul and the poison from your body. A win-win."

"Looking on the bright side of things now? You've grown quite a bit since you first came here."

"I guess, but now I'm kinda back at square one. I've no idea where to go from here."

"Well, maybe I can help you with that. You want to take your home back. But you have no idea where to start. You'll need an army and I think that part will reveal itself soon enough. But there is something I can do. Since it is dangerous to travel alone how about I send someone with you?"

"That is a great idea, Farisah!"

"I'm glad you think so, Samara. I'm sending you with him. I've held you back long enough. It's not fair for me to keep you sheltered here."

"Goddess you have sheltered me. You have protected me and taught me so much."

"Samara, this was the first time you've left Anahail since you first came here. It's time for you to find yourself. I know you've wanted to. Go with him and explore the world. You'll be surprised what you will learn."

"Do I not get a say in this?"

"You have objections, Trace?"

"Not really, but shouldn't Samara get a say? I don't think you should make her come with me if she doesn't want to. Let her choose for herself."

"You're right. Samara what is your choice? Would you prefer to go on your own down a lonely road, stay here and forever regret not leaving, or help Trace save his home?"

"That's not fair you're guilting her into it."

"I am not. I'm just telling her the options. I've seen the outcomes of the first two."

"I can't make that decision now. I'll need to think about it."

"Take as much time as you need, my child."

"Yes, take some and think. Now! We celebrate! The goddess is better and Anahail is safe once more! This calls for a feast! Me and Kai will start planning the feast. Of course, it'll take a few days and if everyone chips in we can definitely make this a celebration to end all celebrations!"

"Tor, you're getting ahead of yourself!"

"Nonsense, Anrael, Tor is right. We need to celebrate our friends, family, the ones that are still here and the others we have lost and our victory we would not have achieved without them!"

"See even Farisah is down to party!"

"Tor, Anrael spread the word, we will have a memorial feast for the fallen. It will take place three days from now."

"Yes, m'lady. I'll get right on it."

"Everyone return to your homes and get some rest. We have a lot to do and not a lot of time to do it."

Samara and I returned to her home. Over the next few days Samara was lost in thought and conflicted over what she should do next. Should she stay or should she go? I tried to reassure her I would be fine and that she shouldn't worry about me. Not sure if it really helped.

The day had finally come, the day of the feast. You could hear the cheers of the people all the way across town. Samara and I made our way to the temple to join the others. It looked like everyone that wasn't preparing for the feast was repairing houses.

"This place is starting to look like home again."

"Yeah, Farisah must be working her magic. Most of the scorched grounds have been fixed." We continued past the memorial on the way and I had my time to pray for the fallen.

"The feast will be starting soon, we should hurry." We made our way to where the walls once stood to be met with a green field covered with flowers. And families with their kids gathering around the tables.

"Wow, this is amazing."

"Hard to believe this was a battlefield a few days ago," Tor said as he brought the last of the cask. "For a second I thought you guys weren't going to make in time. Anrael saved us seats next to Farisah. I'll meet you over there."

We take our seats next to Farisah, and the feast finally begins. It's been a long time since I've seen so many smiling faces. What's it been, about seven or eight years? Seems so much longer than that. I wonder what's happening there? Is Dad still alive? Will there even be a home to save when I get there. What am I talking about? Of course, there's still a home to take back, and my dad is the strongest guy I know. He's there with everyone else, fighting the good fight. Just hold on, guys, I'll be there with backup soon enough.

Static zzzzzztttt zt zzzzzt.

"Anyone hear that strange noise?"

"Yeah I hear it too. What is that?"

"Trace, there's transmission coming over the emergency channel."

"Now? Is it Dad?"

"I'll play the message."

"Everyone quiet down for second."

"Can anyone help us? This is Eli of the Jericho squad. We are under attack by what looks like flying demons, vampires and werewolves. Someone, anyone send hel…"

"I'm sorry and I'd really hate to interrupt your story because it's really great. But it's closing time."

"Awwww. Miranda really?"

"I'm sorry, guys, but the rules are the rules."

"Just another hour."

"No, you have to go."

"Don't worry, guys, this isn't the end of my tale this was just the beginning."

"So does that mean you're coming back tomorrow night?"

"I don't know for sure."

"Please! That was such an awesome story. The demon fighting, the superpowers, the magical creatures all of it was super cool."

"Yeah kind of, I'm actually sorry I called you a drunk. You can tell one hell of a story. Maybe next time you can show us some of your spells. Mors Ignis sounds emo as hell but super metal at the same time."

"Maybe. Will you tell us more about the shaman Samara? She sounds like a badass."

"That is because she is. Out of all the people that I have met over the years Samara is by far one of the strongest. Human or otherwise. But who knows what tomorrow night has in store? If I do come back here where would I start? Maybe with the dragon or maybe with the ghoul ooh maybe the kitsune."

"You could tell us all of them! If you do I will give you free drinks whenever you come in."

"That is a very tempting offer to consider. I'll think about it. Until next time, ladies and gentlemen. Stay safe and good night."

Printed in the USA
CPSIA information can be obtained
at www.ICGtesting.com
CBHW021039241223
2912CB00002B/27